You,
Your Girlfriend
& Me

To Jade,

Thank you

SCOTT BISSETT

Scott Bissett

ISBN: 9798324950781

FOR MAGGIE

To think they gave us six months. You're still the one.

Chapter One: December 23rd

Kate

I'm a Christmas person. Honestly, I am. I love everything to do with Christmas. It's the most wonderful time of the year, after all.

You know those cheesy made-for-TV Christmas movies? The ones where the cynical big business city girl comes back to her small-town childhood home to buy out the cutesy family bakery which is getting in the way of her evil, heartless, corporate bosses and their plans to develop a ski resort, but instead ends up falling for the handsome, widowed, single parent baker and turns her back on her soulless city life to bake cookies? Yup, I love every single one of those movies. Guilty as charged. I will happily sit with a tub of rum and raisin ice cream and a spoon, my knees tucked up inside my beautifully ugly Christmas jumper, and I'll watch those brilliant, silly, heartwarming things back-to-back until I fall asleep on my sofa and the ice cream – assuming I've actually left any, that is – starts to melt.

I love to look at twinkling fairy lights, and I love the smells of Christmas. Gingerbread houses. Real Christmas trees, all sticky and sappy and piney. Turkey and all the trimmings roasting in the oven. Mulled wine. Side note, I could never get a straight answer out of anyone when I asked what 'mulling' was, but all I know is that it makes wine smell just fabulous. All warm and comforting. Give me some mulled wine and the satisfying snap of a German sausage as I stroll around the Christmas Market in Glasgow's George Square, and I am one happy little Christmas elf, all blissed out in my very own personal

Hallmark movie.

Don't even get me started on the Christmas songs. Every year, without fail, as soon as the Take That calendar – don't judge me! – in the kitchen of my flat gets flipped over to the December page, the radio in my car goes off and the 'Now! Christmas' CD goes in. I remember when I was a kid, Dad would put on Christmas records while we decorated the tree. I can still remember the sound of the needle dropping on the record, that little scratch it made, and then Chris Rea's gruff-but-smooth voice, singing about driving home to see the faces of the folk he loved. Mum would roll her eyes at Dad's terrible dancing, and I'd think he was the most hilarious guy who had ever lived as he'd run into the kitchen, grab a wooden spoon from the drawer, and serenade Mum like he was Michael Bublé himself.

Like I said, I'm a Christmas person.

So, if I'm such a holly jolly wee Christmas elf, then why am I sitting on one of the metal tube-framed bench seats outside of the designer chocolate shop in the massive, busy and *extremely* festive Glasgow Fort shopping centre, watching the bustling crowds of holiday shoppers, listening to 'Jingle Bells' being played over the outdoor speakers, feeling the occasional snowflake melt on the tip of my nose and wishing, just wishing, more than anything, that I could be anywhere else in the world but right here, right now?

Kate: Earlier that day

'Look, if you're going to sulk and be such a bloody bitch about it,' I snap at Steph, 'Maybe you should just go for a walk and calm down.'

'Aye, maybe I should,' she yells back at me.

'Just don't slam the door,' I say, closing my eyes.

I seethe in silence as she storms out into the hall of the flat, pausing only to slam the door behind her, and the resulting draught of air causes a handful of Christmas cards to flutter and tumble to the floor. I sink, defeated, into the corner of the white leather sofa and want to cry so badly that the effort involved in holding back the tears physically hurts. My head pounds, my eyes sting, and the lump that catches in my throat makes it almost impossible to speak or even swallow.

It was an argument that had erupted out of nothing, really, but then, that's how they've all started over the last couple of months. Just a series of small, insignificant nothings that we'd allowed to burn out of control, until one or both of us – normally Steph – ended up saying something we'd later regret. And then of course we'd circle each other in unbearable silence for hours until one or the other of us – normally me – would give in and apologise. Or worse, we'd go to bed with tensions still simmering, sleep with our backs to each other, and in the morning grudgingly put it behind us with nothing really resolved, and then spend the day trying to ignore the elephant in the room.

With a deadline approaching and an editor breathing down my neck for the finished article – two thousand words on, irony of all ironies, *"How to keep your partner satisfied on Valentine's Day"* – I'd been hammering away on my laptop in the spare bedroom which served as my office space. As a result, I'd completely forgotten about the three eggs in the pot which had completely boiled dry, resulting in an explosion which left in its wake an awful smell of burnt saucepan, and eggy remains splattered on the wall, door and ceiling of the kitchen, which to be fair, Steph had just spent an hour cleaning in time for the start of our Christmas dinner preparations.

To make matters worse, I'd completely misread her mood and laughed about it.

'That's just bloody typical of you, Kate. Everything's just a big joke to you, isn't it?' she had said, clearly annoyed.

'I'm sorry, babe, I—'

'Don't even bother,' she snapped. 'You're so selfish. I've got so many other things I'd rather be doing than running around after you and cleaning up your mess because you can't even be bothered to keep an eye on a pot!'

'Don't be like that,' I said, as I opened the cupboard where we kept our cleaning supplies. 'I'll clean it up, it's not a big deal. It's just a couple of eggs.'

'It's not about the bloody eggs, Kate. It's about you not paying attention to things. And I'm not talking about the eggs. I'm talking about me. I'd already asked if you wanted me to make you something to eat while you were working, and you didn't answer.'

'I'm sorry, I was completely focused on what I was doing, and—'

'Yeah, you're always focused on what you're doing. Because that's all that matters to you, everything always has to be about what *you're* doing.'

And with that – and with a little prompting on my part for her to take a walk and calm down – she stormed out of the flat and slammed the door shut behind her, purely because she knows how much doors being slammed annoys me. I love Steph more than I've ever loved anyone, but she knows exactly how to push my buttons when we're arguing. And it feels like lately, that's been more often than not.

I spend the rest of the afternoon staring at the screen of my laptop, writing a sentence or two, and then erasing it again, because, honestly, what the hell do I know about keeping my partner satisfied on Valentine's Day, or at Christmas, or Pancake bloody Tuesday or any other time of the year, really? I seem to bounce from bad relationship to bad relationship like some kind of wild, defective pinball made entirely of hormones, chocolate and bad decisions.

Is that *really* how I feel about Steph? Is that how I feel about our relationship? Is she just another bad decision?

I pick up my phone and text her.

> ME
> *I'm sorry, babe. I cleaned up the mess I made.*

Are we still going Christmas shopping tonight?

I stare at my phone for a few seconds, waiting for a response. Finally, it pings.

STEPH
I'll meet you at the Fort at 6:30. Can't talk right now.

I close my laptop over, finally accepting that I'm not going to be able to write anything worthwhile today. Not while I feel like this. I always get this way when we're fighting. I can't focus on anything else. I just want everything to be okay between us again.

Kate

A family of four happily clutching shopping bags filled with gifts stroll past me, their laughter ringing through the night air, and I pull my deep crimson wool coat a little tighter around me, trying to ward off the December chill seeping through my bones. I wish I'd worn my gloves. My fingers are starting to feel a little numb.

'Can we talk?'

I look around.

It's Steph. Perhaps she's seen sense. Maybe she's realised that this has all been blown completely out of proportion, and she wants to apologise and talk things through. And I'm more than happy to apologise for my part in things too, if that's what it takes for us to finally get back on track and be as amazing together as we were at the start, just over two years ago. It's hard to read her expression, though. It's bitterly cold tonight, and she's wrapped up so tightly in the hat and scarf I bought for her right here last Christmas that I can barely see her face.

I motion to the chocolate shop in front of us.

'In there?' I suggest. 'We can have a hot chocolate and get

warmed up. I'm frozen stiff.'

She looks through the window of the shop. The café area inside is busy. There's a long queue at the counter, and not a table to be had.

'It looks too busy,' she says, still not meeting my eyes. 'Let's try the little coffee shop around the corner. We can talk properly there.'

'Okay, babe,' I say quietly, reaching hesitantly to thread my fingers through hers, the way we normally do, but instead, all I find is cold December air.

Matt

It's not like I'm unhappy in my job, you know? Don't get me wrong, I don't think I ever set out to become a barista. I'm pretty sure nobody ever really does. I mean, almost every single one that I know is doing it while... while they wait to become something *else*, I guess. Like Anja who works the early shift with me sometimes. She's the most talented painter whose work you've never seen. She finally managed to convince Dom, our boss, to let her hang a few of her paintings on the wall of the shop, and she's even sold a couple. Not enough to convince herself that she's good enough to make a full-time living out of it, though. And Heather who's working with me tonight. She plays bass in a band, and whilst I've seen them play enough times that I can confirm that they do indeed kick a moderate amount of butt, they always seem to be juggling their various work and University schedules just to play a show.

And then there's me. I'm a writer. In my head, at least. There are probably three unpublished 'work in progress' novels on my laptop at any given time, but I guess that I'm honest enough with myself to know that it'll never amount to anything more than a hobby, because honestly, who even reads books these days? It's not like I'm not happy with my life as it is, either. I like the people I work with. I'm lucky enough to say that I have the most beautiful girlfriend in the world, and for the most part, I enjoy being able to people-watch as I create little Christmassy doodles in the foam of the dozens of chestnut praline lattes that I pour in the course of an average shift here in the shop.

Like the couple sitting at the table just underneath Anja's painting of the city lights sparkling on the river Clyde, for example. I'm trying so hard not to stare – or not to get *caught* staring, at the very least – but they're not making it easy for me. I've seen this play out enough times to know exactly what's going on. The contrasting body language of them both – one of them cold and detached, the other pleading and emotional – and the occasional snippets of conversation that keep filtering through tell me that this isn't a couple on a date. It's a couple in the process of very publicly breaking up.

The girl in the red wool coat with her back to the door of the coffee shop is pretty, but she looks as sad as anyone I've ever seen. I feel kind of bad for her, to be honest. The other girl looks ice cold, and it's easy to see which of the two is still invested in making the relationship work, and which of them has already emotionally checked out. Heather motions at them with her eyes, and I make a slight grimace in return to let her know I'm already following the drama as I wipe the steam wand on one of the machines. I feel a little guilty about watching, I have to confess, but it's like a car crash happening in slow motion right in front of my eyes, and I can't tear myself away from it.

'Please, Steph, can't we at least talk about it?' I can hear Sad Girl plead. Cold Girl simply stares into the untouched oat milk hazelnut mocha in her cup.

'There's nothing to talk about. Don't make this any more difficult than it needs to be.'

'How long has it been going on?' Sad Girl asks after a short pause. I get it now. Ouch, I didn't see that coming. And neither did she, it would appear. Cold Girl's already checked out of this relationship because she's started a new one.

'I should go,' Cold Girl says finally. And just as I think their show is drawing to a close, Sad Girl erupts.

'Just bloody go then,' she yells, tears now streaming down her face, mascara beginning to streak. 'I'm getting used to you walking out on me now. But this time, don't come back.'

Cold Girl stands up, steps back from the table, and in what looks like a final symbolic nail in the coffin, pulls off the expensive-looking scarf from around her neck, bunches it up, and throws it down on the table in front of Sad Girl, who looks devastated.

'I won't. Goodbye, Kate,' she says as she walks away. I half expect Sad Girl to follow her or at least turn around to watch her leave. But she doesn't. Instead, she picks up the discarded scarf and buries her face in it, trying to muffle her loud sobs.

Heather makes a face in my direction, which I can only interpret as meaning *'You're in charge! Do something!'* But I'm not sure exactly what it is that I'm *supposed* to do in this situation. I don't have the first clue what the etiquette is for a scenario like this.

Do I ask her to leave because she's causing a scene?

Do I ignore her and pretend none of this is happening, and hope she's so embarrassed that she just gets up and leaves of her own accord?

I have no idea. So, I grab the first thing that comes to hand and open the hatch on the countertop.

Kate

In between sobs, I'm breathing in Steph's perfume from her scarf. *Under the Lemon Trees* by Maison Margiela. Her favourite. Our favourite. I bought it for her one day during the summer when we went shopping at Buchanan Galleries. She tried it on when we were in John Lewis, and when she let me smell it on her neck, it was all that I could do to stop myself from pinning her down on the glass-topped perfume counter right there and then. And every time she's worn it since, it's had the same effect on me. Except right now. I don't feel like that right now. I just want to clutch her scarf and breathe it in and pretend to myself that none of this is happening and that everything is going to be okay.

Wait.

Her scarf. She's left her scarf. I need to give it back to her. She didn't mean to leave it behind. She didn't mean to leave me behind. She didn't mean any of it. I can fix it. I can catch up with her and we can fix this.

'Are you okay?' asks a quiet, kind voice that doesn't belong to Steph and I jump in my seat a little.

'I'm sorry,' the voice – the male voice – says, having seen me jump. 'I didn't mean to give you a fright.'

I look up. And then I look down at the table in front of me. And then back up at the man standing beside my table. And finally, confused, back at the table in front of me, where a small slice of carrot cake sits on a plate. I stare at it for a second.

'On me,' the man says. 'I didn't know what else to do or say, and you look— well, I mean, you look like you could use something comforting right now.'

I clear my throat and wipe my tears on Steph's scarf.

'Thank you,' I say, forcing a weak smile. I look up at him again. He's wearing a black polo shirt embroidered with the shop's logo, a steaming cup, and a name badge which reads *Matt. Shift Manager.*

'I didn't mean to bother you,' he says. 'I'll leave you alone if you'd prefer. I just wanted to make sure you were okay, that's all.'

He smiles kindly and turns to walk away. I force myself to speak, but it comes out as little more than a hoarse whisper.

'I'm sorry we caused a scene,' I say quietly. 'I feel so embarrassed.' And I do. I really do. I can feel my cheeks burning. There are only a handful of customers in the coffee shop, and I'm thankful for that small mercy, even if I do feel as though they're all still staring at the panda-eyed nutjob sniffing her girlfriend's scarf in the middle of a shopping centre two days before Christmas.

'Nothing a nice wee bit of cake won't cure,' he smiles again and points to my cup. 'And maybe a fresh coffee? That one must be freezing by now.'

I look down at my untouched drink. It's stone cold. I look at the piece of carrot cake, and for just the briefest moment, I think again about going after Steph.

But I don't. I look back at Kind Matt the Cake and Coffee Guy.

'That would be nice,' I say.

Matt

I look up at the clock above the counter as I finish putting the last of the freshly washed cups and saucers away. Midnight. I like my job. I like working here at the Fort, too. Mostly. At Christmas, not so much. I mean, really, I can get behind late-night shopping and all that stuff. Folk who work late appreciate the additional time to get their shopping done without feeling rushed. And it's great seeing the whole place decorated with the lights and the music playing outside and the little Christmas mini market, too. I like all that. I'm not even remotely Grinchy about it. But who in the name of all that is good and holy is still drinking coffee at midnight? Perverts.

'So,' Heather says as she pushes in the last of the chairs against the newly wiped tables, 'Are you going to tell me about it or not?'

'Tell you about what, Hev?' I ask, playing dumb. I know exactly what she's doing, but the mischief maker in me wants her to have to ask. And she knows what I'm doing too.

'You're an arse, Matt,' she grins. 'Those two girls from earlier tonight. What was the deal with them, you reckon?'

I shrug. 'Domestic? How am I supposed to know?'

'See, this is why I wish you were a girl. If you were, you'd have been right in there, empathising with her.'

'And getting all the gossip for you?'

'And getting all the gossip for me, yes. Honestly, it's rubbish working with straight guys sometimes. You're all crap and insensitive! Jason would have managed to find out that girl's entire life story within ten minutes, never mind what happened between her and her girlfriend.'

Jason is the drummer in Heather's band as well as being her flatmate and – her words, not mine – 'aromantic asexual life partner and sistah from a different mistah,' and she is, of course, absolutely correct. Jason is probably the sweetest, funniest, campest guy I've ever met, and is utterly relentless when it comes to digging up hot gossip for his bandmates. Mind you, I imagine it takes a certain level of fierceness to survive when you're the only male in a shouty feminist punk band called Cramping Pussée. And yes, that is pronounced *'poo-sayyy,'* with the emphasis hard on the 'sayyy.'

'What can I tell you?' I say to her. 'I felt really bad for her. Getting dumped in public like that is bad enough, but it's even worse when it happens two days before Christmas. That really sucks. I didn't want to pry. She seemed nice and I didn't want to make her any more upset than she already was.'

'Aw, maybe you're not so crap and insensitive after all. I mean, for a straight guy,' Heather says, punching my arm.

'Shut up,' I reply, rolling my eyes. 'Look, you can shoot off if you want. I'll lock up. Go and enjoy your Christmas, eh?'

'You sure, mate?'

'Yeah, on you go. I've got this.'

'You're an absolute legend, Matt. Say hi to the gorgeous Paige for me? You're both coming to the gig at G2 on Wednesday night, right?'

'She'll be out cold by the time I get back to hers, and yeah, we wouldn't miss it for the world,' I grin, but Heather's already in the office pulling her jacket on.

Chapter Two: December 24th

Kate

I shut myself away in the spare bedroom-turned-office of the flat with a mug of coffee while Steph goes through the rest of it, packing up the last of her stuff. I can't bring myself to watch, because I'm terrified that every time I see her putting something into a box, I'll be reminded of how that thing came to be in the flat, or where we picked it up, or what it meant to us. To me. I guess. I don't know. I don't even know how much of it really still means anything to her at this point. I've even found myself wondering if she'll take certain things or leave other things behind purely to hurt me. It's so messed up. I never thought we'd end up here, in this place. All I know is that I can't bring myself to watch what was 'our life' being turned into 'my life,' because that's all that will be left when she's finished.

What hurts most is that she doesn't even say goodbye when she goes. I hear the rattle of her keys being dropped onto the kitchen counter, her footsteps going down the hall, and then the sound of the flat door as it closes behind her. And in the split-second of that last click, 'we' becomes 'me.'

Ugh. I walk into the living room and stand looking at the bare spot on the wall where her Glasgow University graduation photo used to hang, and all of a sudden, I become acutely aware of the fact that, really, I have no idea how to even be alone. Since I moved out of my parents' house eight years ago, I haven't been single for more than a few weeks at a time. Some relationships lasted longer than others, and the gaps between them varied in length, but there was never any overlap. I am the very definition of a serial monogamist. But right now, feeling like this, I can't even begin to imagine how to do this, how to get back out there, or even how to just be on my own and still be okay with that.

I wander into the bedroom. Our bedroom. My bedroom. She's left the door of her side of the wardrobe open, as if to intentionally force me to look at the utter emptiness of it. And then I look at the bed. It's nothing fancy, nothing big, just a regular double bed. But it looks and feels huge now. I couldn't sleep last night. I just kept reaching out and finding... well, nothing. Just the space where she used to be, the space where she should have been.

I sit down on the bed. Her scarf is still on what used to be *her* pillow. I brought it home from the coffee shop with me. I couldn't bear to throw it in the bin outside when I left. It still has the smell of our perfume on it, and I needed that last night. I know, it's stupid. I'm stupid. I just feel so... stupid. I lay awake all night with her scarf scrunched up and my face buried in it, just breathing her in and pretending that she was right there.

Twenty-six and single again. What a fantastic Christmas Eve this is turning out to be.

It's just occurred to me that there's an important phone call I now need to make. I pick up my phone and tap the familiar photo on my contacts screen.

'Hiya, pal,' Dad says. He always calls me 'pal.' It's his default term of endearment, but it also feels kind of fitting, as he is and will always be my best friend and my number one fan. But right now, there's someone else that I need to speak to.

'Hi Dad. Is Mum there?'

'Aye, she's in the living room. I'm just making us a wee cup of tea. Hang on a minute, I'll put her on.'

I hear him say 'It's our Katie' to Mum as he passes her the phone.

'Hiya, honey. You alright?' Mum asks me, and I immediately burst into tears.

'No, Mum,' I stop sobbing long enough to say. 'Steph's finished with me. She's moved out.'

'On Christmas Eve?'

Cheers, Mum. Nice one. Daughter's crying. Christmas is ruined.

'Want me to come up?' she asks.

'No, it's okay. You don't need to do that,' I say, sniffling.

'I've got a better idea,' she says. 'Why don't you come here? I'll make up the bed in your old room and you can stay here tonight. You were going to be coming over tomorrow anyway, weren't you?'

'Yeah,' I answer. I'm so choked up it's about all I can get out.

'It's settled, then. We'll get Chinese in tonight, open a bottle of wine and watch Dirty Dancing.'

I love my Mum. She always knows the right thing to say, and she's been round this particular track enough times to know that my heartbreak cure is invariably Peking ribs and roast pork chow mein from the Jade Palace, a wee bottle of Chardy, and Patrick Swayze on DVD.

'Dad'll love that, I'm sure,' I laugh.

'Your father can just shut his hole and watch the telly in our room. We've got girl talk to catch up on. Nobody puts Katie in a corner, eh?'

Despite how they sometimes jokingly talk about one another, my Mum and Dad are ridiculously still in love to a sickening extent – and I have to admit that they are completely, as Dad takes great pleasure in hilariously mangling, 'hashbrown couple goals.' Thirty-odd years married now, and Dad still looks at her like she's the wee pigtailed, freckly girl down the street that he used to walk home from school every day. I bet he still sings to her when they're decorating the Christmas tree. Maybe one day I'll find someone who does that for me.

'You just bring your cosy jammies. I'll take care of everything else.'

'Thanks, Mum. I love you.'

'See you in a wee while, honey. Everything's going to be okay. I promise.'

And with that, I hang up, and while I feel a little bit better knowing that no matter what happens, Mum and Dad will always have my back, I still bury my face in Steph's scarf, smell her perfume again, and I cry until there are no more tears left in me.

Chapter Three: December 25th

Matt: Morning

'Merry Christmas, darling.'

I prise my bleary eyes apart, yawn and stretch my legs satisfyingly. Paige kisses the back of my shoulder as she threads her arm under mine and around my chest, and I almost drift blissfully back into a well-earned sleep.

'Merry Christmas, babe,' I reply, squeezing her arm. My phone is propped up on Paige's cute little bedside table. I peer through one sleepy, blurry eye and can just about make out *09:48*. I had hoped we'd have been up a little earlier, what with it being Christmas morning and all, but I take it as a sign that I needed the rest. Christmas is the busiest time of year in the shop, and I've worked the late shift for the last fourteen nights in a row, closing at midnight, and not getting home, either to my place or Paige's, until just after one in the morning. The healthy bonus Dom paid me for my hard work made it all worthwhile, though, and it allowed me to pick up something really nice for Paige's Christmas.

'Fancy a coffee?' Paige asks.

'I think I'll take a break from coffee for one day at least,' I smile, turning around to face her. My God, she is absolutely beautiful. I really am a lucky man. Even with her blonde hair scraped back tight and her face scrubbed free of makeup, she glows. Heather is forever reminding me that I really am punching above my weight with Paige, and if I'm being honest, I find it impossible to disagree with that. I'm a solid five and a half on a good day. Paige is a ten without even trying.

'Tea it is, then,' she grins. 'I'll go and pop the kettle on,' and then she kisses the tip of my nose. She gets out of bed, still wearing one of my t-shirts as a nightdress which barely even skims the top of her thighs, and it's all I can do to stop myself from pulling her right back into bed beside me, tea be damned.

Instead, I dig to the bottom of one of the drawers she's put aside for my clothes for when I stay over at hers – which is more nights than not, at this point – and I find exactly what I'm looking for. The gift-wrapped box containing the white gold and diamond pendant necklace from Chisholm Hunter that she'd fallen in love with one day when we were out shopping. She didn't mention it, but I could see the faraway look in her eyes, and I went back that night before my shift and picked it up for her. I've had it hidden away inside a folded-up pair of my jeans since then, looking forward to seeing the look in her eyes when I surprise her with it today.

I should clarify, though, Paige isn't materialistic in any way, shape or form. I know she'd have been equally as happy with some fluffy pyjamas and a set of her favourite bath bombs from Lush, but this has been a special year for her, having completed her Postgraduate Diploma, and then securing a traineeship with one of the most prestigious law firms in the city. I just wanted to show her how proud I am, and how in awe I am of the hard work she's put in to get where she is.

I throw on a clean t-shirt and a pair of black jeans and put the box in my back pocket as I head through to the kitchen, with nothing more in mind than surprising her with my gift. Those good intentions go out of the window, however, when I walk in. My t-shirt is already in the laundry basket, and Paige is leaning back against the black marble kitchen counter, wearing nothing but a red silk ribbon, wrapped around her and tied in a neat bow over her full breasts, her nipples already visibly stiff beneath it.

'Would you like to unwrap your present first?' she asks me, grinning wickedly, and I decide that the tea can wait after all.

Kate: Morning

I prise open one eye. One side of my face is buried in a pillow, and it would appear that I am completely unable to move my head. I don't understand why that would be the case. I also don't understand why I'm looking at a white wicker chair (which I don't own) and lavender painted walls (which I don't have.) I close my one open eye and take a couple of slow deep breaths in an effort to, I don't know, somehow force my brain to reset itself.

Why do I feel like this? Am I ill? Or have I been drinking? Time for some basic routine maintenance. My tongue is so dry that it's stuck to the roof of my mouth. My stomach is making some odd noises and feels a little like a tumble dryer filled with wet socks. My head isn't doing much better. Those are all pretty good indicators of some serious alcohol consumption.

I manage to roll onto my side and get my head off the pillow. I turn around to ask Steph what's going on. But Steph isn't there. Why isn't Steph there? I enter into some gentle negotiations with my brain. I don't like you very much, and I'm pretty sure you're not my biggest fan either right now, brain, but help me out here, eh?

Steph isn't here, because... *you and Steph aren't together anymore.*

Ugh. Okay. And I don't recognise this room because... *this isn't your room.*

But it looks familiar because... *you spent the first eighteen years of your life in this room.*

Just one last thing, brain... *Oh, for God's sake, Kate. We're at Mum and Dad's house because you had a meltdown yesterday and ran to the comfort of the only place you know you feel completely safe and protected.*

Okay, first of all, rude! All you had to do was say. It's all coming back to me now. Mum opening the front door and me throwing myself, sobbing, into her arms. Sitting on the couch while Dad pottered around awkwardly, just generally being Dad. Peking ribs and roast pork chow mein, followed by the Dirty Dancing DVD with a glass of wine, which turned into a bottle, which turned into an ill-advised second and then into a disastrous third, before the Bacardi appeared. Beyond that, it's all very much a case of *'this file has been deleted and cannot be recovered.'*

Despite feeling like I am very much – and I cannot emphasise this strongly enough – on the verge of an entirely self-inflicted death, I do feel completely safe and protected, because that's what this place is. It's not my home anymore, and somehow at the same time will always be my home.

I sit up in the bed. My bed. Not my bed, of course. That's long since been replaced by the bed which now occupies Mum and Dad's spare bedroom. The room that once belonged to me and my sister Fiona, older than me by eighteen months in actual time, and, oh, a decade or so in terms of maturity. Fi's the sensible daughter. The responsible one. Good, steady job. Married to good, steady hubby Ewan. Nice house, nice car, nice life. A nice girl.

Sorry, that makes me sound a wee bit resentful of Fi, but nothing could be further from the truth. I love her to bits. We're sisters, but even if we weren't, we'd be best friends. I know that I can go to Fi with any problem, and she'll have great advice for me. In fact, I might put that to the test later today when she and Ewan come to Mum and Dad's for dinner. I could do with her insight on what went wrong with Steph, and I know if I can count on anyone to be completely straight with me – no pun intended – it's our Fiona.

But first, though, I think I'd better get a strong black coffee and one of Dad's trademark crispy bacon rolls with brown sauce down me, or this is going to be the longest Christmas Day in living memory.

Matt: Afternoon

This is the first Christmas that I can remember where we don't have any guests for dinner at all. Today is all about just Paige and I, and I'm completely okay with that. When we eventually got around to unwrapping our *actual* gifts to each other this morning, she was totally over the moon with the necklace and burst into tears when she unwrapped it. She had no idea I'd even noticed her looking at it, let alone gone back to get it for her. And I love the watch she got for me, although much like Paige, I'd have been every bit as happy with a box of chocolates and a pair of slippers.

'This is nice, babe,' she says, burying her head in my chest as we lie slumped on the couch watching rubbish TV in a post-turkey fugue. 'All I could ever ask for.'

'Feels a little weird it just being the two of us, though, doesn't it?' I say, kissing the top of her head. 'Not that I'm complaining about that!'

'Yeah, I should probably have made a little less food, knowing we'd have so much left over,' she laughed, a little tipsy from the wine. Or maybe just drunk on love. 'We'll be eating turkey curry for a week.'

'Mum and Derek are coming over tomorrow, though. I'm sure they won't say no to a good feed,' I smile.

Derek is Mum's new friend. Or 'companion' as she likes to refer to him. My Dad passed away three years ago, and Mum thought she'd never love again until she bumped into Derek at a garden centre down in the Clyde Valley one Sunday morning when she was shopping for bulbs for her little garden. And while it's still early days, she looks happier than she has in a long time. Derek's great for her. He's a good, kind man and loves nothing more than sitting with me, having a beer and a natter about music or football or just life in general. He and his late wife never had a family of their own, and I think he secretly kind of enjoys the idea of having a surrogate son.

As for Paige's parents, Martin and Carol, they're currently sunning themselves somewhere in Gran Canaria and won't be back until the middle of January. I think Paige has missed having them around – but only to a certain extent. I get along just fine with them, but Paige finds her Mum a little hard work sometimes. Carol's one of those *'oh, we're more like sisters than mother-and-daughter'* Mums, and Paige finds it a bit much. Carol's a good-looking woman, for her age I mean, but the trouble is, she kind of knows it, too. Paige, on the other hand, is the complete opposite – she's absolutely drop-dead gorgeous, and is completely oblivious to the fact – despite how often I remind her!

My phone pings, and I stretch to reach it from the little table beside Paige's couch. It's a message from Jason, and both the content of the message and the attached photo have me laughing so hard that I feel like I'm either going to cry or be sick, so I pass the phone to a puzzled-looking Paige, and almost instantly, she's in the same condition.

Jason and Heather have taken what can only really be described as the most absurd Christmas selfie I've ever seen. Hev is dressed in a full Santa suit, including beard, and is swigging from a bottle of sherry, standing back-to-back with Jason, who has – voluntarily, I don't doubt for even a second – donned a short, vivid green, 'sexy elf' costume, including candy-cane striped tights, hat, and pointy ears, and is drinking from a bottle of what looks to be the supermarket's second cheapest bottle of champagne.

Paige passes the phone back to me, still howling with laughter, and I look at the message one more time.

> *JASON*
> *Merry Christmas, my favourite pair of*
> *hetero knob-ends. Love H and J xoxo*

Kate: Afternoon

'Gran, for God's sake, you can't say that!' a mortified Fiona admonishes our wee Granny, as Dad chokes on a bit of his turkey and Mum thumps at his back.

'All I'm saying,' Gran continues with neither fear nor shame, 'is that our Katie would maybe be better off finding herself a nice wee boyfriend instead of messing about with lassies. There was none of that carry on back in my day, and we managed all right.'

'You hated my Grampa, though, didn't you, Gran?' I can't resist throwing in a grenade. I've heard all of these rants before, and they make me laugh every time. Our Fi kicks me under the table and I smirk.

'Och aye, hen, I did. He was a hoor-maisterin' arsehole of a man! Thought I didn't know about him sneaking about with that manky wee trollop from McCallum's bakery,' Gran continues, revving up to get started on one of her stories before Mum can put her foot down.

'Mum! It's Christmas Day,' she chides my Gran. 'Can we not have one dinner like a nice, civilised, *normal* family?'

Mum gives me a sneaky side-eye, and I know she's dying to laugh. She knows what I've just done, and I think secretly she's glad to see me joining in and having a bit of a laugh, even if it is kind of at my own expense. I love my Granny to bits, even if she can't quite get her head around the realities of being bisexual. She's from a different time and a different place, and I know that everything she says, no matter how out there, wacky or downright offensive it seems, comes from a place of pure love for her family.

'Christ, Alice,' Dad says to my Gran, still clearing his throat, 'you nearly seen me away there.'

'Aye, chance would be a fine thing, Billy,' Gran winks at him, and the entire table erupts in laughter once again.

After we finish dinner, Ewan insists on helping Mum clear the table, and Fiona ushers me into the living room for a catchup over a barely touched glass of wine, which is still giving me the absolute fear when I look at it.

'Right, come on then, wee sis, tell me all about it,' she says, as we settle into Mum's comfy corner sofa.

'I just didn't see it coming,' I tell her, even though that's probably not entirely true. I think if I'm being honest with myself, I did, and I just didn't want to admit or accept it. I can't lie. Fi knows me better than that. 'Maybe I did. I don't know.'

'And had she been seeing the other girl for a while?' Fi asks.

I shake my head. 'Not long. I don't think so, at least. I suppose I knew on some level that she wasn't really happy. I just didn't want to confront her with it, or even admit it to myself. We hadn't been ourselves for a while. Still, though, I didn't think she'd have moved on so quickly. Two years isn't exactly just a quick wee fling, know what I mean?'

'Cow,' Fi says, and the sharpness of her tone catches me a little off-guard. I think she can see it in my eyes, too. 'Sorry, I shouldn't have said that. Just being an over-protective big sister. You know I always thought the world of Steph, despite all of her,' she pauses for a moment, choosing her words carefully, '...quirks.'

'Her quirks?' I repeat, curious to see where this is going.

'Och, I don't know. Maybe I'm just seeing something that isn't quite there,' she says, trying to put it together in her own mind first. 'It was just something I always sensed was in the background of your relationship. It's like, you've always known you're bi, right? And you were always open with Steph about your past relationship history.'

'Right?' I say, trying to follow.

'Well, Steph hadn't had that experience before you, had she?'

'How do you mean?' I ask, genuinely confused.

'She'd never dated anyone who was openly bi. She's gay. She's always known that she's gay. And all of her previous partners before you were, I'm guessing, gay. I always kind of got the impression that... well, I guess it's as if she was waiting for the penny to drop with you. Like she sometimes struggled to fully accept that you'd been with guys before, too. She loved

27

you, Katie, I don't doubt that for a second. But looking back on it with the benefit of hindsight, I'm not sure she was ever able to be completely one hundred percent secure in your relationship in case, I dunno, in case it was just a phase for you?'

'God, you're good at this,' I say, a little sadly.

'Women are complicated, sis,' she laughs. 'That's why I married Ewan.' She looks through to the kitchen, where Ewan is standing beside Mum, washing dishes while she dries. He drops a plate back into the sink and some soapy water splashes his shirt. She smiles to herself. 'He's as uncomplicated as it gets.'

'Shut up, you,' I laugh, playfully slapping her arm. 'Ewan's lovely.'

'He's going free to a good home. Make me a decent offer!' she laughs.

'Here, maybe Gran had a point after all,' I joke. 'Maybe I *should* just find myself a nice wee boyfriend to settle down with?'

'With your history of boyfriends?' she laughs, her turn to playfully punch my arm, 'I'm not sure you'd make much better choices than you do with women!'

'Oh my God, you're not wrong. Remember Danny?'

'BMX Guy!' Fi shrieks.

'Every time we'd have an argument about something, he'd get his bike out of the shed and go out because he "needed his own space!" He ended up getting back together with the girl who lived two doors down from his Mum because she still had her bike. Which wouldn't have been half as cringe if we'd been eleven, and not twenty!'

'At least he went outside and got fresh air and exercise, even if it was to seek the company of like-minded bike enthusiasts. Not like—'

'Don't say it, Fi. Don't you bloody dare!' I put my hands to my flushing cheeks, mortified at the memory.

'Dungeons and Dragons Guy!' she erupts, almost spilling her

wine on Mum's couch. I squirm in embarrassment and cover my face with my hands. 'The one who used to insist on addressing you as "m'lady" or "fair maiden." Oh my God, Katie, what were you even thinking?'

'His name was Patrick. Even if he did prefer to be known as "Sir Wulfric of Elm's Door, Slayer of Orcs and Liberator of the Silenced."' I shake my head and close my eyes. I can't even with my sister sometimes. Dad sticks his head around the door, having heard the uproar. His Christmas cracker crown is sitting squinty on his greying head.

'Alright in here, girls?'

'Our Fi's making me feel better, Dad. You've to tell her to stop!' I say, giggling myself. But I'm right, she really is making me feel better.

'Fiona, you've to stop trying to make your sister feel better. I'll have none of that business under my roof, do you understand?' he winks and ducks back out, leaving us to it.

I wipe my eyes, not sure I've been crying from sadness or hilarity or some mixture of both, and we settle back on the couch. Fi puts her glass down and takes my hand.

'Just a wee bit of advice, sister to sister?' she says softly and sincerely.

'Mm hm,' I nod. Our Fiona never steers me wrong.

'Don't rush back into anything, Katie. Just take a wee bit of time to heal from this. It's been a shock to the system, and it's going to take you a while to get over it. Any time you're struggling, no matter what time of the day or night, you can pick up your phone and call me, or send me a text. I love you to bits, sis. And so do Mum and Dad. All we ever want is to see you happy. So maybe the best thing for you right now is to spend a wee bit of time learning how to love yourself as much as we all love you.'

And for approximately the millionth time since we were kids, our Fi is one hundred percent correct.

Matt: Night

Paige just stepped out of the shower, and she smells absolutely amazing. She's leaning over her dressing table, moisturising and I am having to fight the urge to do very, very bad things to her. She's wearing that little electric blue satin pyjama set I like so much, the one with the tiny shorts and the lacy, strappy top. She's also wearing the necklace I gave her this morning. She sees me looking at her in the mirror and smiles at me.

'What?' she asks, self-consciously, as if she doesn't light up every room she walks into.

'Nothing, babe. I'm just happy.' And I can say that with my hand on my heart.

'What's making you so happy? The wine? The salted caramel cheesecake you inhaled?' she winks at me.

'You. You make me happy,' I say. 'Although that cheesecake was pretty damn tasty, I have to admit.'

'Oh, it was, was it?' she grins, and then wiggles her bum slightly, just enough that she knows I notice. Tease. She is absolutely glorious. I want her right now.

She slides into bed beside me, and her hand – not completely by accident, of that I'm certain – brushes lightly past something which makes it more than obvious how excited just looking at her makes me. She smirks and raises a perfectly threaded and shaped eyebrow at me.

'Does Santa Baby have one more present to give me?' she giggles.

'Well, now that depends. Have you been an awful good girl this year?' I ask, acutely aware that I am walking a very fine line between keeping the flirting going and lapsing into mood-killing silliness.

'Mmm, maybe you should double check the naughty list. You might find my name on there,' she bats her eyelashes.

'God, I hope so,' I whisper.

'I love you,' she says, as she flicks off the lamp on her

bedside table.

'...to the moon and back,' I finish her sentence in the darkness, and without another word, she pulls me closer to her and we kiss.

Kate: Night

It's just me and Dad now. He's taken Fiona's place on the couch, and we're watching rubbish on TV while Mum soaks in a well-deserved hot bath with one of the huge selection of scented bath bombs she's been given for Christmas. Fi and Ewan have called it a night too, delivering Gran safely home in their taxi before heading back to their lovely little detached house down in the south side suburbs. She didn't realise I saw her nipping Ewan's bum on the way out to the taxi. Fiona, that is. Not Gran. Gran didn't nip Ewan's bum. I wouldn't put it past her, right enough. Especially after a couple of sherries.

'Stay just a wee while longer, pal?' Dad says. 'I've missed you.'

'I've missed you too, Dad,' I say, and rest my head on his shoulder.

'I'm sorry it didn't work out with Stephanie,' he says. 'I liked her.'

'I did too,' I say, sadly.

My Dad looks like a grizzly bear and acts like a teddy bear. He's gruff and he's crotchety and he's possibly the most loving human being I've ever met. He adores Mum, and I know without him even having to say it that Fi and I are his whole world. But he does say it, though. And often. It's a rare thing for men of his generation, but Dad is completely and utterly free with his emotions and with his love, when it comes to the three women in his life. He calls Ewan 'son,' and his heart broke completely when he and Mum had to have Charlie, the wee Cavalier King Charles Spaniel who grew up with Fi and I, put to sleep a couple of years ago. I've never seen a man look so completely and utterly lost as he was without that wee dog.

'Promise me something?' he says quietly.

'Anything, Dad,' I say as I squeeze his hand.

'Don't ever give up on love,' he says. 'I overheard our Fiona talking to you earlier. And I'm not saying she's not right, in a way. It's important that you take a wee bit of time after this, just to learn how to be happy being you. That's a good thing. But you're like me, pal. And I mean this in the best way possible. See people like you and me? We're made to love. We're so absolutely filled with it, that it overflows from us. And for us not to spend every waking second of our lives letting the people that we love most in the world know and feel it, that would just be selfish of us.'

My Dad, Billy McArdle, ladies and gentlemen. Says nothing for hours at a time, quite content just sitting reading his paper, or chuckling away at something stupid on the telly. Then, completely out of nowhere, hits out with something like that. God, I love my family.

I'm in the taxi on the way back to my empty flat, still thinking about what Dad said, when the driver, a chatty middle-aged lady with short silver hair and twinkling eyes, somewhere around the same age as Mum, if I had to guess, looks at me in her rear-view mirror and interrupts my train of thought.

'You had a good wee night then, pal?'

I smile at hearing her call me that. 'The best. Christmas dinner with my parents and my sister. It's just great catching up with family sometimes, you know what I mean?'

'I do, darling. Tell you this, as long as you've got your Mammy and Daddy in your corner, you'll never go far wrong. No matter how old you are.'

I turn the key in the lock and open the flat door. I get inside, turn the hall light on, and lock the door behind me. It's quiet, because as I immediately remember, I now live on my own. I walk into the living room and turn on the Christmas tree lights. For the briefest of moments, I think about maybe taking the tree down and packing it away, because without Steph here, it doesn't really feel like Christmas. But that's not me. That's not who I am. I'm the girl who loves Christmas, even if this one hasn't worked out quite how I'd imagined it.

So, I decide I'm not going to take the tree down. Not just yet, anyway. I'm going to keep it up for a few more days, I'm going to allow myself to feel whatever it is that I need to feel, and I'm going to love myself as unconditionally as my family.

The question is, though, how am I going to do that? I'm not planning on doing any work for the next couple of days, so I won't have that to distract me and keep my mind off my mind. And if I just sit around the flat, I'm going to end up wallowing in self-pity when I look at all of the empty spaces Steph used to fill. I'm going to need something to keep me occupied, so I don't end up doing something I'll end up regretting, because God knows, my brain seems to be intent on telling me to pick up the phone and call her every five minutes.

Without even thinking about it, I *do* pick up my phone, but not to call Steph. I tap *'what's on in Glasgow this week?'* into the search bar and wait for the results. The panto is still running at the Pavilion, but that feels like more of a 'run up to Christmas' event. There's the indoor carnival at the Exhibition Centre which runs right through until January. That's a possibility, I'll come back to that. But then I think about it again, and wonder if it'll be jam-packed with loved-up couples and boozed-up wee neds? I'm not sure I'm ready for that just yet. I need something where I can just be anonymously on my own. Where I can just *be*.

A concert, maybe? Loud music. A dark venue. A couple of drinks to throw a wee blanket of confidence buzz over any self-consciousness I might feel about being out by myself.

This might work.

I start scrolling down the gig guide to see what's on in town this week. The choice is a little more limited than I'd hoped, with most of the venues in town seemingly focusing on either 'late Christmas' or 'early New Year' party and event nights. In fact, there's only one gig which meets my criteria of being cheap, being local and tickets being readily available, and it's on Wednesday night. Just close enough to give me something to look forward to for a day or so. The problem is, I have no idea who the band are, and their name doesn't inspire a huge amount of confidence that it's going to be a fun night out. But it's this or sit and mope at home alone, so we are where we are.

What kind of name for a band is Cramping Pussée, anyway?

Chapter Four: December 27th

Paige

I'm tired, I'm freezing and soaked through, my train is delayed yet again, and I've had a thoroughly rotten day. I knew when I took this job that I'd have days like this, but honestly, all I've ever wanted to do is practice law. Even if it means having to deal with jumped-up, ignorant, misogynistic little knobheads like Connor bloody McCauley. He's a year younger than me, and barely even qualified himself, but because I'm still completing my two-year traineeship period, he technically has seniority to me, and boy, does he like to remind me of that fact.

Today, he deliberately made a big show of highlighting a tiny, relatively harmless mistake I made in order to – what? Make me look small and incompetent in front of everyone? Make himself feel better about his own position? I don't know. What I do know is this. He's made me more determined than ever to not only see this traineeship through, but to dedicate every second of my career to being a better lawyer than Connor bloody McCauley will ever be.

Right now, though, I am just very, very tired, and I can't wait to get home, even if I do still have a ton of work to do when I get there. At least I know Matt will be waiting to welcome me home with a smile and the biggest, warmest hug. That makes everything else worthwhile. I just need to hear his voice.

I take my phone out of my bag and call him as I wait for my train to pull into the low level platform of Glasgow Central station.

'Hi, babe,' he answers. 'How was your day?'

'It'll be a damn sight better when I get home to you, darling,' I sigh.

'Tough day?' he asks. I don't even know where to start.

'I've had better. Nothing I can't handle, though.'

'At least we still have tonight to look forward to,' he says, and I can almost hear his smile through the phone.

'Tonight?' I ask, momentarily confused, and then I remember. Oh, crap. We'd made plans for tonight. With everything that had happened today, I'd completely forgotten. 'It's Heather's band's gig tonight, isn't it?'

'Did you forget?' He sounds a little disappointed. But knowing Matt like I do, he'd never let me see it. He's never been anything less than completely supportive of my career and ambitions, and I genuinely can't think of a single time where he didn't put me first.

'I am so, so sorry, babe,' I say. 'I've just had so much on my plate.'

I feel awful. He's been working such crazy hours, especially in the run up to Christmas, and I know how much he was looking forward to going out tonight. I know how much he was looking forward to us just being able to spend a little time together. In the distance, I can see my train pulling into the station.

'My train is just getting in,' I tell him. 'I'll be home soon, but I have so much work to do. I'm really sorry, babe. I know how much you were looking forward to tonight.'

'Look,' he says, 'don't worry about tonight. It's not a big deal. How about this? I'll text Hev and let her know we can't make it. She won't mind. I'll nip out to *Piccolo Mondo* and order that lasagne that you like, and we can eat that before you get started on your work?'

'Babe, that sounds— well, it sounds amazing,' I say, and admittedly I'm more than a little tempted by his offer. 'But I don't want you going to all that trouble. Besides, I'm going to be terrible company tonight. I've had a rotten day and I still have loads to do. Don't text Heather. You should still go out tonight.'

'I can't go out without you,' he protests. 'I'd feel like an arsehole leaving you at home alone after the day you've had!'

'And I'm telling you it's your turn to relax and have a little fun. I know how hard you've been working these last few weeks. I'll throw on my comfortable clothes, get my work done, I'll have a nice long soak in a hot bath, and then I'll be feeling much better by the time you get home. You can tell me all about the gig, and who knows, you might even get lucky!'

The man in front of me in the queue for the train turns his head around and smirks. I make a face at him and roll my eyes, and he wisely returns to minding his own business.

'Well, since you put it like that,' Matt says, 'I don't see how I can refuse!'

'He's clearly a wise man,' the eavesdropper mumbles, and I accidentally on purpose jab him in the back with the point of my umbrella. He harumphs. That is quite enough out of you, creepy.

'Have fun tonight,' I say, feeling better purely because I've just spoken to Matt, and that's how he always makes me feel. 'Tell Hev and Jason and the gang that I said hi.'

'Of course I will, babe,' he says as I step up into the carriage.

'Love you,' I start.

'...to the moon and back,' he finishes our sentence.

Matt

The stage at G2, despite it being the grungier and more attitude-y little sibling which hides behind the back of the Garage venue on Glasgow's Sauchiehall Street, is still the biggest one upon which Cramping Pussée have played, and Heather sounds uncharacteristically nervous.

'I'm absolutely shitting my knickers,' is how she phrases it, and Jason almost spits his vodka and cola all over me.

'Ever the lady, Hev,' I laugh.

'He's more of a lady than I'll ever be,' she says, nodding at Jason.

'And a fabulous one at that, darling,' he snorts, all hyperactive high camp and full of excitement, like a punk rock Alan Cumming. 'Right, c'mon you,' he yanks at her sleeve. 'I've my hair to get done before we go on. And you'll be needing a fresh pair of scants, apparently.'

'Meet you at the bar when we finish,' Heather says as she's dragged away. 'You know the drinks order by now.'

'Break a leg,' I laugh. 'Or a nail, or something less painful.'

I wish Paige could have made it along tonight. I still feel a little shitty for leaving her at home alone, even if she is snowed under with work. Heather and Jason were completely understanding when I explained. I never doubted it, of course. But still, I wish she was here. Not because I've got any issues standing around like a Billy No Mates when Hev and J are playing their set, but just because I know how hard she's been working, and she deserves a night out. Even if that night out involves a fair amount of jumping around, jostling in crowds, avoiding flying pints of (what I hope and pray is) lager and listening to shouty songs with titles like 'The Ovary Overlords Can Eat Me,' 'Mansplain Me Again and Die' and my own particular favourite, 'I've Got a Castration Fascination.'

I get myself another beer and stake out a decent position just off to the side, and safely out of the way of most of the carnage which is undoubtedly about to occur. This isn't my first time at the Cramping Pussée rodeo. I see a few familiar faces jostling against the barrier at the front of the stage, most of whom are student friends of Luisa, the band's boisterous Portuguese lead singer and all-round force to be reckoned with. She and Heather met when they took a class together, bonded immediately over a shared love of obscure nineties Riot Grrrl bands, and within the week, Cramping Pussée was born.

The lights go down and a few scattered cheers come from the back of the club as Hev, Jason and Shazza, the fourth member of the band, take their places on the stage. Without saying a word, Heather picks out the rumbling bassline to their usual opening number, 'My Uterus, My Rules,' and we're away. I spend so much time having to deal with Hev's goofing around at work that sometimes I actually forget not only how seriously she takes her music, but just how bloody good she is at it. She and Jason have that perfect, almost psychic connection that every good rhythm section needs, which is probably just as well as they spend almost every waking second together.

Jason's drums and Shazza's guitar come crashing in, and then Luisa hits the stage and her adoring support erupts. She's like a whirling dervish, all bronze skin and swirling, whipping dreadlocks in her crop top, baggy camo trousers and oxblood boots, instantly grabbing the attention of the casual observers near the back. I forget that this happens whenever people see the band for the first time. It's the name, I'm sure of it. People read it and don't take them seriously until they actually start playing. I once made the mistake of asking Hev if they'd ever thought about changing it, and you'd have been forgiven if you'd assumed I'd asked if she'd ever considered nailing puppies to a tree.

'Our pu-*ssayyys* will not be silenced by you, Mister Representative of the Patriarchy,' she said as she punched my arm. J simply grinned and shrugged, and I made a mental note to never again raise the matter.

As they rip through the song, I see the grins on Heather and Jason's faces as they look at each other, completely lost in the music. In another universe, they'd be the perfect couple. In this one, they're the absolute definition of platonic soulmates. I catch Hev's eye and she winks at me as I raise my beer to salute them.

I take a mouthful of my drink and do some quick mental gymnastics. Do I have enough time for another one before they finish their set and the serious drinking commences? I run through which songs they still have to play and decide that I do. Before that, though, another item of business needs to be taken care of, and with some urgency.

As I step out into the foyer and make my way towards the bathrooms, a short girl barrels out of the ladies' room with her head down, completely oblivious to anything in her path... which is, essentially, me, and the remains of the beer in the plastic tumbler in my hand. I pause for a moment, not sure what the shock I suddenly feel is. At first, I suspect it's the sudden coldness and wetness of my t-shirt clinging to my chest. That'll be my beer, it occurs to me.

Then I realise that's not what's caught me off-guard. The girl responsible for me now wearing the last of my beer is standing in front of me, looking at up me with a quizzical look in her wet eyes and on her pretty, round, mascara-streaked face.

I can read the look in her eyes. It's same one I have. It's a kind of puzzled semi-recognition.

'I'm so, so sorry,' she sniffs, wiping at her eyes with the heel of her hand. And then, 'Wait, have we met before?'

I'm almost certain that we have. But where? She looks up at me again and her eyes glisten.

'You're the kind cake and coffee guy,' she says, and then it registers with me.

And you're Sad Girl, I think, but don't say out loud.

Kate

Once again, I feel so bloody stupid.

'He's not worth it, sweetheart, whoever he is,' says the random drunk girl with her arm around my shoulder in an effort to console me as I stand looking at myself in the mirror of the ladies' bathroom in G2.

The bottle of wine I'd drunk in the flat before coming out in order to steady my nerves seemed like a good idea at the time, but now I'm regretting it. I'd been feeling anxious all day about going out alone tonight, and more than once I'd seriously thought about just giving it a miss altogether. Not because of any safety concerns about being out in town alone, but just because it's been so long since I've done it.

'He's an arsehole and he doesn't deserve you,' she continues loudly, releasing me so she can touch up her own eyeliner.

All I wanted was to not have to think about Steph for a little while, but that's all I've done since I've been here. I keep going over it, wondering what I did that was so wrong. Wondering why I'm not enough. I'm so stupid. Just a stupid emotional mess. No wonder Steph doesn't want to be with me anymore. No wonder I can't hold down a relationship. Look at the state of me. I wouldn't even want to be with me when I see myself like this.

'C'mon,' the girl says. 'Chin up, tits out, lippy on and get a drink down you. What is it that Luisa always says?'

I look at her blankly. I have no idea what she's talking about or who this Luisa is.

'"We're living in a Fem-ocracy," that's it. You don't need a man, babe. You're better than whoever's made you feel like this. Know your worth.'

I nod and give her a weak smile, largely, I have to admit, in the hope that she'll think it's job done and leave me be. 'Femocracy, yeah,' I agree.

Yet again, I'm left staring at a panda-eyed nutjob in the mirror. This time, thankfully, in this particular crowd, the makeup doesn't look entirely out of place. For a minute, I think about going back to the bar and getting another drink, but I know that would be a terrible idea. I think I just need to get out of here and go home. This was a bad idea. I'm not ready to do this just yet.

I can feel the tears ready to start again. I need to go home now. I turn and open the door, keeping my head down so no-one can see the mess I'm in, and I head out into the foyer. Keeping my head down, of course, means that I'm not paying much attention to anything other than getting the hell out of there and heading home. And I'm certainly not paying attention to whoever it is that I've just run straight into.

I'm startled, but obviously have no right to be. This is entirely my fault. I look up, then back down, seeing this poor guy's t-shirt, soaked with his own drink, then back up. Ugh. Just what I needed. I try to get out some mumbled apology, but I feel as though my throat is closing up. I want the ground to just open up and swallow me now. I try to compose myself.

'I'm so, so sorry,' I just about manage to get out as I look up at the guy. He's head and shoulders taller than me, and for just the briefest of moments, I am very afraid that I'm going to either be punched or thrown out for causing a disturbance. However, neither of those things happen. I look at him again. He doesn't look angry. His face is kind, concerned, and even somewhat familiar, but I have no idea how. I wipe my eyes with the heel of my hand and sniff.

'Wait, have we met before?' I ask, vaguely aware and acutely embarrassed that this could pass for the world's shittest chat-up line. That's not what it is, though. I genuinely feel like I've met this guy somewhere before. It's his eyes. I just can't put my finger on it. Jesus, Kate, you're staring. Say something. Say anything. He's going to think you're a loony.

And, just like that, it's hit me. I remember him now. I know where I've seen this guy.

'You're Kind Cake and Coffee Guy,' I blurt out, and then realise that there's no way he's going to know what I'm talking about. Instead, though, I see a flicker of recognition in his eyes. His warm, kind, smiling blue eyes.

'From the coffee shop at the Fort, right?' I ask. He smiles and nods.

'Matt,' he says. 'My name's Matt.'

His smile disappears as he looks at me again, but for the life of me, I can't read why.

'Are you okay?' he asks. 'Do you need to get some fresh air or something?'

'Yeah, I was thinking about just heading home, to be honest. More than enough excitement for one day for me.'

He looks down at his soaking t-shirt and then back into the

club where the band is still playing. I feel awful. I wonder if I should offer to buy him a drink to replace that one, but I'm worried he'll misread my intentions. Instead, I say nothing. I look down at the floor.

'I think I could use some fresh air myself,' he says.

We head for the exit of G2 and walk out onto Sauchiehall Street, just me and this strange man, and part of me wonders if I'm about to make the biggest mistake of my life.

Matt

I should have worn something warmer than just a t-shirt and a denim jacket tonight. It's bloody freezing. Mind you, I wasn't planning on standing out on Sauchiehall Street with a woman with puffy, bloodshot eyes, shivering from the cold and the beer soaking my t-shirt. I didn't dress for that. I did say I wanted some fresh air, though. Mental note to be careful what you wish for, I guess.

Sad Girl and I are standing outside of the club, and I'm not entirely sure what to say to her. I pull my jacket closed and start buttoning it up. I don't care if it ends up smelling of lager. It'll wash and I'm cold.

A taxi whizzes past us, through one of the thick, icy, grey-brown puddles, sending a splosh of dirty wet slush onto the pavement, narrowly missing us. I step back from the road a little and take a look around. Just behind us, the bright yellow front half of a truck which explodes out of the façade of the Garage, just above the entrance. On the other side of the street, a small, intimate live music venue called Box, where Cramping Pussée played a number of their earliest gigs. A few doors down, the Colonel tempts with his chicken.

A group of well-groomed lads, probably around the same age as us, walk past. Most likely headed to one of the casinos just along the street. One of them looks at Sad Girl as she wipes at her eyes, and I'm almost sure I see him smirk, which makes me bristle a little. Given the numbers, though, probably best to let it go.

Directly across the road from us, two belligerent drunks are getting into a shoving match on the pavement outside Nice N Sleazy, and the bouncers are trying to convince them to either calm down or take their disagreement elsewhere.

I look at Sad Girl for a moment. I don't want to stare. I don't want to look for too long in case she catches me looking and gets the wrong idea. She's tiny, petite, barely a nudge over five feet, if I were to guess. Dark brown hair, dark eyes, accentuated by the now-ruined mascara and eyeliner. She's pretty, I think. Like, 'girl next door' pretty. I don't know. Maybe it's just her sadness and vulnerability. She looks open and honest. I look away again.

I don't know what comes next. I'm not sure what it is that I'm supposed to say now. I just wanted to make sure Sad Girl was okay, and she certainly appears to be now. Better than she was ten minutes ago, at least. And much better than she was the last time I saw her, crying into her girlfriend's scarf in the coffee shop.

'It's freezing,' she says, her own breath coming out in a white puff, hanging in the air in front of her. 'Want to go for a walk?'

I look around us, suddenly very conscious that I'm a complete stranger to this girl. How does this even look? To bystanders, I mean. Vulnerable, upset woman leaves the club with an unknown man. This is *literally* how the report on the news normally begins. 'She was last seen leaving the club with an unknown man.' What's the protocol for this? What if someone saw us leaving together and got the wrong idea? How easy would it be to misconstrue or misinterpret what's just happened? I even think about making my excuses and heading for home, but I look at her again, and I don't think I have it in me to do that to her right now. All I wanted was to make sure she was okay.

'Are you sure? You don't even know me,' I say, trying to find just the right balance between sounding reassuring without giving her the wrong idea. 'I'm a complete stranger. I could be a pervert or a murderer or a Tory or something.'

'And are you?' she asks, almost smiling. 'A pervert or a murderer, I mean?'

'Well, no,' I laugh. 'But then, I probably wouldn't admit to it if I was, would I?'

'That's a very good point,' she says. She looks down at the pavement. I shiver again. She looks back up at me. 'But I don't think you are.'

'Okay. Good. I think. Yeah.'

'What I think you are, Matt, is a good person,' she says, still looking at me.

'Well, thanks. But if you don't mind me asking, what are you basing that on?' I ask. I don't know if I really want to hear her answer or not.

'I'm basing it on the fact that, for the second time in the last four days, you're the stranger who's been nice to me when I've been upset. You saw me when I made an arse of myself in your coffee shop, and instead of asking me to leave because I was causing a scene, or just ignoring how bloody awkward it was, you brought me a bit of cake and a coffee, and you took the time to ask if I was okay. And now, tonight, I've come running into you like a nutter, spilling your drink all over you, I've ruined your night out, and once again, you've gone out of your way just to make sure I'm okay.'

'True,' I shrug. 'And *are* you okay now?'

'Better,' she replies.

'Good,' I say. And I mean that. I don't know this girl, but I'm genuinely glad she feels a little better now. And I have to admit to myself, I'm glad that I was able to help in some small way.

'So now we've established that you're not a pervert and you're probably not going to murder me,' she says. 'There's just one other thing we need to address.'

'What's that?' I ask.

'You're still a stranger,' she smiles. 'But technically, you won't be if you know me.'

She extends her hand for me to shake. I take it.

'I'm Kate.'

Kate

We're walking along Sauchiehall Street, heading back in the direction of the City Centre, and there's another little flurry of snow beginning to fall. In the distance, I can see Buchanan Galleries and the Christmas lights, and for the first time today, I don't feel like a complete and utter wreck. I passed the Galleries on the way down to G2 earlier, and all I could think about were the times Steph and I would go shopping there, and it was all I could do not to turn around and go straight back home to my empty flat. Now here I am. Here *we* are. I don't know what this is, but I know it's not *that*, and right now, that's enough.

It's bloody cold, though. I could have dressed a little warmer, I suppose. That's the thing about nights out, isn't it? You're never quite sure which direction they're going to take. I came out expecting to just listen to some music and then go home. Walking along Sauchiehall Street in the snow with a strange guy I've just spilled a drink over wasn't really on tonight's agenda.

'Do you want to talk about it?' Matt asks.

'About what?' I ask. 'What happened tonight, you mean?'

'Yes. If you like. If not, that's okay, I don't mind. Just making conversation,' he says.

I don't even know if I'm ready to revisit it again. In a way, I feel like I've spent enough time and emotional energy talking about Steph over the last couple of days. First with Mum and Dad, and then with our Fiona. But I don't know. Maybe it would be nice to get a stranger's perspective on it, too? It's not like we're going to see each other again, as long as I remind myself that I can never go back into that coffee shop at the

Fort. I could easily just drunkenly spill my guts about everything, knowing that I won't have the embarrassment of waking up tomorrow morning and going 'Oh my God, why the hell did I say all of that? How can I ever show my big stupid face in public again?'

'Sure,' I say. 'How much do you want to know? I'm a mess, and you might not have enough time for me to cover it all.'

He smiles and shrugs, and it gives me a warm feeling. 'I've got plenty of time.'

The snow is falling a little heavier now. We keep walking and looking up at the lights.

'I thought about you after you left the shop the other night,' he says. 'Sorry, I didn't mean that the way it came out. Just— I couldn't help wondering what had happened. And I wondered if you were okay after you left. I hoped you were.'

'The cake helped,' I smile. 'I feel like I never did get to thank you properly for that. I was absolutely mortified. I just wanted the ground to open up and swallow me. I don't imagine you get drama like that every day.'

'Not every day,' he smiles back. 'And you're welcome. Although my friend Heather was annoyed that I didn't lurk around your table to get the full gory details out of you.'

'It's a man thing, isn't it? You feel more comfortable not being too involved in it all. Not that there's any gory details, really. I mean, other than the fact that she already had my replacement lined up!'

He winces. 'I kinda figured that part out. Sorry. That's a bit crap.'

'It hurt,' I say. 'Not even gonna lie. I knew things hadn't been the best between us lately, but I'd no idea she felt that little for me. I just felt so humiliated, you know? Like I'd been made a complete fool of for all that time.'

He gives me a sympathetic smile. 'Were you together for a while?'

'Two years, give or take.'

'That's rough,' he says. 'What was the final straw? I mean,

breaking up with someone two days before Christmas. Who even does that?'

I'm not sure whether he's completely tactless, or just feels comfortable enough with me to be able to ask a question like that.

'Boiled eggs,' I say, smiling sadly. He looks utterly flummoxed. 'Never mind, long story.'

I can feel myself starting to get a little emotional and reflective, and I don't think I want to go back down that road. At least, not tonight. I think he can see it in my face, too.

'We can talk about something else, if you want,' he offers.

I think about it for a second, but it occurs to me that there's something else that I want more. I didn't eat much of Mum's Christmas dinner, amazing as it was, and if I've eaten much of anything else in the forty-eight hours since, I certainly don't remember it. That's the heartbreak diet for you. For the first time in four days, though, my stomach is gnawing at me and I feel like I could eat. The smell coming from the shawarma place just across the road is making my mouth water, and since, let's face it, it's not like I have anyone to impress by getting naked right now, I think I deserve a little comfort food.

'Are you hungry?' I ask him, motioning across to the takeaway. 'Can I get you something to eat? Just my way of saying thanks, really. For listening to me and for making sure I was okay.'

'Nah,' he says, and I'm surprised that I feel a little twinge of disappointment in his refusal of my offer. 'I'm fine, thanks. But I'll keep you company if you want to get something.'

'What a year this is turning out to be,' I sigh, only half-jokingly. 'Dumped at Christmas, embarrassing myself on multiple occasions in front of a perfectly nice, kind and understanding stranger, and now I can't even buy him some pakora by way of an apology.'

'Well, if you're going to guilt trip me,' he smiles, 'I'm pretty sure I could force a kebab down.'

We cross the street, dodging taxis and trying not to slip on the rapidly freezing road, and duck inside the warm shop, shaking off the snowflakes.

'Two donner kebabs, please, boss,' I say. I think for a moment. 'And a portion of mixed pakora. Better throw in a portion of chips, too. Large. In fact, make it chips and cheese.'

The man behind the counter raises his eyebrow at me as he peers over the counter, probably trying to work out how many people I'm ordering for.

'It's been a rough few days,' I shrug, by way of an explanation, and out of the corner of my eye, I can see Matt grinning.

Matt

'How can you honestly sit there and try to tell me that you enjoy mushroom pakora? Like, you *actually* enjoy it. Like you'd buy a portion of *just* mushroom pakora?' she asks me.

'I would, and I have done,' I reply. 'It's my favourite. Mushroom, then chicken, then the ordinary veg one. In that order.'

'What about fish?' she asks.

'Right, now *you're* just at it,' I laugh. 'Nobody's deliberately ordering fish pakora. If you want deep-fried fish, you get yourself along to a chip shop and get a fish supper.'

That's enough to get a grin out of her, and I'm glad. Smiling definitely suits her more than being sad does. But, really, shouldn't that always be the case for everyone?

We're sitting on a little wooden bench across the street from the kebab shop, our backs to the road, and facing the Centre for Contemporary Arts, which has a number of flyers for upcoming events and exhibitions in the window. There's a tree beside me which is sheltering us from the worst of the snow flurries, but if I'm being entirely honest, I'd stopped noticing the snow quite some time ago. I take another piece of the mushroom pakora which Kate refuses to touch and make an exaggerated show of eating and enjoying it. She rolls her eyes at me. It feels almost wrong in a way. Being almost stone cold sober and eating a meal which, for all intents and purposes, should be labelled *"Do not eat unless the pub is shut and/or it's no earlier than 2am,"* yet here we are, and it's not even 10 on a Wednesday night.

'So,' I say, as I feed myself strips of greasy donner kebab meat from one of the boxes sitting between us on the bench. 'You already know what I do for a living, I guess. What about you?'

'I'm a journalist. A writer. Magazine articles, mainly,' she says, off-hand. I'm impressed.

'No way. Really?' I ask. I don't think I'd ever have guessed that. She has that bohemian, West End, hipster look of someone who works in one of those antique book shops or chic retro clothing boutiques on Byres Road. Or a cook in a vegan café on Great Western Road or the southside, maybe.

'Really,' she says. 'Although I'm making it sound a little more glamorous than it is, really. Mostly I'm just sitting in my spare room eating snacks in my pants and an old curry-stained t-shirt. And that's on a good day when I can be bothered to get dressed at all!'

'Who do you write for? Would I have seen your work anywhere?' I ask, genuinely curious.

'I doubt it,' she laughs. 'Unless you're interested in finding information on fifty ways to satisfy your lover on Valentine's Day, or working out which Disney Prince is your soulmate based on your zodiac sign. You know the ultimate irony, now that I think about it? I wrote a piece last month called *"Is your man cheating? Take this quiz to find out if he's being unfaithful."* Makes me question my own journalistic credentials, that.'

'Still, though. You're a writer. That's impressive,' I say, and she brightens up again. 'Really. I sometimes daydream about being a writer.'

'Yeah?' she replies. She dips into the cheese-covered chips

and eats a handful. She's still looking at me like she's waiting for me to tell her more.

'Yeah. I've always wanted to write a novel,' I say, a little embarrassed at hearing myself say it out loud. I feel a bit pretentious and cringey now.

'So why don't you? Or why haven't you?' she asks.

'I've started,' I reply. 'Quite a few times, really. But that's my problem, I always start them and never finish any. It's like, I get these ideas that I think might be quite interesting, but when it comes down to actually sitting down and turning it into a real story, I don't know. It's like I lose interest or something? Like I can't imagine how I get from the start to the end. I don't even know if that makes sense.'

I feel so incredibly awkward. I've never told anyone about that, not even Paige. I mean, it's not like I can't write or anything. I can put a sentence together. It just feels like something– like an idea that's so stupid and far-fetched that I shouldn't even bother talking about it, because people will just laugh.

'I think you should keep trying,' she smiles. 'Your life is probably far more interesting and full of inspiration than you think it is, you know. You work in a coffee shop in a busy shopping centre. You probably see all kinds of bizarre stuff happening every day.'

'Well, a while back I did see this mad lassie having a bit of a meltdown when her girlfriend broke up with her.'

'Too soon!' she laughs and punches my arm. I'm pleased that got a laugh out of her. That has to be a good sign.

'Yeah, I've got a bit of a problem with that,' I say. 'My girlfriend Paige is forever telling me my filters are completely broken. I sometimes forget that not everyone is a completely terrible person like me!'

'Well, for what it's worth, Matt, I don't think you're a terrible person at all. Apart from your odd taste for mushroom pakora, that is. That's a wee bit of a red flag.'

She dips the last piece of the chicken pakora into the little tub of pink sauce. 'Tell me about your girlfriend. Paige, was it?'

'Sure,' I say. 'Why, though?'

'Because you're distracting me, and if there's one thing I definitely need tonight, it's a distraction. Otherwise, I'd be sitting alone in my flat, drinking Baileys from the bottle, eating salted caramel ice cream from the tub and listening to Lewis Capaldi on repeat.'

'Since you put it like that, I think it would be downright negligent of me not to,' I smile.

'Exactly.'

'Well, she's twenty-five, so a year younger than me. Just graduated from Strathclyde Uni and working as a trainee solicitor for a firm in town. She loves art and music, Italian food,' I think for a second. 'And reading daft articles in women's magazines about how tracking your period can help manifest your destiny.'

'I'll have you know that was a difficult piece to finish!' she laughs, and her eyes crinkle at the corners. 'I kept dropping chocolate down my keyboard!'

She pauses for a moment. 'Is she pretty?' she asks, like she's being careful in how she words the question.

'Oh, God, she's beautiful. I mean, she is so out of my league that it's not even funny.'

'Beauty and brains,' she says. 'And here she is, stuck with your goofy arse.'

I let out a little laugh, because, a: she's not wrong, and b: it's not the first time I've heard that, mostly from my own friends.

'How did you meet?' she asks me.

'Friends of friends, I guess. We met at the birthday party of a girl who worked in the shop part-time, and was in her class at Uni. We started talking in the kitchen, found out we loved loads of the same music and movies, and I guess she couldn't resist my obvious charm. What else can I say?'

'Where is she tonight? How come you're out by yourself?' she asks. 'Sorry, you must think I'm a right nosy cow, asking so many questions!'

'She had a lot of work to do tonight. Her workload can get pretty intense sometimes. I did offer to stay in with her and get her some lasagne from Piccolo Mondo and—'

'Oh my God, I bloody *love* Piccolo Mondo's lasagne!' she interrupts, and laughs. 'Sorry!'

'Anyway, I promised my friends I'd come out to their gig, and Paige didn't want me to let them down on account of her having work to do, so... here I am, I guess?'

'Wait, the band who were playing tonight? They're your friends?'

'A couple of them, yes. The bassist and drummer. Heather works with me in the coffee shop, and Jason is her flatmate.'

'Now *I'm* impressed,' she says. 'Look at you, friend of the stars. I feel a wee bit guilty, though, now I know I've dragged you away from them.'

She finishes the last of the chips, and I gather up all of the wrapping paper and plastic containers to deposit into the rubbish bin a few yards back along the street. As fun as tonight has been, it feels like it's coming to an end. I'm very cold, I'm very wet, and I'm pretty sure that Paige will be soaking in a hot bath by now. The thing is, though, I'm not sure that I want it to end just yet. Sad Girl has turned out to be funny, smart and interesting, and as poorly as the night started, it's ended up being a lot of fun.

'It's that awkward time of the evening now, isn't it?' she says.

Once again, it's like she's picked up on what I was thinking. Or maybe I'm just like a book that's too easy to read, and she's seen it on my face. If this was a date, I'd be trying to gauge whether or not to lean in for a kiss and ask if I can see her again. Or if I was out with a mate, I could just say 'catch you later on,' or something equally non-committal where we both know we absolutely will catch up later on. But this isn't either of those things, is it? I don't know exactly what you can call 'getting to know a random person who happens to be gay and happens to be of the opposite sex and that you've quite enjoyed hanging out with.'

I mean, other than 'making friends.'

So, I suppose that's what it is that I'm about to do.

'Add me on Insta if you're on it?' I ask, and immediately feel wracked with insecurity and awkwardness. What if she thinks I'm coming on to her or trying to take advantage? Instead, she just smiles and takes her phone out.

'Katie Mac is a Writer,' she says, and I quickly search and hit the follow icon when I see her profile picture. Obviously an old one. She's with her ex, the other girl from the coffee shop incident, who I've now learned is named Stephanie. I wonder why she hasn't changed the picture yet. Maybe she can't bring herself to do it? Maybe she just hasn't had time? Maybe part of her is trying to pretend it's not over? Who knows?

'I really am sorry about your t-shirt,' she says.

'All is forgiven. You made up for it with the mushroom pakora,' I laugh. 'And your company. Mainly the pakora, but.'

'Thanks for making me feel better again,' she says, and leans in and pecks me on the cheek.

And with that, she's on her feet and into the taxi she's just flagged down. She waves to me as the cab heads off into the drizzling rain which is now falling, turning what's left of the snow into filthy grey slush. My phone, still in my hand, pings.

HEV
What happened, dude? Where did you go?

Balls. I completely forgot I was supposed to meet Heather and Jason at the bar after they finished their set. I could head back down to G2, I suppose, but I'm soaking wet, I'm freezing, and I'm pretty sure they'll have left by now. They're most likely three shots deep in Box or Nice N Sleazy by now, and I don't think I'm equipped for that kind of night out tonight. I'm going to message Hev back and let her know I'm heading home, and that they were great. Even though I missed most of their set. And I know that I'm definitely not ready to have *that* conversation right now.

Just as I'm about to reply, my phone pings again. Give me a chance to reply at least, Hev.

@katiemacisawriter
Thanks again for tonight. I feel so much better. x

I think about replying, but the rain is really starting to fall now, and all I want to do is get back to Paige. I turn up the collar on my jacket, stick my hands into my pockets and head towards Argyle Street, the train station, and home.

Paige

I swear, the person who invented bath bombs deserves a knighthood. I feel like a completely different person to the frozen, wet mess who came home to an empty house laden down with work four hours ago. I say an empty house, but only in as much as Matt had already left when I got in. But he'd gone to so much trouble to make sure it didn't feel deserted, bless his heart.

The first thing that hit me when I opened the door was the smell of Piccolo Mondo's lasagne which he'd gone out and picked up for me and left in the oven to keep warm. The second thing was the Lush bath bomb he'd left sitting on the coffee table for me. Part of me wished I hadn't insisted he go out, so I could have given him a big, squishy 'thank you' hug for being the best boyfriend in the world.

The positive side is that it allowed me to power through the work in about half the time I'd expected it would take, leaving me more time to soak in that hot bath and enjoy the lasagne with a glass of red wine. Okay, *three* glasses of red wine. Stop judging me.

Now, I'm sprawling out on the sofa in my fluffiest housecoat with an aloe vera facemask on, indulging in one of my favourite guilty pleasures: reading a brilliantly nonsensical magazine article titled *'The Skinny Jeans Butt-Camp: Twerk Yourself Sexy!'*

Stop. Judging. Me.

I hear a key in the door and look at the clock. I didn't expect Matt to be home for a while yet. Not that I'm complaining, of course. I hear him taking his shoes off in the hall, and then the living room door opens. He looks freezing cold and soaking wet.

'Hi babe, you're home early,' I smile.

'Yeah, bit of a weird night, really, and it's getting pretty wild out there. Thought I'd be better off heading home for a bit of comfort,' he grins, looking at the state of me. 'Let me stick these into the washing machine and then I'll tell you all about it.'

He disappears back out into the hall and re-emerges a few minutes later wearing a clean t-shirt and grey sweatpants. He flops onto the couch beside me, and I put my freshly pedicured feet in his lap.

'So was the gig good?' I ask. 'How are Heather and J?'

'What I saw of the gig was good, they were great as always,' he says. 'I ended up leaving before they finished, though. Just don't tell Hev that. She'll kill me!'

'What happened that made you leave early?' I ask. I don't remember Matt ever leaving a gig before the end, for as long as I've known him.

'That's the weird bit,' he says. 'I got talking to this girl—'

I raise an eyebrow as I look up from behind my magazine.

'No, not like that,' he squeezes my toes. 'Okay, so we had this bit of mini drama in the shop a few nights ago, and these two girls had this really wild and emotional breakup.'

'What, like splitting up? Like a couple splitting up?' I ask.

'Yeah, exactly. One of them had apparently started seeing someone else and decided to break the news to the other one over coffee. It all happened right in front of us. She literally just got up and walked out and left the other girl crying at her table.'

'Right before Christmas?' I ask. 'Who even does that?'

'I know, right? That's exactly what I said!'

'And then what happened tonight?'

'I was planning to hang about after Hev and Jason finished and have a drink at the bar with them, but while they were still playing, I bumped into the girl who got dumped in the shop.'

'What, like, she recognised you and said hello?' I ask.

'No,' he replies. 'I mean, like *literally* bumped into her. Or she bumped into me, rather. She came running out of the ladies' toilets, a bit emotional, and knocked my beer all over me. That's why my t-shirt's in the washing machine. Anyway, so she was in a bit of a state. Struggling with everything that's happened, I reckon. She went outside to get a bit of fresh air, and I went just to make sure she was okay. She'd had a bit too much to drink, and anything could have happened to her, the condition she was in.'

I don't even doubt that's exactly what happened. For one thing, Matt's never given me a reason not to trust him, and for another, that sounds exactly like the kind of thing he'd do, is make sure someone is okay and look after them when they're clearly in a bad place.

'She wanted to walk back up Sauchiehall Street to clear her head and get a taxi, and I didn't really feel comfortable letting her go alone, so I walked up with her as far as the kebab shop across from the CCA. We sat on the benches for a bit and ate while she straightened up enough to get a taxi home.'

'A romantic Mediterranean dinner date for two! You dirty big charmer,' I half-tease.

'Oh, yeah, that's exactly what it was,' Matt laughs, but I can see he's a little uneasy about it, so I don't push it too far.

'So, what was she like?' I ask. 'Did she deserve to get dumped, do you think?'

'Probably not under those circumstances,' he says. 'But you never really know what goes on behind closed doors, do you? She seemed nice enough, I guess. Funny. Eats like a bloody horse, I can tell you that much.'

'Is she pretty?' I ask and immediately wonder if that's an insecure girlfriend question too far.

'She asked me the exact same question about you,' he laughs. 'You women, I swear. I can't even with you.'

'You told her about me?' I ask, feeling a little relieved. That's my Matt.

'Babe, I tell *everybody* about you. I wake up every day feeling like a lottery winner. Hang on.'

He pulls his phone out of his pocket and swipes Insta open. He shows me the profile photo from an account called @katiemacisawriter. It's a picture of two girls, smiling, cheek to cheek.

'Which one is her?'

'The one on the left. The other one is her girlfriend. Ex-girlfriend now, I guess. She's the one who entertained us with the big dramatic exit in the coffee shop.'

'And her name's Katie?'

'Kate, yeah,' he replies.

'You added her on Insta?' I ask. It's not that I mind, I'm just genuinely curious.

'I felt bad for her,' he says. 'I don't know if maybe she doesn't have a lot of friends or something. I know she works from home, and she was out on her own tonight, so— I dunno, it just felt like the right thing to do? She seems like a nice enough person who's had a bit of a crap time lately. Just the vibe I got from her.'

'Well, now I feel bad for her too,' I say.

And I actually do. I mean, I know Matt's not built for cheating, and I'm secure enough in our relationship that I don't feel the need to scratch the eyes out of any female who comes within fifty feet of him. He's known Heather longer than he's known me, and I know how important her friendship is to him.

Maybe that's part of the equation, though. His relationship with Hev pre-dates me, so it's like I don't really have the right to comment on it, just as Matt would never question me being friends with some of the guys from Uni that I've known longer than him.

But even taking that into consideration, I look at Kate's picture and I don't see a threat. And not just because she happens to be gay. She really just does look like a nice person, and God knows we all need more of those in our lives.

'I'm so lucky,' I say.

'How?' he asks, confused.

I smile at him.

'Because my boyfriend is the kindest, most thoughtful man in the world.'

And I mean that too.

We chat idly for a little longer, just going over my horrendous day at work and finishing the last of the bottle of wine before we head to bed. I kiss Matt goodnight, and as he drifts off into sleep, I pick up my phone from my bedside table and search for Katie Mac on Insta.

Chapter Five: December 28th

Kate

Mental note to self: wine is not your friend, especially when you need to actually get some work done the following day. What on earth was I thinking, going out during the week? Oh, right. I remember what I was thinking. I was thinking 'let's do something that doesn't involve sitting at home alone, eating stupid amounts of ice cream, listening to Lewis bloody Capaldi, and crying because I've been dumped yet again.' Ugh.

At the very least, I've managed to get *"How to Keep Your Partner Satisfied on Valentine's Day"* finished and turned in ahead of the deadline. Now, I'm staring at a screen which is completely blank apart from the title: *"Don't Text Your Ex!"*

I swear to God, even my own career choices are mocking me. I am dangerously unqualified to be advising other women how to get their shit together. I mean, right now, if I had to come up with a list of article topics that I could write honestly and with any kind of authority about, it would look like this:

"Elastic waists are fine. Stop pretending you're a size 6."

"4 ways to blow your own mind in bed."

"Eat the whole pizza if you want, you're a grown adult."

"I forgot to shave my legs for a month and the world didn't end!"

I wash down two paracetamol with a mouthful of energy drink, get up and out of my leather office chair and step away from my desk. I stand in front of the full-length mirror and take a long hard look at myself. My hair looks like a mop-head that's just come out of the washing machine. The less said about my skin, the better. And don't even get me started about my outfit for today's workday. I literally put my hand through the hole in the armpit of the t-shirt I'm wearing as I pulled it over my head this morning, and then decided it was still good enough. Also, I think I'm wearing knickers. I *think*. I'm not one hundred per cent on that, though.

I know, I know. I'm quite the catch. Form an orderly queue, ladies. The Hot Mess Express is now boarding at platform one. Please have your tickets ready for inspection.

I pad barefoot through to the kitchen to investigate the contents of the fridge. Wine doesn't count as lunch. Wow, look at me, being all grown-up and sensible. I take out a tub of cream cheese, pop the two halves of a pre-sliced bagel into the slots on my toaster, and look out of my kitchen window. Last night's rain has washed away all of the snow.

My phone pings from beside the fridge, where I've left it. I walk across the kitchen and retrieve it. I have one unread message. I swipe Insta open.

> *@justplainmatt*
> *Hey, hope you got home safe last night.*
> *Thanks for the kebab and company.*

Oh God, he must think I'm a complete train wreck. I mean, he wouldn't be completely wrong if he did. What the hell was I thinking, just unloading everything like that in front of a complete stranger? Well, a semi-almost-stranger. Still. I am such a red neck. It's all coming back to me, too. I spilled his pint down him, dragged him up Sauchiehall Street in the snow and rain, and made him keep me company! Argh! And why do I have him on Insta now? Did I follow him? Did he follow me? How has that even happened? He probably felt sorry for me or something. Or maybe he's just actually a nice guy and enjoyed my company— despite my many and various quirks?

I don't know how to respond to his message. I don't even know *if* I should respond to it. I look at his profile and the photos he's posted. It's quite a mix. It's definitely not like one of those super-fake 'curated' accounts where every photo is carefully framed, filtered, and perfectly captioned to eliminate any suggestion that it might belong to an actual, real, flawed human person. Matt's isn't like that at all. There are photos of particularly pretty coffee art that he's been proud of, sure, but there are just as many self-effacing ones where his artistic attempts haven't quite hit the mark, and he's happily poking fun at himself. There are goofy, unflattering selfies where he looks quite ridiculous and just a little endearing, I have to admit. There are photos of him with and without his girlfriend, and lots and lots of her alone, and—

Oh. His girlfriend.

Wow.

He wasn't lying or exaggerating at all. She really is quite beautiful. I don't know if these are filtered or not, but even if they are, she's still pretty. And you can just tell she's a nice person, too. For one, she just has that look about her. Like there's no pretence there. And besides, from what I can remember of our conversation last night, he doesn't come across as being the type of guy who would be with a woman for just her looks— even if she does look like a bloody supermodel!

They look amazing together. You know the type, those couples who just 'fit.' They're very different people, but their differences completely complement each other. I bet they're like that. I chomp into my bagel and drop crumbs down my t-shirt, right between my modest— *modest*, I maintain, not *small*, unholstered boobs. I bet Perfect Paige doesn't have this trouble. I make a mental note to go back and have a little look at her profile later, because of course what I really need right now is that kind of boost to my already crumbling self-esteem!

Before that, though, I should reply to his message.

@katiemacisawriter
Home safe, thanks for checking in. Still mortified!

I close the app and try to get myself into some vague semblance of a work-ready mental state. I'm still slightly hungover, my boobs are already being irritated by bagel crumbs, and I've got a half can of energy drink left to power me through churning out 1000 words of sage-like wisdom about why late-night booty calls are not, and I repeat, *not* in your best interest.

Let's do this.

<u>Matt</u>

I smile and stick my phone into the back pocket of my work trousers. We're in that weird period between Christmas and New Year where most people are still off work, spending most of their days full of cheese, confused about what day it is, and debating whether or not it's still too early to start drinking again. Unless you happen to work in a retail environment, that is, particularly one where the Christmas sales are in full flow. It's been full-on so far this morning, but we're experiencing a little bit of a lull now, and Hev and I are taking full advantage of the brief respite to catch up.

'I still can't believe you skipped out early and ditched us, you arsehole,' she says. 'You were supposed to be waiting to adore me and tell me how amazing I was when I got off stage. And don't even get me started about J. You know he's even more needy and attention hungry than I am! I had to put up with him pouting all night because his mancrush bailed on him.'

She grins, but I do still feel genuinely bad about ditching them last night.

'Where did you even go, anyway? Please tell me you're not turning into one of those "have to be home and tucked up in bed by nine" guys!'

'Quite the opposite, Hev,' I say. 'I'll have you know I had quite the adventure last night. You're not gonna believe who I ran into at the gig.'

'Well, I'm pretty sure Taylor Swift wasn't cutting about Sauchiehall Street on a wet Wednesday night in December, so you're going to have to help me out here.'

'That girl Kate from the other night.'

She looks blankly at me. I would have thought she'd be all over the prospect of more gossip, particularly as she's normally the first to tell me off when I don't get it for her.

'Remember that couple who had the fight in here? Her girlfriend dumped her and stormed out?'

'Ohhhh, yeah. Right. The one with the panda eyes and the snottery scarf.'

I roll my eyes.

'I definitely wouldn't have imagined she'd be a fan of the band,' she says, and then I can almost hear her brain whirring as the questions start to form. 'Wait, what am I missing here? How did that cause you to duck out on us?'

'Well, I didn't exactly run into her,' I say. 'She ran into me. Like, *actually* ran into me. She spilled my beer down me. She was in a bit of a state.'

'Riiight?' Heather says slowly, still trying to piece things together.

'So, we went for a walk to get some fresh air, got something to eat—'

'Whoa, hang on,' she interrupts. 'If you're about to tell me something happened between you and this girl, I don't think I want to know, Matt. We're mates, but even I have limits.'

'No, it's nothing like that,' I say, consciously aware that I'm in danger of sounding like I'm protesting just a little too much. 'She's gay and I've got a girlfriend, in case either of those very important facts had slipped your mind. We literally just got a kebab and sat on a bench eating and talking until she sobered up enough to get a taxi home. I couldn't just let her wander about the streets alone in the state she was in, could I?'

'Well, no, I suppose not since you put it like that,' she says. 'What's she like?'

'She's nice enough, I guess. Funny. Pretty laid back. Doesn't take herself too seriously.'

'Must have been a pretty in-depth conversation you had?'

Suddenly, I don't feel entirely comfortable with the way this conversation is going.

'Hev, we've been friends for a long time. I know when you've got something on your mind. If you've got something to say, let's hear it.'

'It's not about what I've got to say, Matt. I'm more curious about what Paige would have to say about you cutting about Glasgow at night with a strange, drunk, emotional single woman.'

'Don't make it sound like that, Hev. You know me better than that. Or at least I hope you do.' If I sound a little annoyed and sharp with her, it's because I am. More than that, though, I'm a little bit disappointed in her. It must be showing in my eyes, too. 'But since you're that concerned about it, I told Paige all about it as soon as I got home.'

'I'm sorry, Matt. You're right. That was out of order of me. You know I just think the world of Paige, and I'd hate to see her get hurt, even if it is completely unintentional. I know you'd never do anything like that. That's not who you are.'

While I'm a bit ticked-off about how clumsily Heather handled that and how quickly she jumped to a conclusion about me, I know that it didn't come from a bad place. In a way, I can even understand her concern. It really *was* an odd situation to get into, no matter how innocent, even I can't deny that. Still, though, a wee bit irritating.

'Please just promise me one thing,' she says quietly as a young couple enter the shop and shake the rain off.

'What's that?' I ask.

'That you'll be careful, Matt,' she says. 'Just be careful. That's all.'

Chapter Six: December 29th

Paige

I love when Matt's not scheduled to work over a weekend, especially around Christmas and New Year. It means we can actually make plans to spend a little quality time together. I've never been so happy as I was earlier this evening when I turned on my 'Out of Office until January 3' message and shut down my laptop, because I know Matt's done for the next five days too.

The first thing on the agenda is a decent 'date night' meal tonight, as we haven't really had a chance to sit down and eat together properly since Christmas Day. I love to cook. I find it so relaxing and therapeutic, especially when I've had a rough day at work. I know that sounds odd. Like you'd expect after a bad day, all I'd want to do is kick off my shoes, throw my feet up and order a takeaway, but I'm the complete opposite. When I'm stressed, I just want to get into the kitchen and get creative. Is that weird? It's weird, right?

In between work calls, I've spent the afternoon browsing Nigella's date night recipes – have I ever mentioned how much I absolutely love Nigella? I think I own every book she's ever written, I've seen every show she's ever presented, and I'm at least ninety per cent certain that, given the opportunity, I'd run away with her. I realise that this makes me sound like a terrible, awful person, but in my defence, Matt's already told me that he would ditch me 'in a heartbeat' for his celebrity crush, Emma Watson, and I'm pretty sure she wouldn't be as liberal with butter, cream and wine in her dinner as my Nigella would be. That's my defence and I'm sticking to it.

In the end, I decided on scallops with Thai scented pea puree to start, followed by chicken schnitzel with bacon and white wine and – assuming we're still able to move – chocolate peanut butter fudge sundae for dessert, and I'm not going to lie, I think I could live forever in a house that smells like this. Thanks again, Nigella. I'm ready whenever you are, doll.

Matt sticks his head around the kitchen door. He's just stepped out of the shower, his sandy hair all ruffled and damp, with only a towel wrapped around his waist. I look at his bare torso, and the way the towel sits on his hip, and just like that, all of my thoughts of Nigella dissipate.

'Babe, something smells amaaaaaazing,' he virtually purrs, but I'm not even thinking about cooking anymore. All I want to do is rip his towel off and smack his tight little bum with a spatula for teasing me after all the work I've put into this meal. In fact, I think that's exactly what I'm going to do. I pick one up, and lunge after him, chasing him around the breakfast bar in the middle of the kitchen until we're both on the verge of collapsing from laughing so hard.

After dinner, I'm lying on the couch with my feet on his lap, sipping on the last of the Sauv Blanc I'd used in the chicken dish. Matt's got his long legs stretched out in front of him, head tilted back and eyes closed, completely blissed out. This is what contentment looks and feels like, I think.

'Babe?' I say.

'Yeah?' he replies, his eyes still closed.

'We're still doing New Year's Eve here on Sunday night, aren't we?'

We'd planned on hosting a very small-scale party to see in the New Year. Nothing too rowdy. Just a few friends, some drinks, some food, some music. Matt's been spending more and more nights at my place lately, and we've been discussing the practicalities of him even bothering to renew the lease on his flat, when there's more than enough space in my house for us both. Ostensibly, it's just a party to celebrate the New Year, but the unwritten and unspoken subtext of it is that's really our first official party as a fully-fledged, almost living together, proper grown-up couple.

'Yeah, unless you'd rather it was just the two of us?' he says, sounding a little disappointed. 'Don't get me wrong, I'd be more than happy with that as well, but I think it would be nice to see in the New Year with our friends too.'

'I was hoping you'd say that,' I smile. 'I've been thinking.'

He opens his eyes. 'Uh oh. I'm not sure I like the sound of this,' he grins.

'Shut up,' I laugh, poking my toes into his side. 'I was just thinking, maybe it would be nice if you invite Kate round, if she doesn't have any other plans, that is?'

He turns around a little to face me, my feet still in his lap.

'Why?' he asks.

'Because if my man is going to be friends with a strange woman, I want to vet her first,' I laugh, reminding myself that I am – kind of, sort of – joking. He rolls his eyes at me.

'No, but seriously,' I say, 'I just think it would be a nice thing to do. You said it yourself, she's been through a bit of a crap time lately, and she might be feeling a bit down if she has to see in the New Year on her own. She might enjoy the company. And all joking aside, I would actually quite like to get to know her too. I could always use a new gal pal. Everyone I know seems to be marrying or having kids or settling down.'

'Okay,' he says. 'I'll message her tomorrow and ask if she has plans. It's a little late to do it now, and besides, I can think of one or two more important things I could be doing.'

He runs his hand softly up my calf, past my knee, and grazes my inner thigh, and I have to admit I agree that sending out party invites can wait.

Chapter Seven: December 30th

Kate

Bloody stupid bloody Christmas tree.

I'm standing here just staring at the thing, trying not to cry, and trying to fight the urge to just open the living room window and toss the whole thing out into the street. Why the hell did I think that today would be a good day to just take it down and be done with this whole stupid bloody Christmas season for this year?

Because I can't. I can't take it down, I mean. And not just because I'm apparently physically incapable of successfully unwinding the fairy lights and wrapping them up carefully, like an actual, proper grown-up, so they don't get tangled when it comes time to doing this all over again next year, although that does indeed appear to be the case. I'm standing here looking at it, looking at the baubles Steph and I picked out together. Because that was going to be our thing. Picking out special baubles for each other and decorating the tree together. Why, oh why do I have to be a bloody 'Christmas person?'

I've already donated our matching ugly Christmas jumpers – yes, the ones with the little Rudolphs and their LED light-up noses – to a charity shop, because I know I'm never wearing that again. I've boxed up all of the little ornaments and put them back in the cupboard in my spare room. The only thing left to do now, is take down this bloody stupid bloody Christmas tree that's standing in the corner of my living room, silently mocking me.

The most wonderful time of the year, my big fat arse.

'I give up!' I wail as I flop to my bum on the floor,

completely and utterly defeated. 'You win, tree. You can stay up today. But I'm warning you, if I get full of wine and regret tonight, I can't guarantee your physical safety. There's every chance you're going to sail past my downstairs neighbour's window, so on your own head be it.'

I'm talking to my Christmas tree. I realise that now. We've now reached this point in my inevitable slide into weirdo cat lady lunacy. Brilliant. Just brilliant. I'm only a few more short steps away from becoming the man who argues with the dustbins behind the newsagents near my Mum's house.

I let out a lengthy, dramatic sigh, for the benefit of nobody but myself and the tree, who I've just decided should be called Terry, on the grounds that if it has a name, it makes this whole scenario marginally less sad and demented. Right?

'I'm sorry, Terry. It's not your fault. We'll try again in a few days when I'm feeling like less of a complete failure.'

Once again, I'm talking to the tree. This can't be a good sign. I wonder what Steph's doing now. I bet she's not sitting on the floor of her new bloody girlfriend's fancy place, talking to inanimate objects. No wonder she chucked me. I'm such a loser.

Right, no. Stop that. That's enough of that. You're not a loser, I tell myself. You're a strong independent woman with her own flat, a decent career, a car which starts almost every single time, and until very recently, you hardly ever argued with Christmas trees. Now, like you're forever telling your readers, it's time to get your shit together.

It's pretty hard, though, isn't it? The whole 'getting your shit together' thing? Especially if your shit was already more of a tangled mess than these bloody bastard Christmas tree lights that are still mocking me.

It's Saturday morning. Second last day of the year. Just need to get through today and tomorrow, and then it'll be Next Year, that strange, nebulous time construct where everything is suddenly, miraculously different and somehow better. 'New year, new me,' all that jazz. The new issue of the magazine hits the shops today, and it's full of all that shite. I know, because I'm responsible for writing a fair portion of it. Because I'm an expert. Clearly.

I'm pondering getting myself up off this floor and paying the fridge a visit. I know there's no point, though. Everything worthwhile that was there has been demolished, and unless I fancy a delicious breakfast of pickled red cabbage and a tub of raspberry jelly which might well have passed it's 'sell by' date quite some time ago – and haven't we all? – then I should probably get my bum up off this floor, run a brush through my hair, put actual outdoor real person clothes on, and go and do some food shopping.

Just as I do that, though, my phone pings.

Matt

On a day off from work, you'd be forgiven for thinking the last place I'd want to be would be a coffee shop, yet here I am. It's the last Saturday of the year, and instead of lazing around in bed and enjoying the rare opportunity to recharge and do as little as possible, Paige and I have been out and about for a while already, doing some food shopping and getting everything we need ahead of the party tomorrow night.

Now, though, we're sitting in a little café on Woodlands Road, enjoying bacon rolls, hot drinks – a double-shot mocha for me, a caramel cappuccino for Paige – and just watching the world go by. It's one of my favourite parts of town. Vibrant and student-heavy, artsy and hip, nestling in the shadows of Glasgow University, Kelvingrove Park and the Art Gallery.

'You're sure we've got enough wine?' Paige asks, not for the first time. I smile. I think we could go into the yacht-christening business and still have more than enough left over at this point.

'We'll be fine, babe,' I try to reassure her, but I can see the wheels are still turning. I know how important this party is to her. To me, too. I want everything to be perfect because I know how happy it'll make her. We've had friends over to Paige's house before, but this time it feels— I don't know, just different somehow. Like this is the start of the next chapter for us, I guess.

'I love you, you know,' she says, threading her fingers through mine on top of the table.

'I love you too,' I smile.

I take a photo of our interwoven fingers beside our coffee cups, slap an arty black and white filter on it – because I'm classy that way – and post it quickly on Insta. Within seconds, Jason has added an 'Ugh, get a room!' comment, and I smile again. Being on Insta jogs my memory, and I remember I have something to do. I open my messages.

> *@justplainmatt*
> *Hiya. How's your Saturday going?*

I hit send and put my phone on the table. I'm toying with the idea of turning my breakfast into an impromptu brunch with a piece of one of the home-made cakes the café has on offer when my phone pings.

> *@katiemacisawriter*
> *Lost fight with Xmas tree. Need sausages.*

As responses go, it's as quirky as I would have expected from her. I know I've only spent an hour or so in her company, but from what I remember of the conversation we had, that reply strikes me as being completely on-brand for her. It elicits another little smile from me.

'What are you smirking at?' Paige asks me. I show her the message and she looks at me, clearly puzzled.

'I have no idea what it means either!' I shrug.

'Don't forget you've to invite her to the party,' she says.

'I'm getting to that, let me at least say hello first,' I laugh.

I take another drink of my coffee and return to the

messages.

> *@justplainmatt*
> *Got any plans for tomorrow night?*

I turn the phone around and show Paige. She smiles and nods her approval. There's no immediate reply this time, so I go over to the counter and order two pieces of the tempting carrot cake. What can I say? I can't resist a good piece of cake with my coffee. And since it would be rude of me not to, I order a second mocha to wash it down.

'I'll bring them over to you, my honey,' the woman behind the counter smiles.

I sit back down at our table, and Paige raises an eyebrow at me.

'Oooo, my honey,' she teases.

'Hate the game, not the playa, baby,' I wink, and she thumps me on the arm. My phone pings.

> *@katiemacisawriter*
> *Eating and drinking too much, followed by*
> *weeping and feeling like crap. It'll be a*
> *pretty action-packed evening, I'm sure.*

I'm not entirely sure how much of that is meant to be her self-deprecating way of laughing her current situation off, and how much of it is serious. I suspect it's finely balanced.

> *@justplainmatt*
> *Come to a party at ours. You can still eat and*
> *drink too much. No judgement.*
> *Seriously, though, you'll have fun. I promise.*

I hit send again, hoping I haven't completely misjudged her tone. This time, though, the reply comes quickly.

@katiemacisawriter
Won't your girlfriend mind?

I look across the table at Paige. I smile and show her the message. She grins and sticks both thumbs up, and it's all I can do to stop myself from laughing long enough to snap a photo of her. I reply to Kate's message, with the photo attached.

@justplainmatt
Completely her idea. She practically insists.

Almost immediately, the little heart emoji appears against the message.

@katiemacisawriter
Well, in that case...

Chapter Eight: December 31st

Kate

'Look, all I'm saying,' our Fiona continues, 'is that you'd be more than welcome here tonight. You don't even need to go home. You can crash in the spare room and then we can all go to Mum and Dad's together tomorrow. Why see the bells in with a bunch of strangers instead of family?'

'I think that's exactly what I need, to be honest, Fi. I love you and Ewan to bits, you know I do, but I shouldn't have to rely on you to babysit me because I don't have a social life.'

I love the very bones of my big sister, but I don't think she gets this at all. I suppose I can see it from her perspective. I know she worries about me, and part of me suspects that she might even think I'm making this party invitation up so she doesn't think I'm completely pathetic and that I'm actually going to spend tonight alone getting drunk in front of the TV as I work my way through the entire Jade Palace menu. I mean, that might well have been my original plan for this evening, but mind ya business, you know?

'I need to start meeting new people and making friends of my own, Fi. I'm actually looking forward to it.'

She puffs in exasperation, completely forgetting that we're video calling, and that I can see her expression. It gives me a little chuckle.

'Explain it to me again,' she says. 'Who is this guy?'

'Just a guy I met at a gig the other night,' I tell her. It's not the entire story, but omission isn't *really* lying, is it?

'And his girlfriend is completely cool with all of this?'

'Yes! I told you already! Inviting me to the party was her

idea.'

She pauses for a moment, and I can see thoughts forming in her head.

'Wait. They— they're not, like, *swingers*, are they?'

'For God's sake, Fi!' I squeak, a little mortified at hearing that come from my sister.

'Well, you never know, do you? They could be trying to lure you to one of those pervy suburban sex parties you hear about, with the pampas grass and everything.'

'Ooooo, here, you think? What's the dress code for those?'

'Shut up, halfwit,' she grins.

'Peephole bra and edible panties, maybe? Rubber dress and no knickers?' I can't even contain my laughter, and tears are rolling down my cheeks.

'Right, I'm away,' she laughs. 'See you at Mum and Dad's tomorrow afternoon for steak pie. You'd better not be too hungover to eat, you know what Mum's like.'

New Year's Day steak pie dinner at Mum and Dad's is a family tradition which started when Fi and I were kids, and never stopped even after we'd both grown up – although I use that term very loosely in my case – and moved out into our own places. Mum is what could most politely be described as 'generous with her portions,' but I prefer to refer to her as 'a feeder.' Her special occasion dinners, like Christmas and New Year's are absolutely ridiculous. When she runs out of plate space, she simply starts stacking it skywards, and I don't have any reason to think tomorrow will be different. I love it, though. It makes me feel like a kid again. Just the thought of the smell of the steak pie coming from the kitchen when I walk in the front door tomorrow is enough to set my mouth watering.

The thought of just turning up at this party tonight, on the other hand, is absolutely filling me with anxiety. I've already thought about messaging Matt to tell him I can't make it, and digging out the Jade Palace menu, but I actually meant what I said to our Fi. I can't go on the way I've been going. When I was with Steph, all of our friends were really all of *her* friends. That's how it's always been with my relationships over the years. Then, when they invariably come to end, so do all of the so-called 'friendships.'

For the first time that I can remember, I may have a chance to make friends of my own. And that is a scary thought. This is when all of my self-doubt and self-esteem issues start running wild on me. I mean, I've known Matt for what, about an hour? I've seen photos of Paige, but never spoken to her. And I don't even know who else will be there. Matt just said there would only be a few people, some of their closest friends, all people our age. But what if they don't like me? What if I don't have anything in common with anyone? If I get too self-conscious, there's a very real danger that I'll stay in close proximity to all of the alcohol, and the night won't end well.

Most of all, though, I am absolutely terrified at the prospect of meeting Paige. I know Matt said it was her idea to invite me, and that she's super chill, but there's a part of me that worries she thinks I'm after her man and that this is an attempt to either scope me out or warn me off. Not that she'd have anything to be even remotely concerned about. I mean, look at her. I spent an hour going down an Insta rabbit hole the other night, looking at her posts and photos. She's clearly super-smart, being a lawyer and all, and frankly, she's model gorgeous. I mean, like, to a ridiculous extent. Matt was joking that his friends always say she's out of his league, but when I looked at her photos, I completely get it. She's one of those women who other women just find intimidating. I know I do. She's like someone spliced Margot Robbie and Sydney Sweeney's DNA together and turned the confidence dial all the way up to ten.

Ugh. I look at myself in the full-length mirror in my spare room. I look like a potato in comparison. I should know better than to fall into the comparison trap. God, I've even written articles about how unhealthy it is, yet here I am. I've spent all afternoon trying on outfits and then having tantrums and throwing them onto the bed. Nobody ever tells you that the biggest downside of meeting new people is the having to get ready to meet new people! I decide to send Matt a message. I start to type in 'can't make it,' but then erase it.

> *@katiemacisawriter*
> *What's the dress code for tonight?*
> *I have no idea what to wear!*

He messages me back almost instantly.

> *@justplainmatt*
> *Eh?*
> *What do you mean 'dress code'?*
> *Have you never been to an actual party before?*

He follows it up with some laughing and winking emojis, and I am now teetering on the edge of a full-blown anxiety attack. What does he mean? Like, what kind of party? Do I wear a little black dress like I would to a cocktail party? God, I hope not. I've had way too much ice cream over the last week or so for that. Maybe I should just brass neck it and wear the 'swingers party' outfit I suggested to our Fi? That thought is enough to get me laughing, and I can feel myself relaxing a little. My phone pings from the bed, and I pick it up.

> *@justplainmatt*
> *Sorry. :)*
> *Paige slapped me for being, and I quote, 'a big meanie.'*
> *Dress casual, we're not fancy.*
> *See you tonight. 8ish?*

I sigh in relief. Okay, I can deal with casual. I dig out my favourite jeans, the ones which make my bum look the least terrible, and a lovely new top I picked up in the sales in New Look when I was at the Fort the other day, a floaty, black marble print, tie-front blouse. I hold it in front of myself as I look at my reflection. Not horrible. Not horrible at all.

Now all I have to worry about is my hair, my make-up and my propensity to make a complete rip-roaring arse of myself in public.

Paige

I'm so excited. I can't help but feel that this coming year is going to be huge for us both. Like we're about to take the next big step in our relationship. Not that the last two years haven't been great, too, but like, things are just going to be— well, *amazing* this year, you know? I always get like this at the New Year. Just full of optimism. I know, I know. That's such a cliché, that whole 'new year, new start, new me' thing. But right now, everything just feels right. I can't wait until Matt finally moves in with me officially. I'm just sitting here, at the breakfast bar in the kitchen, glass of wine in hand, watching him chatting away with our friends, and it makes me feel all warm and gooey inside.

The doorbell rings, and I see him about to break away from his conversation to get it, and I motion to him to carry on. It might be the pizza delivery we ordered forty minutes ago. A little quicker than I expected if it is. On New Year's Eve, I'd expected it to take a little longer.

I walk down the hall and immediately know that it's not our takeaway. I can tell by the silhouette through the frosted glass pane on the front door. I open it, and I immediately recognise Kate from her pics on Insta. She's much prettier in person than I expected, too. She's tiny and petite, almost doll-like, but even wrapped up in a hat, scarf and warm coat – crimson wool, just gorgeous – I can see she's pretty. She appears a little worried as she looks at me, but I can't put my finger on why. We stare at each other for a moment before I remember my manners.

'Hiya,' I greet her, trying to sound as warm and welcoming as I can to put her at ease. 'You must be Kate? Come on in out of the cold, babe.'

She steps inside and I give her a friendly, welcoming hug and a peck on the cheek. I hope I haven't misjudged this and come across as totally forward.

'I love your coat! It's absolutely gorgeous,' I say. 'Can I take it for you?'

She freezes. 'Um, aye, it's just, I—'

I look at her, wondering what I'm missing. She sighs and then unbuttons her coat, and I immediately understand why she looks like she wishes she could be anywhere but here right now. She looks at my top in horror. I look at hers. I laugh.

'New Look sales? I couldn't resist it either.'

'It looks amazing on you,' she sighs.

Yes, we are wearing the *exact* same top, and poor Kate looks absolutely mortified. I feel so awful for her. Matt's absolutely right. She has a 'frightened, lost orphan' look about her. I just want to give her a big hug and tell her it'll all be okay. Instead, I do the next best thing.

'Let me show you through to the living room,' I smile. 'Matt can introduce you to everyone while I nip into the bedroom and throw another top on.' I put my arm around her shoulder and give her a little squeeze, and I lead her through. Matt lights up when he sees her and gives her a friendly hug before he begins making the introductions, freeing me up to make a quick outfit change to save any further awkwardness.

When I return, Matt is telling Jason about Kate running into him and spilling his beer all over him, Heather is quizzing Kate about her music taste and which bands she's seen playing in town, my work colleague Leah is talking to Matt's mum about some reality TV show they both watch, and Matt's mum's 'special friend,' as Matt insists we refer to him, appears to have commandeered the CD player and is currently looking through my collection to work out his DJ set for the evening's entertainment. I bring a fresh bottle of wine in and begin topping up glasses.

After the stack of pizzas have been demolished, I settle down in the quietest corner of the living room with Kate, who now thankfully seems much more comfortable, despite being surrounded by an assortment of strangers and nutters.

'I'm so glad you decided to come,' I say to her, clinking my glass against hers. She smiles, sweetly. She really is very pretty, and for a second, I actually feel a little insecure. She has the most gorgeous big brown doe eyes that I could easily imagine a lot of men would find difficult to resist.

'Can I let you into a secret?' she says. 'I almost didn't. Right up until the second the taxi pulled up outside, I was having second thoughts.'

'Really? Why?' I ask.

'This is gonny sound so weird,' she says. 'Like, I'm pretty sure Matt has told you about how we first met, what happened at the coffee shop, but still, I had this thing in the back of my mind that you were just inviting me to— I don't know, to make sure I wasn't out to steal your man, or worse, that you were going to claw my eyes out!' She laughs nervously but I'm actually seriously impressed that she's able to be so honest. I give her a little squeeze of reassurance.

'I will admit I was a little bit curious at first,' I say. 'When Matt came home the other night and told me about you, I mean. It's not something that happens every day. But I've known Matt long enough to know how he is with people.' I hope that doesn't sound like I'm marking my territory.

'He was just so incredibly kind and understanding,' she says. 'I was an absolute shambles, and he just wanted to make sure nothing bad happened to me. He's so nice. You're a lucky lady, Paige. And he's a lucky man to have you, too.'

I can't argue with that, really. I top up her glass and we spend the next little while talking about our respective jobs. She listens to my many gripes about my work enemy, and I'm shocked to learn that I've actually read a huge number of her magazine articles. She picks my brain about the finer points of setting up as self-employed to allow her to do more freelance work, and I try to convince her that she should think about starting a blog or making more use of her social media to make her work a bit more visible.

The old year ebbs towards the end, the drinks continue to flow, the conversations get a little more animated and the oddest dynamics are in play – Jason and Derek are now co-hosting what has turned into something of a mini karaoke session, and Derek is wearing Jason's hat at the jauntiest of angles. As Derek finishes a hearty rendition of the Scissor Sisters' 'I Don't Feel Like Dancing,' J emerges from the pile of CDs as if he's clutching the Ark of the Covenant.

'Right, troops,' he says. 'It's nearly twelve, and it's time to really get this party started. I know just the song, but I'm gonna need the lady of the house to join me and give us all a wee tune. Mon, Paige, hen. Up you come, ya wee Dancing Queen, ye!' he grins, brandishing the ABBA Greatest Hits CD.

'Right, well, if I'm making an arse of myself,' I laugh, 'I'm not doing it alone,' and I grab Kate's hand and drag her up from the couch and across the floor with me. Within seconds of the infectious intro of the song playing, everyone is clapping and singing and dancing, Kate and I are barely able to sing for laughing as we dance, and for the first time tonight, she looks completely relaxed.

The song finishes and someone turns the TV on, just in time for the countdown to the bells. I top up everyone's glasses with champagne, apart from Derek, who's happy with his single malt. The lone piper is playing up on the ramparts at Edinburgh Castle as the final seconds of the year tick down. I feel Matt's arm snake around my waist, and I look up at him.

'I love you,' I mouth silently at him.

'I love you too, babe,' he replies. He smiles and the corners of his eyes crinkle that way they do, and I go a little weak at the knees. He has that effect on me.

As the bells chime to ring in the new year, hugs, kisses and the very best of wishes are exchanged. I can see Kate looking out of my kitchen window, watching the fireworks explode in the night sky, and as I approach her, she sees my reflection in the window and dabs at her damp eyes, desperately trying not to let anyone see, and my heart breaks a little for her.

'Happy new year, Paige,' she says, forcing a smile.

'Happy new year, Kate,' I reply. 'And it is going to be a happy one, I promise. For what it's worth, it's her loss, not yours,' and I give her a hug.

Chapter Nine: January 1st

Matt

I'm surprisingly not in the slightest bit hungover, despite the amount of beer and champagne that was consumed last night. I even remember enjoying a drop of Derek's malt – at his insistence – as he cuddled me and told me how much he enjoys Mum's company, and how lucky he feels to have met her when he did. There's nothing quite like a Hogmanay party in Scotland to make people feel less guarded with their emotions. Although I'm pretty sure that the alcohol plays just the tiniest part in that too.

I'm trying to keep the clinking to a minimum as I tidy up the seemingly never-ending pile of empty glasses and bottles from the kitchen and living room. I'm putting the bottles and cans into a box to go out to the recycling bin, and the glasses in the dishwasher, very conscious that Paige may well have the slightest headache this morning. It was an enjoyable night, though. But then, any time is a good time when you're surrounded by the people you love most in the world, and new friends too.

I did wonder how Kate would feel about being surrounded by strangers last night, but to her credit she seemed to enjoy herself and certainly made an impression on the other guests. Jason, naturally, was completely fascinated by her job and seemed to be convinced that she knew loads of celebrities but was keeping it all under wraps. He even took me aside at one point to tell me that – strictly hush hush, of course – she's so fabulous that, were he so inclined, he'd ditch Hev and run away with her. Coming from J, I think that's the highest

84

compliment one human can pay another.

Heather herself gave Kate the seal of approval, once her lingering suspicions had been put to rest. At some point, long after Jools Holland had packed his piano away in the ridiculously small hours of the morning, I've taken a photo of Hev with the crook of her arm around Kate's neck, giving me a wide grin and a 'thumbs up' gesture. To be fair, it may be the most aggressive display of affection that I've ever seen, and I'm still not entirely convinced that she *wasn't* trying to apply some kind of headlock.

The funniest message I've had so far this morning came from Mum, informing me that Derek is claiming he may have picked up some kind of terrible winter bug, as he's woken up with a pounding headache and a sore throat. I mean, I'm by no means a qualified medical professional, but I'd feel quite comfortable in betting that the headache might be a direct result of his little liquid visit to Glenfiddich, and the mystery sore throat might somehow be related to his enthusiastic rendition of 'Hi Ho Silver Lining' at around 2am. I already liked Derek, but I have a new appreciation for him this morning, seeing not only how fun and comfortable he is around my friends and family, but how much he obviously thinks of Mum.

And Paige. My beautiful Paige, who admittedly might not feel so beautiful when she eventually surfaces. I never expected anything less, but she really was the perfect hostess last night. I watched her just existing last night, in her very element, floating from conversation to conversation, from guest to guest, making sure no glass ever went empty, and I just felt completely in awe. I mean, I already know I'm the luckiest man in the world, but last night was just... I don't know, it was a different level. I don't think I can imagine what my life would look like without her in it anymore. I don't think I'd want to even try.

Not that I doubted this either, but it was great to see how she and Kate got along, too. I knew they'd click once they got to know each other. They are very, very different personalities –

really, they couldn't be more polar opposites – but where it really matters, in terms of being nice, being warm, being funny, and just generally being good human beings, it's like they could have been separated at birth.

When Kate was waiting at the front door for the taxi to take her home, long after Mum had poured Derek into a taxi back to her house and Heather and Jason had called it a night and gone their own way, Paige had insisted that Kate text her the minute she got home to let us know that she was home and safe, which she did. That's my Paige for you.

'She's so awesome, babe,' she had bubbled enthusiastically as we'd waved her off. Between them, they'd agreed we should all hang out together again soon, starting with our weekly pub quiz night on Thursday. How could I say no to an offer like that?

I take one final look around the living room and kitchen to make sure I haven't missed any more empties. Looks good now. I open the windows to let a little cool, fresh morning air in and the smell of stale booze out. Just one more thing left to do before I take the empties out to the recycling bin. I click the switch on the kettle, because I suspect someone is going to be in desperate need of a strong cup of coffee sooner rather than later.

Kate

Despite the fact that I'm up before ten on New Year's Day, having had more to drink than I had planned, I feel fantastic. A damn sight better than I did when I woke up in my old room at Mum and Dad's this time last week. I mean, I know I said that the whole 'new year, new me, new start' thing was a big steaming pot of pish, but weirdly this morning it— well, it actually kinda feels true. I've woken up not feeling absolutely hanging, which is always a good start, but it's more than that. I feel optimistic. I feel like things are on the up. I feel like I could actually tackle that bloody Christmas tree again today, and this time not feel like I want to throw the whole thing out of the window. Baby steps, innit?

Right now, though, I'm perfectly content sitting here on *my* couch, in *my* flat, drinking *my* coffee from *my* 'Sip Happens – Write On!' mug, and not even thinking about she who must not be named, not even a little bit, not even at all, because this is a new year, and no matter what happens, I am going to move on. I can't get what Paige said last night out of my head. Like, when she told me this is going to be a happy new year. She's right, kind of. It's going to be as happy as I allow it to be. As happy as I allow myself to be. So, that's my new year's resolution. I'm not going to commit to eating healthier, or drinking less, or getting myself a booty to die for, because frankly, those are unrealistic goals and a surefire way to make myself miserable again. But training myself to be happy? I can do that. I can do *that*, right?

I enjoyed last night. Much more than I thought I ever would, actually. I already knew what kind of guy Matt is, but I'm not gonna lie, I had the absolute worst social anxiety about meeting Paige and all of their friends. Paige, most of all. But she's nothing like I expected. I mean, other than the fact that she's like, ridiculously, intimidatingly gorgeous. When you see women like that, ones that are really put together, you kinda expect that they'll be— well, that they'll be a wee bit bitchy, let's be honest. You expect them to be frosty, snotty cows, but she couldn't have been any further from that. She's just bloody lovely. Infuriating, innit? Looking like *that*, and she has the bloody cheek to be lovely as well! Cow. Kidding. Sorta.

Right, Terry the tree. You and me. Square go, round two. You're going down. Literally. I'm going to put you in a box. Literally. You're going— eh... back in the cupboard, I suppose. Sorry, I'm all fight metaphored out. Some writer I am. Mind you, that guy Jason seemed impressed with my skills. Oh God, wee flashes from last night keep coming back to me and making me laugh. That guy was absolutely hilarious.

Focus, Kate. God's sake. You're going to end up sitting here with your Easter eggs under this bloody bastard tree at this rate. My phone pings.

@justplainmatt
Hungover?

I type out a quick reply and toss my phone on the couch behind me so I can least pretend to be serious about taking this bloody tree down.

@katiemacisawriter
Fresh as a daisy!

I mean, it's all relative. I probably couldn't go out and get a five mile jog in or anything – not that I could before, I should clarify – but I do feel good.

Before I realise it, I've not only got both sets of fairy lights untangled and completely free from the tree, I've got each of them wrapped around a plastic coat hanger just ready to go straight onto the tree next Christmas without the agony of having to untangle them like a ball of yarn that's lost a fight to a gang of hyperactive kittens looking to commit a mugging to fund their catnip habit.

Terry looks back at me, naked and conquered. I extend both middle fingers like I'm 'Stone Cold' Steve Austin, and then buckle into a fit of hysterical laughter at how ridiculous I am. For some reason, I find myself singing 'Hi Ho Silver Lining' as I start removing and smoothing down the branches and placing them into the box on the floor. I have no idea why. I don't think I've heard that song in years. My phone pings again. I stop my victory lap to check it.

@justplainmatt
Still on for the pub quiz on Thursday?

I smile. I'm not sure if I'd forgotten about that invitation, or if I'd just convinced myself it was one of those things that you say in the heat of the moment and the exhilaration of a good night, without meaning to really follow through on it. Kinda like when you say 'I'll call you' at the end of an underwhelming date, knowing that you never will. I guess I'd just assumed Paige was being nice because that's how she is. Apparently, I was wrong, and I'm a little pleased that's the case. Because as I found out last night, I genuinely enjoy being around them, and it would appear that I'm not a complete social disaster who should be hiding in the attic eating from a bucket of fish heads instead of being in civilised company. Who'da thunk it?

@katiemacisawriter
I'm in. See you there.

Within minutes, Terry is boxed up, put away neatly in the cupboard for another year, and I'm getting ready to jump under a hot shower before I head to Mum and Dad's for the comfort and familiarity of some family time, and the best steak pie in the west of Scotland.

Chapter Ten: January 4th

Paige

The Lock isn't the trendiest or the most flash place in town, but it's cheap enough, it's lively, there's a reasonable enough range of cocktails, and on Thursday nights when it's quiz night, it's our local. On warm summer evenings, Matt and I love to sit out on the terrace which backs onto the Forth and Clyde Canal, enjoying a drink and some pub grub, but tonight, a particularly grim and icy first Thursday of January, it's quiz night, and we're cosy and warm in the bar, sitting at a mezzanine table with our guest and new team-mate.

'You don't need to come up with a new team name on my account,' Kate laughs, sipping on her strawberry and lime cider.

'What do you mean? Of course we do,' Matt says. 'We can't very well use our usual team name with you here! "Matt and Paige" doesn't really work when there's three of us. And besides, all of this lot have funny team names.'

He sweeps his arm around, motioning at the little groups huddled over answer sheets around their tables. He's not wrong. In our midst, we have the regulars. 'Quizlamic State' are here as usual. And there are the three blonde girls who compete as 'Quiz-teama Aguilera.' I mean, most of them are 'quiz' related puns, with the obvious exception of my favourite, the particularly creative 'Sorry, I Thought This Was Speed Dating Night.' We do need a name which perfectly sums us up, though.

'How about "The Brainy Beauties... and their sidekick Matt?"' I wink. He rolls his eyes at me. Git.

'The Love Triangle?' he suggests.

'Doesn't that sound— well, a wee bit "swinger-y?"' Kate laughs. She's not wrong. People might get the wrong idea about us.

'Decide between yourselves, then,' he says. 'I'll get some more drinks in before we get started.'

When he comes back to the table with a pink gin and lemonade for me, a cider for Kate and a lager for himself – and three packets of salt and vinegar peanuts between his teeth – Kate and I have come up with a fitting name for our newly expanded team.

'Three's Company,' Kate and I say in unison, and he grins.

'So, what's your area of expertise?' Matt asks her. 'Paige is pretty good on news and politics, and I'm an expert on sports, films, music and general trivia.'

'Excuse me, sir, you are no such thing,' I laugh.

'What do you mean?' he exclaims in mock offence.

I look him dead in the eye. 'To the question, "Which iconic band were referred to as The Fab Four?" what did you say in response?'

'Shut up,' he grins.

'Come on, Professor, tell Kate what your answer was.'

He rolls his eyes again, and mutters 'One Direction.' She almost chokes on a nut, and I swear a little cider comes out of her nose.

'Stop ganging up on me, you two,' he says, and takes a drink while Kate composes herself.

By the time we're three drinks in, the quiz is progressing nicely and Kate has surprised us with her surprisingly in-depth knowledge of 1980s movie soundtrack hit songs, one of which has triggered Matt badly.

'Dirty Dancing? Really?' he recoils in horror.

'Yes!' she exclaims. 'It is absolutely my favourite movie of all-time, and I won't hear a word against it.'

'Oh, for the love of-' he says. 'What is it with women and that film?'

'If you go into this rant of yours about Patrick Swayze again, *Matthew*,' I warn him, 'I swear I won't be held responsible for my actions!'

He holds his hands up in a gesture of surrender. 'Fair enough. We can't have you causing a scene while we have company. She won't want to come out and play with us again.'

Someone shushes us from somewhere behind me, and Kate and I both giggle.

'If you lot are finished up there,' Big Andy the Quizmaster grumbles, 'We'll continue, shall we?' and Matt shrugs and waves apologetically.

The sport round comes and goes, and a series of correct answers from Matt has us sitting in second place, just a few points behind regulars Big Head Bill and Shy Sam – I have no idea if their names are, in fact, Bill and Sam, but that's what we've come to refer to them as. 'Bill' is big and broad, loud and boisterous, but most of their correct answers seem to come from 'Sam', who whispers them to him to write down but never seems to speak himself.

'You've a cheek to talk about us women with Dirty Dancing,' Kate says to him. 'But what's the deal with you men remembering pointless facts and nonsense about sporting events? I mean, when are you ever going to need to know who scored the winning goal in the 2012 World Cup Final?'

'First of all,' he says, 'It was the 2010 final, and secondly, we needed to know tonight, didn't we? It was Andres Iniesta.'

Kate and I look at each other and shake our heads. Although, I do have to admit that sometimes having a boyfriend who remembers the most irrelevant trivia does have some benefits – particularly the free round of drinks to the winners of the quiz!

For a little while, it actually feels like that prize might just be ours, but we manage to snatch defeat from the jaws of victory thanks to Matt's insistence that 'The Scream' was, in fact, painted by Bob Ross, 'during the short period when he got tired of painting happy little clouds.' Although, by that point I think we'd all completely given up on being serious about the quiz because we were just having so much fun making each other laugh.

'That concludes our quiz for this week, folks,' says Big Andy. 'Congratulations again to our winning team, Big Cook Little Cook, and I'll hopefully see you all again here next Thursday night for our next quiz!'

Huh. Big Cook Little Cook, eh? I think I prefer our name for them.

'That was fun,' Kate says. 'You guys having another round?' she motions to the empty glasses on the table. It's getting late, and while part of me wants to head for home and get some sleep for work in the morning, I also don't want the evening to end so soon.

'I think I could force another one down,' I smile.

'I was hoping that's what you'd say,' she replies, returning the smile. 'How about we sample some of these fancy cocktails?'

That sounds like a recipe for disaster, and yet I find myself agreeing. This feels like it's going to be a 'tomorrow' problem, not a 'right now' problem, and I'm completely fine with that.

Chapter Eleven: January 13th

Matt

Normally, the thought of getting out of bed early on a Saturday morning to go traipsing around a shopping centre wouldn't exactly have me overflowing with enthusiasm, but oddly, I don't feel like that today. Look, don't get me wrong, it's not that I have anything in particular against shopping centres – I work in one! – or even against shopping trips in general, but I think I have that typical male mentality about them. Like, that 'I know what I need to get, I know where I need to get it, so let's get in, get the job done, and get out' kinda thing, you know?

Paige doesn't subscribe to that same way of thinking, unfortunately. She's definitely a browser. She likes nothing better than going in with no idea what she's looking for and then being pleasantly surprised when she finds something she likes, no matter how long it takes, or how many times we have to circle back around the same shop so she can try on the first thing she found again.

So, yeah. Normally, would I be full of the joys of the morning right about now? Probably not. But today, I suspect we'll have a laugh, because our newly installed third wheel is tagging along with us, and pretty much every time we've hung out so far, that's what's ended up happening. We've had another couple of nights out since the quiz night. Last Saturday, we took a trip to the cinema to see a new rom-com Paige had been excited to see – I'm more of a horror fan, but Paige knows if she plies me with enough nachos and a slushie, I'll generally behave nicely. The funniest thing for me was the discussion about movies on the way there, when Kate revealed that her favourites are those ridiculously cheesy made-for-TV movies that only seem to show on those free cable movie channels, or during the daytime schedule. I mean, honestly, how can anyone take those things seriously?

Then on Thursday, we had another go at the quiz night, and honestly, there was so much hilarity and messing around that we stood no chance of winning. A small price to pay for what ended up being the most fun I've had in forever. Do I remember what was so funny? Absolutely not a bit of it. Just a series of random, silly, hilarious stories and anecdotes, punctuated by what felt like co-ordinated attempts to wind me up. All in all, a fantastic night.

So here we are, the three of us, in Paige's car winding our way down the motorway to the Silverburn Centre on the outskirts of town, via the drive-thru for some road coffees. Which – not to blow my own trumpet – aren't a patch on mine, I hasten to add.

'How's the coffee, Kate?' Paige asks.

'I've had better,' she replies. See? Didn't I tell you. Not a patch on mine.

'That place at the Fort, am I right?' I say, grinning.

'Meh. It's over-rated,' she smiles. 'And don't even get me started about the guy who works there! What an absolute roaster he is.'

'Rude! Last piece of sympathy cake you get, lady.'

'Children,' Paige smiles. 'Play nice or so help me I will turn this car around.'

'Sorry, Mum,' Kate and I say in unison, and then crack up laughing.

The main car park is exceptionally busy when we arrive, even by Saturday morning standards. We eventually find a spot and make our way towards the centre. The bitter winter wind whips all around us, and I zip up my jacket and stick my hands in my pockets. Paige links her arm through mine and smiles up at me. Kate walks on my other side, handbag slung over the shoulder of the red wool coat she was wearing the first night our paths crossed.

We're in either the third or seventeenth clothes shop of the day, and I am getting hangry. I'm sitting on one of those little seats they kindly provide for exhausted and frustrated partners, scrolling on my phone while Paige and Kate *ooh* and *aah* over the various outfits they're trying on. I'm pondering my life choices. I could be in bed right now. This isn't turning out to be quite as fun as I'd expected. They can't all be winners.

'Matt,' Paige snaps her fingers. I was in a world of my own.

'Huh?' I ask.

'I was asking what you think of that one?'

I look around, still getting my bearings, and then I look at Kate. Then I look back at Paige. And then at Kate again.

'It really suits her, doesn't it?' Paige says.

I'm still looking at Kate. She's wearing a dark green sequin wrap mini dress which is completely unlike anything I've seen her wear before, and yes, it absolutely suits her. Like, to a ridiculous extent. The colour makes her dark brown eyes pop, and the fit really flatters her. She's tiny, but the length shows her legs off, and she looks... yeah.

'Nice, yeah,' I stammer. 'Nice.' Smooth, playa. I look at her again. Huh. I didn't expect that. I nod my head and pull my best indifferent 'guy face,' and I have to tear my eyes away from her before she thinks that I'm gawking at her. Which, it occurs to me, I am.

'Ignore him,' Paige grins at Kate. 'You look *hot* in that, babe. I mean, like *tsssssssss!*' she adds, making the universal *sizzle* sound and gesture.

'Where would I even wear something like this?' Kate asks her, now admiring herself in the mirror. Paige has obviously given her confidence a much-needed bolstering. Not that I think there's anything wrong with her – I mean, look at that dress! But the way she puts herself down sometimes, I don't get it at all. I've passed the point where I even attempt to figure women and their self-esteem issues out, I guess.

'Can we eat soon?' I plead, distracting myself, because hangry is the safe option right now.

'Aw, babe, have we shopped you to near starvation?'

I can't lie, the food court is calling my name right now, and not just because all I want is for Kate to get out of that dress. That didn't come out right. That's not what I meant at all.

'Yeah, I could eat,' is all I can manage.

We're sitting at one of the tables in the food court eating lunch from the noodle bar, and Kate has changed back into her oversized wool jumper and jeans, still riding the feelgood endorphins from how good she felt in the new outfit which she's purchased – plus a pair of strappy heels to complement the dress. I'm not sure if it's a result of that confidence boost, or just the fact that she's becoming so comfortable in our company that she feels able to open up, but for the first time since the night we sat on that bench on Sauchiehall Street with the kebabs, she's talking about her ex.

'It still feels weird being alone in the flat,' she says. 'Like, I keep looking at all of these wee spaces that she's left behind. Places where her stuff was, you know?'

'I get it, babe,' Paige says. 'Has to be hard, when you're trying to get your life together and start moving forward and you've got all of those reminders around you.'

'Have you thought about redecorating?' I ask, looking up from my Teriyaki beef noodles.

'Not really. You think?' Kate asks me.

'It might be just what you need, actually,' Paige says. 'Even if it's just a fresh coat of paint and a few wee bits and pieces from Ikea to change things up a little. Make the place your own again, you know?'

Paige looks at me and smiles. We really are a great team.

'We could come over and help,' I offer. 'If you want?'

'You'd do that?' she asks, choking up a little.

'We'd love to,' Paige smiles.

Chapter Twelve: January 14th

Paige

I'm sitting under the cover of the pickup and drop-off point at Glasgow Airport, anxiously fiddling with the car radio. I'm anxious not because the clock is ticking and the charge for waiting goes up every fifteen minutes – although it is and it does – but because I'm waiting on Mum and Dad coming out through the Arrivals door with their bags. Don't get me wrong, I love my parents to bits, and I've missed them over the holidays, but it's just that—

Mum can be a bit much sometimes. I know that. They had me young, and as a result, Mum still thinks of herself as a 'cool young Mum,' even though she's now beginning to edge into middle-age. Or be dragged kicking and screaming into it, might be a little closer to the mark. She's already started getting little bits of work done, although she strenuously denies it, and Dad won't be drawn into *that* conversation for love nor money. They're good together, though, Mum and Dad. Chalk and cheese, but kind of in a good way. Not quite the way Matt and I are, where our little differences really complement one another, but still, their relationship is solid.

I see them before they see me. Enjoy the last couple of moments of quiet, Paige, they'll be the last for a little while. It's blowing a gale and it's been drizzly all morning, but Mum clearly hasn't dressed for Glasgow. It was in the mid-twenties when they left Gran Canaria this morning and frankly, I'm boggled that she expected Glasgow to be anything other than grey, wet and bitterly cold in mid-January.

She opens the back door of my car and pours herself in,

leaving Dad to put their cases into the boot.

'Hiya, Paigey Doll, like my tan?' She stretches out an impossibly long, brown leg in the back. 'You could maybe do with a wee bit of sun yourself, hen. You're looking like a ghost, and you've not got the cheekbones to pull off the Twilight look.'

Outstanding, Mum. Not even a minute in the car and you've already made me feel like the Kristen Stewart you get when you order off a dodgy Chinese website. Just fantastic. And a happy New Year to you too, you old—

'Happy New Year, Mum,' I say, stopping myself. Dad closes the boot and gets in the front beside me. He kisses my cheek.

'How was your Christmas and New Year, sweetheart?' Dad asks, somehow managing to not say anything offensive. Take note, Mum.

'Great. Obviously just Matt and I on Christmas Day, but Matt's mum and her friend came round on Boxing Day, and then we had a few friends round for the bells. The usual crew. Heather and Jason, Leah from work, our friend Kate, Matt's mum and Derek again. It was a good wee night. Got a bit messy when the karaoke started right enough.'

'Kate? That's a new name,' Mum pipes up from the back. Ugh. I should have known better. I've triggered her 'nosy cow' alert.

'Yeah, she's lovely,' I say. 'A good laugh.'

'How do you know her?' she digs, drawing the question out. Here we go. She's like a dog with a bone when she gets started on something.

'Matt met her at work—'

'And he just decided to bring her home?' she says, sitting forward now. I hate when she gets like this.

'It's nothing like that, Mum. Stop it. She's dead nice.'

'It wouldn't matter how nice she was, I wouldn't be very happy if your dad started palling about with another woman, I'll tell you that.'

'Mum, she's just split up with her girlfriend. That was how

her and Matt met in the coffee shop. Her girlfriend dumped her. Kate's gay.'

'Aye, they all say that until the right man comes along. If I was you, I'd be making sure I marked my territory, that's all I'm saying.'

'For God's sake, Carol,' Dad says.

'Mum!' I snap. 'I'm not going to pee up Matt's leg to warn Kate off. I told you, it's not like that. She's our friend.'

Ugh. Just like that, she's managed to completely sour something good in my life. I spend so much time working that I don't get many chances to make new friends, let alone one I happen to like as much as I like Kate. And now it feels like she's made it, I don't know, something to be ashamed of, or worried about. Something *dirty.*

'Okay, whatever you say. You won't hear another word from me on the subject.'

If only that were true. It would be the first time, if that was the case.

We drive the rest of the distance back to their place in Newton Mearns in a tense silence, and I remember why I don't spend as much time with Mum as I probably should.

Because every time I do, I inevitably end up feeling like crap.

Chapter Thirteen: January 20th

Kate

I'd never imagined redecorating would have been this much fun. I'm not even gonna lie, I was really nervous that I'd make a mess of things. But then I reminded myself that it doesn't really matter if I do. I live by myself, who's even going to see it? As it happens, though, I haven't made a mess of anything at all. I watched a couple of tutorial videos on YouTube, and I've got Paige and Matt here keeping me right, too. What else could a girl ask for?

I'd mentioned to Dad that I was planning to redecorate in an attempt to try and put Steph behind me, and bless his heart, he asked if I needed any help. I'm not really sure that he totally understood why it was so important for me to do this, but I love that he offered anyway. He really is the best.

We've got quite a nice little rhythm going now and we're making real progress. Paige is up on the steel stepladder painting the parts that my short arse can't reach, and I'm working my way along the bottom half, painting up as high as I can. I was tempted to go a little crazy and splash out – if you'll pardon the pun – on some bold colours, but in the end common sense took hold and I settled on a gorgeous silver grey that really gives the living room a more intimate – and uncharacteristically classy - feel. I'm perfectly happy taking interior design tips from Paige. I'm a complete and utter disaster when it comes to that kind of stuff, and Paige's place, as I noticed at New Year, is every bit as perfectly co-ordinated and put together as she is.

As we continue painting, I pause to reload my brush and

notice Matt sitting in the centre of the floor, with his tongue poking through his teeth as he attempts to put together the new dark grey wood effect coffee table I picked up in the sale at Ikea. I nudge Paige quietly and motion at him, sticking my tongue out like his. She giggles a little. Matt raises his head.

'What?' he asks.

'You were making your concentration face again,' Paige laughs.

'Is that a thing?' I ask her.

'Honestly, he does it every time. The first time I saw him do it, I thought I was going to pee myself,' she grins.

'Quit bullying me, you pair of absolute clownshoes,' he smiles, sticking his tongue out even further and then returning to his furniture assembly duties.

I enjoyed the little shopping trip the three of us took to Ikea after Paige finished work the other night, even if I did end up spending a little more than I'd originally intended. The thing is, that was *our* thing, Steph and I. Wee jaunts down to Ikea at Braehead for knick-knacks for the flat, I mean. That was a thing that we always did together, and there was a very real danger that if I didn't reclaim it for myself, it would end up becoming one of those things I'd never be able to do again, because her memory was inextricably entangled in it. And if there's one thing that I am completely unwilling to sacrifice upon the altar of Steph-memories, it's a plate full of Ikea meatballs. Besides, I don't remember Steph and I ever having an epic pillow fight in Ikea like the one I had with Paige. We're all about making new memories this new year, right?

'Pass me that bottle of water up, Kate,' Paige says. 'I'm parched here.'

I pick the bottle up from the floor and reach up with it, and as I do, she reaches for it and then *boops* the tip of my nose with her paintbrush.

'Oops,' she grins.

'Cow,' I laugh, and run my own brush up her bare arm. Matt rolls his eyes and carries on being the responsible adult on the floor. I'm beginning to come to the realisation that this is what I've been missing lately, even before Steph and I officially called it quits – well, Steph called it quits, I suppose. We'd been missing this dynamic for a long time, and I hadn't even noticed it had gone. That playfulness. Being able to mess around and have a laugh. Everything had just become so serious, so workmanlike, so routine and pedestrian. Somewhere along the line, we'd just stopped having fun.

We're sitting on the floor around my newly assembled coffee table, Paige and I with our backs against the front of my couch on one side, and Matt leaning against the bottom of my armchair on the other side, none of us able to move as a result of the dinner I'd ordered from Jade Palace as a little thank you not just for their hard work today, but for the kindness they've shown me by helping me get through these last few weeks.

'Does it feel like your own space now?' Paige asks. I look at the new lamp, still in its box, and imagine how it'll look in the corner once the paint has dried.

'It's starting to,' I say, and for the first time, I think that I mean it. Just the simple act of throwing up a couple of coats of paint and adding a couple of pieces of furniture is making me feel like I'm taking control of my life again. I can see the living room starting to take shape. I think I can even feel myself starting to take shape. It's all going to be okay.

'Thanks for today, guys,' I say, as I see them to the door. 'You've both been amazing.'

Paige gives me a warm, squeezy hug, and I feel like I could cry. But not sad tears. I close the door and walk back into the living room. Back into *my* new living room. I take my new lamp out of its box, switch it on, pour myself out another glass of wine, and flop back onto the couch. I hit the button on the remote control and turn the TV on. I feel like watching a movie tonight. The cheesier the better, and without a single hint of guilt.

Chapter Fourteen: January 25th

Paige

Ugh. I'm already exhausted and it's not even lunchtime yet. My email inbox is seriously about to explode, I've still got a stack of document revisions to get through, and my desk is a certifiable disaster zone. I can see Connor bloody McCauley out of the corner of my eye. I know he's just waiting for me to make a mistake that he can pounce on to make himself look good. Weaselly little shit, so he is. Right, forget him. Focus on your own stuff here, Paige. One task at a time. Let's start with Mrs. MacDonald's latest revision to her will. Assuming I can find the notes from yesterday's meeting, that is. I really need to tidy this mess up.

I slip my feet out of my stupid impractical heels under my desk. Some days, I wish I could work like Kate does. Just roll out of bed, grab the first piece of clothing that comes to hand, and away you go. I'm not sure the partners would appreciate me rocking up in a baggy t-shirt and a pair of Matt's boxer shorts, though. Talking of which.

'Paige, fantastic work on those filings for the Docherty case,' says Mr. Sneddon, one of the senior partners, as he sticks his head around the door. 'Very persuasive argument and a great use of citations. It's come back from the KC completely unaltered, which is the highest compliment a trainee can get. Keep up the good work. Catch up with me tomorrow and we can talk about you shadowing me in the High Court next week. You'll enjoy the experience.'

I don't even have to look around. I can literally feel Connor bloody McCauley seethe silently behind me. He's constantly fawning around Mr. Sneddon and Mr. Turnbull, trying to get their attention and approval. I bet hearing that is absolutely ripping him apart.

'Paige, can you hurry up with Mrs. MacDonald's papers, please?' he huffs. 'I've got more important things to do than sit around waiting on you.'

Normally I'd be annoyed at his snarky tone, but right now I feel absolutely bulletproof. It's not just the praise from a partner, amazing as that is, it's the fact that it's got so deep under his skin that's giving me such a buzz.

'Right on top of that, Connor,' I smile. Oh my God, I think he might actually cry, he's so raging.

I know full well that he's in no rush for the papers, he's just trying to make a point and re-establish his place in what he thinks is the pecking order. With that in mind, I slip my shoes back on, grab my jacket, and decide to take an early lunch break. Leah winks at me as I pass her desk. She loathes Connor's arrogance, entitlement and misogyny almost as much as I do.

I'm standing at the queue waiting to order my sandwich, so I decide to call Matt to tell him about my exciting morning. He's working the late shift tonight, so he'll just be starting to get ready.

'Hi, babe, how was your morning?' he answers the phone.

'Oh my God, wait until you hear this,' I bubble. 'I got properly praised up by one of the partners in front of Connor. He was absolutely livid.'

'Brilliant!' I can hear him laughing. He's had to put up with my 'Connor bloody McCauley' rants often enough in the evening that he understands exactly how happy I am right now.

'What are you doing? Out grabbing some lunch?' he asks me.

'Yeah, just a sandwich. I might be a little late getting home tonight, though. My desk is an absolute state. I need to get it sorted out.'

'How about I put something together and leave it in the slow cooker for you? That'll save you having to make something when you get home.'

'Have I ever told you that you're the best boyfriend ever?' I grin.

'You have, but you can tell me again!' he replies.

'While we're on the subject of dinners,' I say. 'How about inviting Kate over for a bite one night next week? You can dazzle her with your culinary prowess!'

'Sounds like a plan. I'll give her a ring once I get dressed.'

'Love you, babe,' I say.

'To the moon and back,' he replies.

'Next please,' calls the sandwich artist at the counter, and I step up to place my order. I am so going to enjoy this victory lunch. I know, I know, I'm petty. What can I tell you?

Matt

I'm in my flat when Paige calls to tell me about her morning and to ask me to invite Kate round for dinner one night next week. I've been spending less and less time here lately, and it just makes perfect sense for me to officially move in with Paige now. I'm there more than I'm here, and besides, her place is so much nicer than mine! I emailed the landlord with my notice just after the party at New Year, and in less than two weeks, I'll officially be living with the woman I love instead of just playing house. I can't even begin to describe how excited I am about it. Even though it won't be all that different in practical terms, it'll just make things feel 'real,' you know what I mean?

I pull my black work polo shirt over my head and tuck it into the waistband of my jeans. I don't mind working the late shift sometimes, even though Paige is normally tucked up in bed for work by the time I get home. I make my way into the kitchen, past the pile of half-packed boxes containing the few bits and pieces I'll be taking with me when I move out. Most of my furniture has already been advertised as free to a good home, as I doubt I'd get very much for it.

I pick my phone up from the kitchen counter and dial Kate's number.

'Hey, Matt. What're you up to?' she asks breezily.

'Just getting ready for work. You?' I reply.

'Got a two thousand word piece to write about the Life of a Professional Honeytrapper.'

'I'm sorry, what?' I ask. 'What on earth is a Professional Honeytrapper? Is it something to do with keeping bees?' I immediately regret even asking the question because I know she's going to answer it.

'They're women who get paid to chat up other women's boyfriends to test their loyalty.'

'Come on,' I say, dumbfounded. 'There's no way that's a thing. Is that an actual thing?'

'It is,' she says. 'I interviewed one for the article. I had no idea either. It's nuts. The idea is, the women who suspect their boyfriends or husbands or whatever might be messing about pay these other women to approach them so they've got actual proof. They give them their men's socials, and the Honeytrappers follow them, slide into their DMs, and see if they take the bait.'

'Seriously, you're winding me up, right?' I ask.

'No! One time this woman I interviewed reported back to the client, and it turns out the snake was messaging this girl while his partner was beside him in bed!'

'And this is her job? Like, her *actual* job,' I ask. 'She can make a living doing it?'

'You'd be amazed how much they make!' she says. 'The girl I spoke to charges thirty quid per trap, and she's almost reached the point where she'll need to start a waiting list, because she's struggling to keep up with the demand.'

'I don't even know what to say to that. I had no idea there were so many rats out there.'

'What can I say? They're not all good guys like you, Matt,'

she says. 'Remind me the next time we hang out, and I'll show you the screenshots she sent me.'

'That's why I called, actually. You got any plans for next week?'

'Well, I was thinking about alphabetising my DVD collection, but Steph took most of the good ones when she moved out, so I don't imagine that'll take me very long. And I was planning on trying to beat my own personal record for number of hours spent slouched on the couch watching bad reality TV. My diary is pretty packed, unless you can make me a better offer.'

'How about dinner at ours? I'm cooking, so I've been told.'

'Hmm,' she says, pondering the offer. 'A decent home cooked meal and the chance of some mildly amusing banter, or a tub of ice cream in front of Love Island. What's a girl to do? Aye, go on then, I'm in.'

'*Mildly* amusing?' I laugh. 'Scrub it. Invite's off the table. You're officially disinvited.'

'I take back what I said, then. You're not a nice guy after all!' she says.

'How's next Friday for you, then? I'm off on Friday night anyway, so I'll have all day to whip up a culinary masterpiece.'

'Works for me,' she says.

'Right, back to your Honeytrapper,' I laugh. 'Talk to you later.'

And with that, I hang up, having learned a new word for the day and something interesting to blow Paige's mind with tonight.

Chapter Fifteen: February 2nd

Paige

'I actually thought about phoning to ask what you were wearing before I left,' Kate says, referring to the last time she was invited over. It makes me laugh and I give her a hug as she enters.

'Matt's in the kitchen, stick your head in and say hi,' I say as I hang her coat up in the hall, trying to make her feel as at home as I can. As ridiculous as it sounds, the truth is that I can't get Mum's stupid comments out of my head. I know that I have nothing at all to worry or be even remotely suspicious about, but yet again, I've let her get to me. I always do this.

'Can I get you a drink, babe?' I ask.

'Wine—' Kate says.

'Beer—' Matt says at the same time, and they both laugh. I roll my eyes.

I get a bottle of lager out of the fridge and pop the top off before I sit it on the counter beside Matt, who is busily stirring one pot as he shakes another with his free hand. I pour a glass of red wine out for Kate and hand it to her with a smile.

'Come through and get comfortable,' I say to her, nodding to the living room. 'We'll leave Jamie Oliver there to get on with it.' He's got his 'concentration tongue' poking out again, and I can't even begin to take him seriously.

We haven't had time to hang out over the last week or so, and I couldn't wait to see her again. I've just been dying to have a bit of girl talk, I think. God bless Matt, he tries, but it's not the same as having another woman to catch up with. She tells me about some of the articles she's been working on for the next few issues of the magazine, and I tell her about some of the more interesting and unsavoury characters and stories I've come across while I've been shadowing Mr. Sneddon at the High Court. We then move on to the latest trashy reality TV we've been watching, and over the second glass of wine, we compare notes on who we secretly fancy on this year's Love Island.

'Oh my God, Paige,' she laughs. 'Does Matt know you ogle that snakey wee rat?'

'We've got a celebrity "free shag" pact,' I explain.

'Sorry, a *what?*' she splutters.

'We've each got a set of celebrities we're allowed to drool over, no guilt attached, because let's face it, Henry Cavill probably isn't going to come and kick the door down to whisk me away any time soon, is he?'

'Fair point,' she nods.

'Matt's current number one is Emma Watson, obviously.'

'Ooh, she's stunning,' Kate agrees. 'I'd let her use her magic wand on me,' and it's my turn to splutter into my drink. Matt sticks his head around the door.

'Everything okay in here?'

'Emma Watson,' Kate says, winking and giving him the thumbs up. He just grins goofily, nods his head, and ducks back into the kitchen, out of harm's way.

'Who else is on his list?' she follows up. 'It sounds like we have similar taste in women!'

'Well, there's Gal Gadot,' I say.

'Yes!' she squeals.

'I should probably confess,' I say. 'When I was growing up, I had a gigantic crush on her too. For a while when I was a teenager, I had actually convinced myself that I might be gay, or bisexual at least. In the end, it turns out that I wasn't actually in love with Gal Gadot, I just *reeeeeally* wanted to be Wonder Woman.'

For a minute, Kate is completely expressionless, and I worry that I might have overstepped or overshared. But then she bursts into uproarious laughter, and I feel a surge of relief that I haven't offended her. She's almost in tears by the time Matt tells us that dinner's ready.

Over dinner we talk about recipes we've seen or enjoyed making, and I learn that Kate's as infatuated with Nigella's cooking as I am. She sends me a link to a website she's found full of the most amazing Middle Eastern recipes, and I return the favour by pointing her at my favourite site for Mediterranean dishes. I'll give Matt all the credit he's due tonight. He's pulled out all the stops with the meal. Everything was fantastic, and he's enjoyed playing host too, making sure the wine glasses are kept topped up. I've obviously got him well-trained. I can't wait until he's moved in here full-time with me.

'Can I ask you something?' I say to Kate as I savour the last mouthful of my cheesecake.

'Aye, of course,' she replies.

'Maybe it's too soon, and feel free to tell me if I'm being a nosy cow, I was just thinking. Well, wondering really. Have you thought about getting on to some of the dating apps? You know, for when you're ready to put yourself back out there again?'

'I'd been thinking about it. I mean, there's no harm in looking, right?' she says. 'It's just— it's been a while since I've had to even look, know what I mean? I don't think I'd even know where to start. I mean, what do you even say about yourself on those things?'

'I could help. If you like, I mean?'

'You wouldn't mind? That— that would be great, honestly, Paige.'

'Get your phone out, girl,' I laugh, topping up her wine.

Matt gets up from the dinner table and starts gathering up our plates as I shift my seat around. We've got girl business to take care of.

Kate

'Can I ask you something?' Paige asks me as I take another sip of my wine.

'Aye, of course,' I nod.

'Maybe it's too soon, and feel free to tell me if I'm being a nosy cow, I was just thinking. Well, wondering really. Have you thought about getting on to some of the dating apps? You know, for when you're ready to put yourself back out there again?'

I have toyed with the idea, don't get me wrong. I don't know if it's too soon. I mean, Steph didn't waste any time in moving on from me, I guess, so what's the harm? I can just sign up and have a look around, right? It doesn't mean I want to jump into bed with the first person I see. Not that I haven't toyed with that idea either, when I've been at my lowest. I know I'd hate myself afterwards, though. I've been lonely, but never *that* lonely.

'I'd been thinking about it. I mean, there's no harm in looking, right?' I tell her. 'It's just— it's been a while since I've had to even look, know what I mean? I don't think I'd even know where to start. I mean, what do you even say about yourself on those things?'

'I could help. If you like, I mean?'

'You wouldn't mind? That— that would be great, honestly, Paige,' I say.

'Get your phone out, girl,' she laughs, topping up my glass.

Matt stands up quite abruptly and starts stacking up our empty plates. I guess he'd prefer not to be involved in the girl talk. I can't say I blame him, I guess. Paige shifts her chair around a little closer to me, and I get my phone out as he heads into the kitchen.

'First things first, let's get a photo of you that'll have the girls queueing up to get to you.'

Oh yeah, I bet I'll have to beat them off with a stick. I always joke that I turn more stomachs than I turn heads. But then,

I've seen Paige's Insta, and I know that she knows how to take an incredible photo. Of course, she has better raw materials to work with than me, but still. Let's see how much of a magician she is. She starts primping and foofing around with my hair, and I immediately feel completely self-conscious. She takes my phone and messes around with a few of my camera settings, stands up, holds the phone at a really strange angle, and presses a button. She makes a couple of swiping motions, hands me my phone, smiling, and then sits down again. My eyes open wide.

'I— uh. How have you done that?'

'Not too bad, eh?' she smiles.

Not too bad? This woman is a miracle worker. I'm looking at the picture she's just taken, and I can barely believe I'm looking at myself. And not in that way where you can look at some girls' profile pictures, and you just know they've been filtered more than Matt's coffee. It looks like me, but on my very best day. I can't believe it. Maybe it's the wine. It has to be the wine. I'm not *that* pretty. Am I? I just can't get my head around it. I look at her.

'I'll feel like such a catfish if I use that pic!' I say.

'What? Why?' she asks.

'Look at it!' I say. 'I actually look like a human in that. I mean, I look... pretty.'

'You're kidding me, right?' she asks. 'You are. You're gorgeous, babe. You don't see that?'

'Well... no. Not really. Or at least I'm not used to hearing it from someone who isn't a blood relative, anyway. I can't remember the last time Steph told me-' I cut myself off before I start choking up.

'Well, you'd better get used to it, lady,' she smiles. 'Once we get this profile put together, you're going to be hearing it a lot.'

You know what? I think I actually like the sound of that. What the hell, I could use a wee bit of a confidence boost. I can hear Matt clattering about in the kitchen, and I'm about to ask if he needs a hand, but Paige interrupts my train of thought.

'Right, let's get started. What are you looking for, besides someone to make your bed rock?' she laughs.

'Well, that would be a pretty decent starting point,' I grin.

Matt

I put the pile of dishes down on the kitchen counter with a clatter and pull the door of the dishwasher open. I grab myself a bottle of beer from the fridge because I don't want to go back into the living room to get my wine and I can't even explain why. I pop the cap off the bottle and drink the entire beer in two gulps. I put it into the box to go out to the recycling bin later and grab another one from the fridge.

I load the dirty plates into the dishwasher and close the door again. I pop the cap off the second bottle and take another swig.

What the hell *was* that, Matt? What are you doing? Take a breath. What's going on? Are you...? Is that...?

Are you actually *jealous*, Matt? What the hell? Where is that coming from? What, because Paige is helping Kate sign up for a dating website? Really? That's messed up, dude. Think about this logically for a minute. Kate is your friend. Kate is gay. And even if she wasn't both of those things, you're with Paige. You love Paige.

So just what the hell is your problem, and why are you getting so bent out of shape? Why would it matter to you whether or not Kate thinks she might be ready to start a new relationship? And who even says that she is? All she's doing is signing up to a dating site. That doesn't even mean anything.

Okay. Got that. So, let's tackle this question again. What the hell was that? Are you scared that if she starts seeing someone else, you won't be able to hang out with her as much anymore? Or could it be that—

Don't say it. Don't say it, Matt. Don't you dare even *think* it.

Are you jealous because you think you've got feelings for her that go beyond friendship? Because that would be ridiculous, and stupid, and dangerous.

Damn it.

Heather warned you about this, you idiot. You literally had one job. You've never looked at her like that before now. And the fact that you're even friends at all was your decision. You could easily have walked away from the bench on Sauchiehall Street, and that would have been that. But now you're friends, you've been happy with that, and what? All of a sudden, you want something else? Something more?

Give your head a wobble, dude. You're acting like an arse because of something that you can never have, something that you should never even *want*.

I finish tidying up around the kitchen, and then I drain the remains of that second beer and put it into the recycling box. Now I'm going to go back into the living room, I'm going to sit down at the table with my friend and the woman I love more than anything else in the whole world, and I'm going to have a glass of wine and act like I didn't just have to have this conversation with myself.

And that is exactly what I do. I sit quietly while Paige and Kate put the finishing touches to Kate's profile, and I sip my wine, nodding and laughing along with their conversation, but not contributing very much beyond that.

When Kate decides that it's time to head for home, sometime just before midnight, the three of us stand in the hall, waiting for her taxi and making plans to hang out at the pub quiz again next Thursday night. When it eventually arrives, Paige gives Kate a hug and a kiss on the cheek, and when Kate leans in towards me to do the same again, I give her an obviously platonic hug which couldn't scream 'we are friends and nothing more!' any louder if it tried.

As I close the door, Paige squeezes my hand and asks if I want to finish off the rest of the wine, and while there's nothing I would enjoy more than spending the last little bit of the evening with her, I'm not particularly enjoying my own company right now.

'Nah, I'm not feeling too hot,' I only partially lie. 'I might be coming down with something. I think I'll just head to bed.'

Chapter Sixteen: February 3rd

Kate

I flick the switch on the kettle to make myself a cup of tea and walk back into the living room while I wait for it to boil. Saturday morning, and I'm not even feeling the slightest bit rough despite the amount of wine the three of us put away last night. Probably just as well, though, as I've got a ton of work to get through and deadlines are looming. I really need to start getting my workload better organised. I always seem to keep putting things off until the last minute.

The button clicks and I put a teabag into my favourite mug and fill it to the brim with boiling water. Last night was fun. I mean, it always is when I hang out with Paige and Matt. I just genuinely enjoy their company. I've noticed something recently, though. As much as I enjoy it at the time, when it's over and I'm back on my own, here in the flat or wherever, I've been getting this feeling. I can't quite put my finger on it or even explain properly what it is, let alone what's causing it. It's like a little twinge of something. I don't know if it's sadness, exactly. And if it's jealousy, it's not because I'm jealous of either Paige or Matt. Nothing could be further from the truth. I absolutely adore them both, and they're clearly perfect for each other. But maybe that's what it is that I feel a little envious of. What they have together. I see how easy and effortless their interactions are, how they bounce off each other and support each other so beautifully, and I miss having what they have. Having that person in my life that I can share that with. I really thought that Steph was that person for me, in the beginning at least. Towards the end, I should have seen the signs sooner.

We were never right. I didn't see that at the time because I didn't really know what 'right' was until I met Matt and Paige. They're the very definition of 'right together.'

I've been thinking this over all morning. Maybe Paige was right. I mean, it's not even been two months yet since Steph and I split up, but maybe it's time I at least start to think about putting myself back out there. I don't have to dive headfirst back into the dating pool, but at the very least there's no harm in dipping my toe into the water, right?

I really should be getting some work done, but I need a distraction to keep my mind off my mind. And I know just the person.

'Hey, sis,' Fi says as she answers the phone. 'How was your dinner party with the suburban sex swingers last night?'

'Oh my God, Fiona, you are, like, *sooo* funn-eh,' I drawl, making sure she gets the sarcasm.

I hear her giggling, and I can just imagine the smile on her face. Cow.

'Good night, though, eh?' she asks me, composing herself.

'Yeah, it was, actually. I feel like I'm getting to know Paige a little better now that she's getting comfortable with me, because,' I put the emphasis on the next part, a little for my sister's benefit, but mostly for humorous effect, 'now she knows I'm not out to steal her man!'

'So what did you all get up to, then? Since, you know, no kinky party stuff.'

'Shut up, halfwit,' I laugh. 'It was just a nice fun night. Good food, some laughs, some girl talk. It's nice to have someone I can talk to that gets me.'

'Well, I remember when that used to be me,' she says, and to be fair, she does sound a little bit hurt, and I feel bad.

'Och, you know what I mean. You're still my bestie, and you always will be. But there are probably conversations that I can have with pals that you might not want to hear. I mean, who wants to hear their wee sister talk about her sex life?'

'Oh my God, Katie, naw, I'm sticking my fingers in my ears,

la-la-la-la-la-la, I can't hear you!'

'Aye, see? That's why I'm glad I've got Paige to talk to now. You know, she even helped me set up my profile on one of those dating apps last night. She took a photo of me that I don't look like a complete munter in. Who knows, I might even end up getting my hole out of it!'

'Right, that's it, I'm away. Back to your swinger pals with that patter, young lady,' she says, and we both laugh.

'Love you, Fi.'

'Love you too, hen. Despite your best efforts.'

I end the call, and despite a pressing need to get back to my laptop and get to these two articles that I promised I'd have finished by Monday, I don't. I open up the dating app on my phone, and I start swiping through the photos which appear.

Chapter Seventeen: February 4th

Paige

The worst thing about getting out of bed early on a Sunday when Matt is on the morning shift, is that I inevitably end up getting all of the housework done before most folk have even got out of bed and gone to the newsagents for their Sunday morning rolls. So far today, I've unloaded the dishwasher, cleaned the bathroom, vacuumed the living room, ironed my clothes for work, and put another load into the washing machine.

I mean, I suppose I could go back to bed and get another couple of hours sleep, but I'm already a coffee deep and I feel a bit too wired for that. I could get a jump on some of the upcoming week's work, but I'm probably not wired *enough* for that just yet. I could even have a crack at following along with that new yoga video I saw online the other day, but, well— Look, I can't actually think of an excuse not to do that off the top of my head, but if you give me a minute or two, I'll come up with something plausible enough. I'm a lawyer. It's what I do.

I briefly consider taking a walk along to the tanning salon down the road and getting in a session on the sunbed, because I've let Mum get inside my head again. That comment she made about me looking like the lassie from Twilight has been living rent-free inside my head for weeks now, and I know that I shouldn't let her get to me like that, but she just has this way of doing that. Like the time she just happened to mention in passing that I might have to think about cutting back on the wine a wee bit, or else just give up and move up a dress size. I was absolutely devastated, and no matter how much Matt tried to talk sense into me, she had me convinced that I was a fat, unlovable mess, without even saying anything of the kind. Unbelievable. The thing is, though, I don't think that she means to be nasty at all. I don't believe she ever sets out to say things that genuinely hurt me, I just think she's completely oblivious to how people take things, you know?

Maybe I'm just making excuses for her because she's my mum. I don't know. One thing that I am very sure of right now, is that I need another coffee, and maybe even one of those croissants with the chocolate and hazelnut filling. I'll worry about fitting into my dress later, if that's quite okay with you, Mum?

While I'm waiting for the kettle to boil for my second coffee of the day, I ponder what else I can do to pass the time until Matt gets home tonight. I don't particularly feel like spending the day slouched on the couch vegging out in front of the TV, and I've already talked myself out of being productive and getting some work done. I take my phone out of the pocket of my sweatpants and call Kate.

'Hiya, Paige,' she answers, sounding a little stressed. 'Everything okay?'

'Yeah, I'm good,' I say. 'Just wondered if you had any plans for today?'

'I've got some work to do, but I can't get myself motivated at all,' she answers.

'I can relate to that. Fancy taking a break and coming out for some lunch with me?'

'Just the two of us?' she asks.

'Just us girls,' I say. 'Matt's working all day, and I could use some company. We can have a bite to eat, go for a wee wander around some of the shops, maybe have a look at your dating app and check out some of the likely suspects? If you can get away, I mean.'

'I'd like that,' she says after a little pause. 'Work can wait.'

'I'm going to jump in a shower to get freshened up and then

I'll pick you up. About twelve?"

'Sounds good to me,' she says.

I hang up and decide against that second cup of coffee. Instead, I start looking for lunch recommendations in town while I wait for the shower to warm up.

Kate

Today's work in progress is titled *'Business on Top, Party Below the Desk: Dress for Success When You Work from Your Couch,'* and I wouldn't be lying if I said that was an area in which I have considerable expertise. Although, if I'm being entirely honest, neither half of me looks particularly dressed for success on this Sunday morning. Comfort, certainly. Success, not so much. I'm wearing a long baggy t-shirt which doubles as a nightdress, and what I can only describe as my 'big pants.' In addition, I'm absolutely rocking the 'natural look,' which is a kind way of saying that I couldn't be arsed putting make-up on. Or brushing my hair, come to think of it. Quite the catch, Katie babe, aren't we?

Come to think of it, calling the article 'work in progress' is being a bit liberal with the truth too. It's in progress to the extent that I've typed out the title. I just can't get myself into the right frame of mind to work today. Maybe if I took my own advice and actually dressed like I intended to, oh, I don't know, do some work, I might be a little more productive. Dress for Success? Dress to Depress is probably closer to the mark for me today.

I need a break and I'm relieved and just a little surprised when Paige calls to ask if I want to go out to lunch. She says she'll swing by to pick me up around twelve, which should just about give me enough time to shower, dress and try to mould myself into something that vaguely resembles a functional adult human.

I see her car pull up outside, so I throw on my jacket and

head downstairs. I open the door and slide in, and immediately I feel completely and utterly inadequate and hideous. Paige looks absolutely and sickeningly immaculate. She's straightened her long blonde hair, and her makeup looks completely natural and effortless. She's wearing a pair of retro stonewashed ripped jeans, paired with her chunky wedge sandals and the most gorgeous olive green short-sleeved top. I, on the other hand, look like a pig who's got trapped in a potato sack and put some lipstick on while wearing a blindfold.

'Oh my God, I love your dress,' she smiles, leaning in for a side hug from her seat. 'That's so pretty on you! You look amazing, babes.'

Under any other circumstances, I'd want to hate her with all of my heart, but I know that she's being genuine.

'Where are we going?' I ask.

'We'll head up Great Western Road, I think. There are a few places along there that I've been dying to try. We'll park up and just walk along and see if anything takes our fancy?'

'Sounds like a plan to me,' I say, and we're off.

In the end we decide on The Loveable Rogue because we'd both read rave reviews and had been keen to try the Sunday roast menu. We settle into one of the booths by the window, ideal for people-watching on a lazy Sunday afternoon.

'You sounded a little stressed when I called,' she says. 'Everything okay?'

'A bit of writer's block,' I reply. 'Or maybe just feeling a bit out of sorts. I don't know, it's like I've been struggling to get myself motivated when it comes to work recently. I mean, I love my job and stuff, and it's great that I can do it from home, but it's just so—'

'Quiet?' she says.

'That's exactly what it is, I think. I've been so used to working while Steph pottered around in the background, just doing stuff around the flat. It's taking me a while to adjust to being on my own so much.'

'Any luck with the dating app yet?'

'I'd swiped on a couple of girls that I thought were pretty interesting,' I say. 'But no matches yet.'

'Give it time,' she says. 'It's only been a couple of days.'

Our food arrives, and it looks incredible. We both decided on the chicken and ham terrine to start, followed by the full roast beef dinner with all of the trimmings.

'I'm going to have to lie on the back seat of your car on the way home,' I joke. 'I won't be able to fit in the front after this.'

'Aye, I should probably re-think my diet too,' she replies, straight-faced, as she looks down at herself.

'You're joking, right? Tell me you're joking.'

'Yeah. No. Och, I don't know. I'm letting my mum get inside my head again, I think. She makes these snidey little comments sometimes, and I always end up totally taking them to heart and feeling shit about myself. I really should know better. She just says these things without thinking.'

'Obviously I don't know your mum or anything, so feel free to tell me I'm out of line, but you shouldn't make excuses for stuff like that. I mean, first of all, eh – look at you! You're bloody drop-dead gorgeous. I'd literally kill to have a figure like yours. Of course, I'd probably need to kill Mr. Haagen *and* Mr. Dazs to have a figure like yours, but you know what I mean,' I say, trying to lighten her mood at my own expense. She smiles. Go me.

'Thanks, babe,' she says. 'You're so sweet. I think I needed to hear that.'

It makes me a little sad for her that her mum would make her feel like that. More than that, it makes me feel so appreciative of my mum. She's never been anything less than completely supportive of me, no matter what.

We continue chatting as we eat, and I show her a few of the girls on the app that I'd swiped right on to see what she thinks. She gives a couple of them the thumbs up, and I notice that more than one of them have a passing resemblance to— never mind.

'You've a got a little— hang on,' she says, as she reaches

across and gently wipes at a smudge of sauce from the brisket mac 'n' cheese just at the side of my mouth.

As her fingertip barely brushes my lip, I feel a surge of electricity shoot through every nerve in my body, jolting my very senses into life. In this moment which seems to stretch out into the ether, my heart skips a beat, and almost immediately, a flush of warmth spreads across my cheeks, to my chest and down, down, downwards.

'There,' she says, smiling. 'Got it.'

But I can barely hear her above the sound of my heart thrumming in my own chest.

Matt

'Mate, what is the matter with your face? You've spent this whole shift looking like somebody's shit in your kettle.'

Leave it to Heather to say it like it is. I mean, she's not wrong, I suppose. I just can't get out of my own head today after what happened on Friday night. I know it was completely wrong and inappropriate, and it's been playing on my mind since. I'm glad I had to work yesterday and today, because to be honest, I'm not sure I'd have been able to look Paige in the eye and not tell her what was bothering me. Not that I'm any further forward in working out exactly what it is that's bothering me.

'It's nothing, Hev,' I lie.

'Aye, pish, Matt. Come on, I know you better than that. You're usually a sickening ray of sunshine in here. Out with it. What's the score?'

'You really want to know?' I ask.

'I wouldn't have asked if I didn't, would I?'

'Promise not to go mental?'

'The fact that you've had to preface it with that makes it obvious that what you're about to say is going to cause me to go mental, so no, I'm not promising that at all.'

I shake my head. 'Never mind, it's fine.'

She gives me a shove in the arm as she continues wiping down the counter at the end of our shift.

'Tell me,' she says, her tone softening. 'It can't be that bad, whatever it is.'

It is that bad, though, as far as I'm concerned. Because I'm not that guy. I've never been that guy. I'm steady, reliable Matt, the guy who loves his girlfriend more than anything in the world. The guy who would never do anything to cross a line or hurt anyone he cared about. I need to get this out. I need someone to talk sense into me, and if I can rely on anyone to do exactly that, it's Heather.

'I'm an idiot, Hev. I had a bit of a meltdown on Friday night.'

'What? Have you and Paige had a fight or something?'

'No, it's nothing like that. Look, I'm going to tell you something, but I need you to promise you won't breathe a word of this to anyone. This has to stay between you and me, okay?'

'Matt, what have you done?'

'Nothing, I swear. I haven't done anything. I just— I can't really explain it.'

'This is about that Kate lassie, isn't it?'

I can barely even look at Heather, I'm so ashamed of myself. 'Yeah. It is.'

'For fuck's sake, Matt,' she snaps. 'What did I tell you? Please tell me you haven't done something you're going to regret?'

'No, I haven't done anything,' I say.

'And you're not going to, right?'

'Right. Yeah. No, I mean. I don't know. I don't know what's going on. We were all having dinner on Friday night, everything was going fine. Then Paige offered to help Kate get registered on a dating app, and I just—'

'Got jealous? Is that what you're going to say?'

'Aye, I think so. I guess so. I don't know. I told you it's hard to explain. I'm trying to tell myself it's because I enjoy hanging out with her, and if she starts seeing someone else, she won't want to hang about with me— with *us*, anymore.'

'You'd better hope that's all it is, Matt, because so help me God, if you tell me that you're falling in love with her—'

'No, it's not that,' I try to convince us both.

'I'll tell you this then, mate. You need to get your head on straight, and quickly. Because if you don't get on top of this before it becomes a thing, you're going to end up losing everything. You're one of my best friends in the world, Matt, you know you are. But I hope that you'd never do anything behind Paige's back, because if you do, I'll wash my hands of you. I'm sorry if that sounds harsh. But I love you both.'

'I know,' I say. 'I promise I'll sort myself out.'

Even as the words leave my mouth, I know it's a half-hearted promise, and I hate myself just a little bit more.

Kate

Lunch today was amazing, but that's the last thing on my mind as I sit alone in my living room. My dress is off, thrown over the back of the couch, bra too, and I'm back to wearing just my favourite baggy t-shirt and pants, and all I can think about, over and over and over again, is that feeling. That electric, electrifying feeling that almost bloody set me on fire when Paige touched my face. I don't know where the hell it came from, but I know exactly where it *went*, and it made me feel something deep down in a place where I haven't been touched in months. It made me feel... alive. But it made me feel more than that. It made me feel guilty. Shocked. Mostly, it made me feel confused.

I'm so stupid. I don't know why I thought any of this would be a good idea. I know it doesn't mean what I think it means. It wasn't intended to make me feel the way I did. It was just a friendly gesture, nothing more, but what I felt was visceral, almost animal. It lit up every synapse in my brain, and now I can't shake it off. I'm sitting here replaying the moment over and over in my head, trying to work out what the hell is going on with me. Paige is my friend, and that's all she'll ever see me as too, so why on earth am I even feeling this? I'm so confused.

And then there's Matt. Oh God. Matt. What the hell are you doing, Kate? That poor guy has been nothing but kind to you. Twice, he went out of his way to look after you and make sure you were okay, when he could just as easily have walked away and left you to deal with your own shite. Then he risks introducing you to his girlfriend, which could have gone all kinds of wrong for him. He's welcomed you into his life, into his world, he's helped you decorate your flat in an attempt to make you feel better... and this is how you repay him?

I get it. It's because you're lonely, that's all. That's it. That's all it is. It's some kind of weird transference or something. You've seen how incredible his relationship with Paige is, and you want that too. But not with Paige. Not her. She's just a representation of what you want from a relationship in your life. This isn't about her. It's not about her. Right?

Yeah. You're lonely. That's what it is. We can fix that, though. We can do something about that which doesn't involve burning someone else's relationship to the ground.

I pick up my phone and swipe open the dating app. See? It doesn't have to be Paige. There are plenty of single, available, *complication-free* women who would be lucky to have someone like you. Here's Susan from Carntyne. She's pretty. Loves dancing, Chinese food, craft beers and self-deprecating humour. Swipe right. Or how about Jacqueline from King's Park? Gorgeous red hair. Sings in an ABBA tribute band, into vegan food and true crime podcasts. She'll do just fine. Swipe right. Look! Here's Claire from Cathcart. Incredible boobs. Into yoga, cycling and hiking. Hmm. I don't know if I like the sound of all that activity. Pros: she's into yoga, she'll be flexible. And her boobs really *are* spectacular. Cons: Hiking. I hate the feeling of sweat in my bum crack. The boobs, though. Swipe right.

And with every single swipe right my confusion and self-loathing both deepen – and I'm ashamed to say that there are a lot of swipes. Like, an almost indecent amount. So much that, if I were a dude, I'd be slagging myself off for being a man-whore. I think at some point I stopped even looking at the locations and the bios and just kind of mentally sized up how likely I'd be to just drag them into bed. This has not been my finest evening by a long shot, and I can't help but feel I'm going to regret a lot of it tomorrow.

But I still don't regret going out for lunch with Paige today, no matter what. Because right now, that's all I can think about. Whether Susan from Carntyne or Jackie from King's Park or Claire from Cathcart or any of the other dozens of anonymous women I've just swiped on will be able to light me up the way Paige did today.

I'm still so confused when I go to bed that, in the midst of crying myself to sleep, I find my hand wandering, wandering, and with every delicate touch, every slight brush and graze of my most warm and sensitive flesh, I feel my guilt and confusion dissipate and my pleasure grow, and as my body shudders around my fingers, I surrender myself helplessly to ecstasy and eventually sleep, no longer feeling any shame at all, and the last face I see as I close my eyes belongs to Paige.

Paige

Matt's not home from work yet by the time I get back from my lunch with Kate, but I'm sure he won't be too far behind me. I'm still feeling absolutely stuffed, but I know he'll be hungry when he gets home, so I've swung by the supermarket and picked up a nice piece of steak for him. I've already got a jacket potato cooking in the oven to go with it. Oh, and a nice bottle of Argentinian red wine, now that I'm done driving for the day. I'm looking forward to Matt getting home so I can tell him about the day. It was all such a last-minute thing, that I'd completely forgotten to tell him I'd gone out to The Loveable Rogue with Kate.

We should definitely go out for lunch there, just Matt and I. I know he'd absolutely love the Sunday lunch menu. The roast beef was cooked to perfection, and I know he'd die for that brisket mac 'n' cheese they served on the side. When we do, though, I'll make sure I'm not driving. That way we can try some of those tempting cocktails I had to say no to today because I had the car.

You know, as nice as the food was today, the best part about it was the company. Kate is just so bloody lovely. I mean, despite the weirdness of the circumstances that we've met under, she's so nice that it's impossible not to immediately become best friends with her. She's warm and friendly, she's super funny and doesn't take herself at all seriously, and she's so incredibly intelligent and well-read. I could listen to her talk all day about books she's read and enjoyed, or about articles she's been working on for the magazine. I suppose when I think about it now, about all of the articles of hers that I'd read before we even met, there was never any doubt that we'd become great friends, because she was making me laugh long before I even knew her.

That's why I can't get my head around the fact that she's single now. That ex of hers, Steph or whatever her name is, I don't know what the hell must have been going through her head. I mean, I get it, like Matt says, you never really know what goes on behind closed doors, but for the life of me, I can't imagine what she gets elsewhere that she wouldn't have got from Kate. It's such a shame. I feel so bad for her. She really deserves to be happy. Any girl would be lucky to have someone like Kate around.

I wish I could do more to help her. I mean, I know I helped her set up the dating app and stuff, but still. I need to have a think about what else I can do for her. I'm pretty sure I must know someone who would be good for her. Maybe I'll reach out to Heather too. I'm sure between us, we can find someone for her.

I hear the front door close. Matt's home. I pour out two glasses of the wine. I know he'll appreciate it. Sundays can be so busy in the centre.

'Hi, babe!' I call out from the kitchen. I get out the frying pan, and a portion of the home-made cowboy butter that I got from a TikTok recipe. 'Got you some steak?'

He doesn't answer. Normally, I'd expect him to come sprinting into the kitchen at the merest mention of steak and cowboy butter. I hear water running in the bathroom. I poke my head in the open door and Matt is standing over the sink, splashing cold water on his face.

'You okay, babe?' I ask.

'Yeah, just had a bit of a rough day,' he says.

'Will a nice bit of steak and a glass of wine help?' I smile.

'Maybe later, babe. Right now, all I want to do is sit down.'

Wow. This isn't the Matt I know and love. I've never known him to refuse a steak and wine dinner. I put my hand on his forehead.

'I hope you're not coming down with something,' I say.

'Nothing I won't get over, babe,' he says, finally smiling.

Chapter Eighteen: February 11th

Kate

I open up the dating app on my phone in the hope that I'll have some matches. Even just one would do right now. I'm not greedy at all. I just need something – someone – to distract me, to give me something else to think about apart from—

I haven't spoken to Paige or Matt since my lunch date with Paige last Sunday, but I'd be lying if I said I haven't thought about them. In fact, it's all I've been able to think about, and that's been a factor in why I haven't spoken to them.

When I say I've been thinking about them, I'm ashamed to say that the thoughts haven't exactly been purely platonic. The problem about working from home, and working alone like I do, is that you have a lot of time on your hands to think about things, and worse, over-think things. And sometimes, that turns into daydreaming. Or worse, fantasizing. And that's where things start to get confusing. Deeply, shamefully confusing.

Like last Sunday night, when I got home. I kept thinking about that feeling I got when she touched my face. I let myself imagine what it would have felt like if she hadn't stopped there, and it wasn't just my face which felt flushed. Every square inch of my flesh tingled and came to life. I imagined what it would have felt like if I'd invited her to come back here to my flat, if we'd kissed and I'd tasted her, if I'd slowly undressed her, taken her to bed and—

I know it's wrong. I do. But I can't help myself. What made it even worse, though, was when I thought about Matt. About how nice he's been to me since that first night we met. About how badly hurt he would be. How betrayed he would feel. I thought about how terrible I am. What a horrible friend, what a horrible person I would be. But then that opened up an entirely new Pandora's Box for me. I started to imagine what it would be like if I could be with them. Like, both of them. Together. How good the intimacy of our touches would feel. Our hands all over each other. Our mouths, our lips, our tongues. I wonder, I wonder, I wonder. The worst part of it all is that I hadn't even thought of Matt in that way until Paige's touch opened a door in my mind which should have stayed closed, and now it's all I can think about.

That makes me sound like I'm blaming Paige for this. I'm not. This is all on me. This is all my fault. I should never have allowed myself to get into this situation. And right now, the only way I can think of to get out of it is to just not see either of them. The downside of that is I feel so very, very lonely right now, but maybe that's just what I deserve. Loneliness isn't just the cause of this mess, it's also the end product.

I hate myself so much right now. I mean that. You have no idea how awful I feel, and neither of them has the slightest idea about it. And I can never tell them, either of them, not under any circumstances whatsoever, not ever.

The writer in me thinks that this would make the most fantastic article for the magazine. I could probably even get a cover story out of it. But the same thing that prevents me from writing about it also prevents me from even pursuing the idea in my imagination, let alone in real life. That is, that I have no idea how the story ends, but I suspect it wouldn't be a happy ending for anyone involved.

Chapter Nineteen: February 14th

Paige

It kind of feels like forever since Matt and I last had a date night, just the two of us, between how busy we've both been with work since New Year, and the nights out we've had with Kate tagging along – I shouldn't say it like that, that sounds so mean. I really do love her company, we both do, but it's so nice just the two of us being out for dinner tonight. It's nice to just have a chance to dress up for each other and spend a little time reconnecting, you know what I mean?

Matt finally moved the last of his stuff into my house – *our* house – last week and handed the keys to his flat back to the letting agent, so as of last Friday, we are now officially living together, and I couldn't be happier. Matt booked the table for tonight, but didn't tell me where we were going, just that he wanted to take me out to celebrate finally moving in with me – as well as it being Valentine's Day, of course! I'm over the moon with his choice, though. We're in my favourite Greek restaurant in town, the one which serves the stuffed vine leaves that remind me of our first holiday together in Santorini. He really does make me feel like the luckiest girl in the world.

It's good to see Matt looking a bit happier and more relaxed too. I have to admit I've been a little worried about him over the last couple of weeks. He's been so stressed out trying to get everything wrapped up with his flat before the move, and having to arrange things around his work hours, that it's been hard to even get a conversation out of him sometimes. I'm happy that he's back to his normal self tonight. He's chatty, he's relaxed, he's happy, he's funny and charming. In other words, he's back to being my Matt.

You know, I'd even tried giving Kate a call to see if Matt had maybe mentioned to her that he'd been struggling with anything, but I haven't been able to get a hold of her. I guess she's been pretty snowed under with work. I know that she had some deadlines looming when we went out for lunch last Sunday afternoon. She mentioned that she was struggling with motivation and a little bit of writer's block. Or who knows, maybe she's managed to get lucky from that dating app we set up for her? I'd be thrilled for her if she has, she deserves a little happiness.

'How's the moussaka, babe?' Matt asks me.

'Oh my God, it's soooo good!' I smile. 'Thank you so much for tonight. I really needed this.'

'Yeah, I know. I did too,' he smiles back, and my heart flutters.

'It's nice to see you smiling again. I've been worried about you lately,' I confess.

'I know, babe. I'm sorry. I've just had a lot on my mind over these last few weeks. It's been a lot to deal with. I'm sorry if I've been shutting you out. We're good now, right?'

'We're good, babe,' I reassure him.

I mop up the last of my delicious moussaka with a piece of garlic bread and then take a sip of my wine. Maybe it's the wine, maybe it's the romantic atmosphere, but I'm looking at Matt and all I can think about is taking him home. Back to our home. I feel a little quiver, and my cheeks flush slightly. I love that he still makes me feel like this.

'Have you heard from Kate this week?' I ask him.

'Not since we had her over for dinner,' he answers. 'I should probably give her a message at some point. She might think we're ignoring her or something.'

'Nah, I doubt that, babe,' I say. 'I know she's been busy with work too. When we were out for lunch last Sunday, she mentioned she was struggling for some inspiration with her writing. Between you and me, I think the reality of living alone is starting to take a bit of a toll on her.'

'Oh? Did she say something?'

'Not explicitly. I just kinda got that feeling from her. I don't think she was having much luck with that dating app either.'

'Right.'

'I was thinking, actually,' I say.

'Yeah?'

'It was just an idea more than anything else. I was thinking we could maybe set her up with someone. Maybe we could all go out on a little double date, or something?'

'Have you got anyone in particular in mind?' he asks.

'Not really. I was thinking about reaching out to Heather to see if she could suggest anyone. I know she has a few friends that might be Kate's type.'

'Maybe. I don't know.'

I have a little flash of inspiration.

'What about Sam?' I suggest.

'Sam from University?' he asks.

I don't know why I didn't think of Sam sooner. Of course. She'd be absolutely perfect for Kate. She's funny, she's super smart, she's kind, and I'm absolutely positive that Kate will agree she's very easy on the eye. I think they'll get on like a house on fire.

'Okay, babe. Whatever you think,' Matt says.

I raise my glass and Matt clinks his against mine.

Chapter Twenty: February 16th

Kate

I may have been living like a hermit for the last week or two, but at least I've been a productive hermit. I've managed to get all of my pieces in before their deadlines, and I've even had time to start work on setting up the personal blog that Paige suggested at New Year. There's not much to it just yet, but I'm hoping that I'll be able to build that and my new 'professional writer-y' business Insta account into something that's actually... well, something, I suppose. At the very least, it'll give me an outlet for some of the stuff that's not 'on brand' with the magazine – and by that I mean my smutty meanderings and random nonsense. Who knows? It might open some doors for me to pick up some other freelance bits and pieces. Lord knows I could use the extra cash now I'm living on my own again!

Our Fiona's on the phone. I've only seen her a couple of times since New Year's Day at Mum and Dad's house, and I think she still worries about me sometimes. Scrub that, I know she does. Like I'm still her snottery wee sister who constantly trails about behind her, usually filthy and in need of some kind of attention. Okay, look, that's probably still quite close to the mark, but, you know, rude! Shut up.

'Have you even left the flat since the last time I saw you?' she laughs.

'I'll have you know that I have, you cheeky cow,' I say. 'Paige and I went out and got some paint and redecorated my living room. And then we went up Great Western Road for a bit of lunch last Sunday. I've been a bit busy with work this week, that's all.'

'Hm,' she says.

'What?' I ask.

'Nothing. It's just that everything you do seems to revolve around Paige lately. It's like every time we talk, you mention her.'

'Och, for God's sake, Fi,' I laugh, 'I've already told you, she's not going to replace you!'

'I'm more concerned that you're going to replace her man, the way things are going, Little Miss Steal Yo Girl.'

'Oh, ha ha, very funny. Mind you, at least you won't have to worry about me getting into kinky swingery suburban threesomes then, will you? It'll just be straight-up hot girl on girl action.'

'Ew, you actual give me the dry boak, Katie,' she laughs. 'You smelly wee tramp.'

'Bye, sis. Love you!' I laugh as I hang up on her.

Ugh. Now Fiona's got me feeling a little self-conscious. I know she didn't mean anything by it, but what she's just said has got me questioning myself. Have I been going on and on about Paige too much lately? If I had, I didn't even notice. Like, I find her fascinating and fun and everything, but... am I making it too obvious? I mean, it's not like I can even help it. She's just so cool to be around. She's funny and smart. She's really great to talk to. She's so empathetic. And, like, the way she talks about her work and how passionate she is about that, too. It's inspiring, and when you're friends with people like that, it's only natural that you want to share it with everyone, right? But now Fi's got me heavy paranoid that I'm overdoing it.

Oh my God, what if she's noticed? Have I been acting like a complete fangirl in front of her? What if she's starting to think that maybe, just maybe, I'm starting to get a wee bit of a crush on her? God's sake, Fi, why did you have to come out and say that? Now I'm terrified that I'm going to make things awkward or uncomfortable and lose the only friends I've got right now.

Maybe I do need to dial it back a bit. Maybe I need to be a bit more subtle, more casual. Yeah, that's it. I'll tone it down. Play it cool. No more gushing about her every move, no more dissecting every single conversation we have, looking for hidden subtexts. Just act natural, like she's any other friend.

Except she's not, is she? She's something else entirely, and no amount of internal pep talks is going to change that. So, what else is there to do except just ride this out, hope it passes, and that maybe, just maybe, it's not as obvious as our Fiona thinks it is.

<u>Matt</u>

'I can't believe we're actually getting you all to ourselves tonight, Matty doll,' Jason says as he passes me another beer. 'I'll maybe need to get the handcuffs out and chain you to the radiator to stop you abandoning us for street urchins again.'

'Don't you threaten me with a good time!' I laugh. Anyone else would be moderately terrified if they knew, like I do, that J does in fact have a pair of fur-lined handcuffs in his bedroom and could conceivably attempt to follow through on his threat.

It's that most rare of occasions, a Friday night when I'm left to my own devices. Paige is on a well-deserved night out with her workmates, and while I *could* have texted Kate to see if she wanted to hang out, two very important factors led me to organising a night in at Heather and Jason's place instead. Firstly, I haven't seen much of them since New Year and I still feel bad about ditching them the last time we were actually out in town, and secondly, I'm still not entirely sure I'd feel comfortable hanging out with Kate alone after how I acted when she came round for dinner. I think I'm still trying to convince myself that it's more about reason one than reason two.

The other thing that I wasn't sure about was how Heather would be tonight. We haven't really spoken much since she gave me some tough love in the wake of my semi-confession at work, and I didn't know if she'd told Jason about it afterwards. Thankfully, she doesn't appear to have, and having said her piece to me already, there's no lingering tension and the atmosphere tonight has been back to how it's always been between the three of us – full of good-natured wind-ups and general banter. J's been ranting and raving about a budding rivalry with a newcomer at his work which he's absolutely convinced is because of the unresolved sexual tension between them. Heather's been talking about the gigs she's been to over the last couple of weeks, and played some rough recordings of a couple of new songs the band has been working on, with working titles 'Queer Eye for the Rrriot Guy' and 'No More Mister Nice Femme.'

'Where is the third wheel tonight anyway?' Jason asks.

'She's been really busy with work lately,' I say. Technically, it is true. I can see Heather bristle in her seat. I need to defuse this. 'Paige has been talking about setting her up with one of her old Uni friends, and the four of us going out on a double date kinda thing.'

'That'll be nice,' Hev says cooly. I can't read her. It could be that she genuinely thinks that'll be a nice thing to do, or even a good idea, but I suspect that's not the case.

The security entry buzzer in their flat goes off. Rescued by the takeaway delivery we've been waiting on.

'Well it's about bloody time,' Jason says. 'I'm absolutely Hank Marvin here.'

He bounces up out of his seat and walks out of their living room to collect the food from the delivery driver, most likely in the hope that it's Ian, the skinny, tattooed guy with all of the piercings who occasionally delivers to theirs. J is a sucker for a Machine Gun Kelly lookalike.

Hev shifts over in her seat and whispers, conspiratorially.

'Are you sure this is a good idea, Matt? This whole double date thing, I mean?'

'I need it to be, Hev,' I say. 'I need to do something. It

would be different if I hadn't introduced her to Paige. Then I could have just patched her, shitty of me as that would be, and that would have been that. But Paige likes her and likes hanging out with her. I can only keep making excuses not to hang out for so long, and then I'll need to explain myself. Maybe if I see Kate happy with another girl, that'll straighten my head out and everything will be okay.'

'And if that doesn't work out?' she asks.

I don't have an answer to that question. Not yet, anyway. All I know is that I need to do something to get these thoughts out of my head. Thankfully, I'm spared being forced to answer it, for the time being at least, because Jason is back, laden down with enough boxes and bags to feed way more than just the three of us.

'Right, who's ready for a mouthful of something hot?' he grins.

Chapter Twenty-One: February 18th

Kate

As nice as it is to have friends like Matt and Paige, there's nothing quite like the relationship I have with our Fiona, and I do feel a little guilty that I haven't seen much of her over the last couple of months – and it doesn't help that she reminds me of that fact repeatedly. When we were kids, we were absolutely inseparable, and even though she was older than me, even if just by the eighteen months, she never minded or once complained when I would tag along with her and her pals. Then when Chantelle McCafferty started bullying me in high school, calling me 'lezzy' and 'dyke,' it was our Fi who put a stop to it when she rag-dolled her and made her apologise on the way home from school. From that day onwards, she really was – and will always be – my hero.

I love the life that she's made for herself, even if it couldn't be more different from mine. She's got her dream job in software development, she's married to a man who worships the very ground she walks on, and she's got this lovely wee semi-detached down in Cowglen where we're gathered for our first Sunday lunch as a family since we were at Mum's on New Year's Day.

Dad's worked through his full repertoire of horrible dad jokes which we all pretended we don't secretly love and is now helping Ewan wash Fi's car out in the driveway, Mum's faffing about in the kitchen because she just can't sit on her arse for five minutes, and Fi and I are sitting out on the back patio with a glass of wine enjoying an unusually mild and sunny afternoon.

I'd given her the *'we need to have a serious convo'* face, which she immediately clocked and got the wine out. We've developed a whole set of these useful silent facial expressions over the years.

'What's the chat then, sis?' she says. 'Out with it.'

'It's just— something you said the other day. About Paige.' I take a gulp of my wine, steeling myself.

'Which part? About you stealing her away from her man, what's his face?'

'Matt. Aye, about that.'

'Och, I was only winding you up,' she says.

'No, it's not that. I mean, it is that, but— see, the thing is, you weren't wrong.'

'Wait, what are you telling me, Katie?' she asks. 'Are you telling me that you're starting to— what, catch feels for this lassie?'

Ugh. I hate that expression. I actually make myself cringe when I have to use it in an article, because marketing says our readers can relate to it.

'Aye. No. I don't know. Maybe?' I non-answer.

'Right, okay. I see,' she says, takes a big gulp of wine herself, and then tops both of our glasses up. Yes, it's a coping mechanism, and yes, it's unhealthy. We're perfectly aware, thank you. Stop judging us.

'You know it can't happen, right?' she says. 'You can't let this turn into a thing or you're going to end up wrecking their relationship as well as your friendships, and you're better than that, hen. That's not how Mum and Dad raised us.'

'I know, Fi, I know,' I whine. 'And I'm trying, I promise.'

'How has this even happened? Has she given you any indication that— has she said anything?'

I think about all of the conversations that Paige and I have had. Has she? Have there been any little subconscious hints that have got me feeling like this? For the life of me, I can't think of a single one. Sure, she's paid me compliments, but that's just innocent friendship. Right?

'No, she just— it's hard to explain. She makes me see myself in a different light, you know? I feel confident. I feel good about myself. It's like she makes me feel like I'm worth something. And god alone knows how much I've needed someone to make me feel like that.'

It's like I see a little flicker of understanding in her eyes now. I think she gets it.

'So what are you going to do?' she asks me. And I genuinely don't have a clue how to answer that question.

'Well, the way I see it, I only have two options, really.'

'Okay, let's weigh them up, then,' she says, taking another drink. 'Option One...'

'Option One is I completely bury my feelings and pretend that none of this is happening. I keep hanging out with them and I force myself to learn to accept it and deal with it, and hopefully at some point I end up meeting someone through one of these dating sites and then it all becomes a non-issue.'

'I've got doubts whether or not you're going to be able to just accept it and fake being happy.'

'Aye, so do I,' I say mournfully.

'Which leaves Option Two.'

'Option Two is that I stop seeing both of them completely before I end up doing damage that can't be repaired. To them and to me.'

'Which is it going to be?' Fi asks me. I take a glug of wine.

'I honestly don't know, Fi.'

Matt

I nudge Paige and nod. She grins and makes that *'Oh my God that is so wholesome!'* face that I love so much, all big puppy dog eyes and petted lip.

It's a gorgeous Sunday, considering it's still only mid-February, and I've just seen Mum and Derek sneakily holding hands when they think they're out of our sight. We're at one of the myriad of garden centres that snake along the length of the Clyde Valley tourist route because Paige has decided that one of our 'something to do together' projects now that we officially live together is to transform our garden from being merely functional to actually pretty. Of course, she hasn't taken into account that neither of us are anything even remotely close to being considered green-fingered, hence why we've invited Mum and Derek to join us. Not only is this where they met, they both have stunning little gardens, and Derek built a nice little two-seat wooden bench for Mum's last summer with his bare hands. That's just the kind of man he is.

We've already enjoyed breakfast, coffee and a slice of cake in the café, and now it's time to get down to the business of finding whichever flowers and plants will be the most difficult for Paige and I to kill. I've already had a text from Heather this morning giving me dog's abuse for 'furthering the heteronormative agenda' by, I presume, conforming to society's demands that suburban couples aren't supposed to have gardens that resemble rubble-strewn nuclear test sites.

It *is* kind of wholesome, though, seeing Mum and Derek in their natural habitat, living their best lives and generally enjoying the second bite at the cherry that life has given them. Some people don't get to be that lucky. Derek's a good man, and he makes Mum happy. I couldn't ask for any more than that for her.

While the lovebirds are out of sight, I have a chance to talk to Paige about something I've been thinking about for the past few days. If the conversation with Heather on Friday night did one thing, it kind of solidified this in my mind. I need to be open to this double date idea in the hope that Kate finding someone will kill this bloody stupid notion that keeps going round in my head about having some kind of, I don't know, feelings for her, or something. The only thing I know for sure is that I can't let that continue, because I'll end up losing the person that matters most to me in this world.

She's just pottering around, sunglasses perched on top of her head, looking at some of the water features and garden ornaments, and all I can do is take her in. God, she's absolutely stunning. She's got a sundress and sandals on, and she's curled a little wave into her long blonde hair, and she just *looks* like summer. The slightest bit of sun brings out a little line of freckles across the bridge of her nose. I am completely and utterly in awe of her, and in love with her, and for just a minute, I completely forget that anyone else even exists and I don't understand why I'm being so stupid with so much to lose.

'Babe,' I say, taking her hand.

'Mm hm?' she smiles.

'I was just thinking. That idea you had about us maybe inviting Sam along to see how she gets on with Kate?'

'Yeah?'

'I think that's a great idea,' I say. 'You should definitely give her a call to see if she'd be up for it.'

'Yeah? You think so?'

Her face lights up. I've never known anyone who gets as emotionally invested in a love story as much as Paige does. Doesn't matter whether it's trashy reality TV – which I'm ashamed to admit she's got me hooked on – or those cheesy Hallmark movies – and I'm sticking to my guns on those, sorry, babe. If there's any kind of prospect of two people falling completely and unabashedly in love, my Paige will be their number one cheerleader. I know that if anyone can wave a magic wand and make two people fall for each other, it's her.

'What's the worst that could happen, right?' I ask.

Chapter Twenty-Two: February 21st

Paige

The first time I met Sam, I knew we'd be friends long after Uni was behind us. We'd been paired together in a mock law firm for the practical elements of our Postgraduate Diploma, and immediately formed a bond in opposition to the two privately educated 'alpha' boy brats who'd also been assigned to our group. Sam saw through them right away, and being more confident and assertive than I am, quickly educated them in what behaviours and attitudes would and wouldn't be tolerated.

Our late-night study sessions, whether in person or through our webcams, invariably extended long beyond the completion of the work and usually descended into gossip and laughter, and on the odd occasion, the consumption of a cocktail or three. We sailed through the Diploma and went our separate ways after graduation, to our respective firms to begin our two-year training contracts, but stayed in touch, and still often bumped into one another in court or on the way to meetings around town.

We'd been talking for ages about needing to arrange something one night, and I knew that she'd split up with her girlfriend towards the end of last year, but it hadn't even occurred to me that she and Kate might get along well. What better opportunity than this to kill two birds with one stone?

'Hiya, my honey,' she answers my call. I'm standing in a bus shelter on Hope Street, taking cover from the wind and drizzling rain long enough to make this call before I pick up my lunch from the sandwich shop just around the corner.

'Hi, sweetie, what are you up to?'

'On the way to court, what about you?'

'Just grabbing a bit of lunch,' I say. 'And wondering if you've got any plans for next weekend?'

'Not that I know of,' she replies. 'Want to do something?'

'Actually,' I smile at the thought, 'I was going to ask how you'd feel about a double date?'

'Are you suggesting that I'm so hard up and desperate for a date that I need someone to fix me up? Because, I mean, yeah, you'd be one hundred per cent correct. What's the story?'

'Her name's Kate, she's a friend of mine and Matt's. She's a journalist. She's so lovely. She's smart and funny.'

'And cute?' she asks me, then bursts out laughing.

'She's super cute, yes. You'll like her, honest. It won't be anything too heavy or demanding. We're thinking about maybe going bowling or something.'

'Yeah, you know what, I haven't had a fun night out in forever. Count me in. What's the worst that could happen?'

'That's exactly what Matt said!'

'Text me the details when you get it arranged. And send me a pic of this mystery cutie!'

'You got it,' I laugh. 'Talk to you later, babes.'

That was easier than I thought. If Kate is as easy to convince, this should be fun. I knew watching all those seasons of *Married at First Sight* would come in handy eventually. I scroll back up my contacts list and find Kate. I hear it ring, and just when I'm about to hang up, she answers.

'Hey, Paige,' she says.

'Hey, you,' I reply, happy to hear her voice. 'I haven't caught you at a bad time, have I? I feel like I haven't spoken to you in forever.'

'Ugh, I'm so sorry,' she says. 'I've been so snowed under with deadlines. I just can't afford to turn down any work at the moment, you know?'

'I get it, no need to worry, I'm not easily offended,' I laugh. 'Hey, look, I won't keep you long, I just wanted to run something past you.'

'Sure, what's up?' she asks.

'Have you had any more luck with that dating app yet?'

'No. A couple of them messaged back, but the conversations didn't really go anywhere. I'm giving serious thought to joining a nunnery.'

'Don't. It's a hard habit to get out of,' I joke.

'Oh my God. Did you— you didn't just hit me with a dad joke, did you?'

I shrug and grin. 'Yes. Yes, I did.'

'I'm hanging up now. That was atrocious!' she laughs. I've missed hearing that sound. She has the cutest little giggle when something tickles her.

'Wait, don't! I haven't finished. I'm here to be your fairy Godmother and tell you that you shall go to the ball, Cinderella.'

'Huh?' she says.

'I might have suggested to a friend of mine that I might just happen to know a lovely, wonderful, cute journalist that she might get along with.'

'I'm listening,' she replies. 'Go on.'

'Just a girl I went to Uni with. Her name is Sam. I think you'll like her. We're talking about going bowling, so it won't even be like a "date date," just friends hanging out and getting to know each other... with the unspoken hope of getting to see each other naked at some point.'

'Aye, you had me at naked,' she giggles.

'Yay! You're in?'

'What's the worst that could happen?' she asks. I roll my eyes.

'Why does everyone keep saying that?'

Chapter Twenty-Three: March 1st

Kate

Right, Katie, you've got this. Just breathe. It's just a first date, no pressure. In fact, it's not even a date, it's just people hanging out and having some fun bowling, and getting to know each other, and maybe even seeing each other in the scud, eventually, if everything works out. Ugh! No! Scrub that last part. You've not shaved your legs yet, so you can forget that part for the time being at least! Just calm the eff down. You've had your wee sneaky browse through her Insta, she seems nice, and you're interested in a lot of the same stuff. And it's not like she's not a bit of a hottie too. This isn't a big deal, so don't start psyching yourself out before you've even met her. If it goes well, great, and if not, no big deal, you at least gave it a shot. What matters is that you were brave enough to at least put yourself out there. You look cute, you feel good, and you're ready for a fun night out. Don't overthink this, don't dwell on the what-ifs. Just enjoy getting to know someone new. Be present in the moment and let things flow naturally, and all that other happy-clappy shite you feed your readers. And just remember, if you're feeling first date jitters, there's every chance she'll be shiteing herself too. You've got this. Now take a deep breath and go and knock her dead!

I'm just getting out of the taxi in the car park outside the bowling alley at the Quay. And yes, I am absolutely feeling first date jitters. At least, I think that's what it is. I hope that's what it is, and not the fact that this will be the first time I've seen Paige and Matt for a few weeks. I'd tried ducking them, because I wasn't sure how I was going to feel, but the truth of the matter is, I really missed hanging out with them. Both of them. It had crossed my mind that maybe I'd just got too emotionally dependent on them too fast, and maybe I was mistaking that for love, or lust or some kind of crush. The truth is, I don't know. One thing I do know is that, either way, I need this date more than anything right now. Because if nothing else, by the end of the night, I'll probably have a better idea one way or the other about what I need to do. Even if it's the hardest thing imaginable.

I toyed with not picking up the phone when Paige called me last week. I'd managed to avoid speaking to her for a couple of weeks under the pretence of being loaded down with work, but being honest, that was just a convenient excuse. The thing is, though, within just seconds of answering, I felt happy again, just because I was talking to her, and able to laugh. And, of course, she described me as 'cute.' Ugh, I really am pathetic, aren't I?

God's sake, Katie. Focus. Relax. Tonight isn't about Matt or Paige. It's about you and Sam. I hope she thinks I'm interesting enough. I know I can talk rubbish when I'm writing an article, but that's because I don't have to look my audience in the eye while I'm doing it! I hope I just don't say anything too stupid to mess this up. Just relax and be yourself, right? She's obviously seen something she likes in you, and Paige has probably given her the big sales pitch on your behalf already. This will all be fine. Be cool. You've got this. Here we go.

I arrive just the right side of fashionably late, and they're already there, waiting in the bar area for me. I see Matt at the bar ordering drinks, and sitting at one of the tables just behind him are Paige and a pretty girl that I immediately recognise from the Insta-stalking as Sam. They both look completely put together, casual and effortlessly stunning, and for just a second, I feel so intimidated that I consider just making an about turn and leaving and texting an excuse from the taxi home, but it's too late, because Paige sees me and springs to her feet, waving me over.

'Hiya, babe, I've missed you!' she smiles, pulling me into a big, warm hug and then looking me up and down, 'Oh my God! You look absolutely gorge! Here, let me introduce you.'

Sam stands up from the table and smiles at me. She's cute. She's got big Audrey Hepburn eyes and an uber-cool *Emily in Paris* vibe about her. Hair pulled back into a high ponytail, just enough makeup that she still looks natural, and even dressed casually, in dark jeans and a floaty top, I can tell she has an amazing figure. Oh my God, what must she think of me? I feel like a potato in comparison.

'Kate, this is Sam. Sam, Kate,' Paige smiles. Sam leans in and gives me a hug, not quite as warm as Paige's, but still, I feel a little shiver of excitement run down my spine.

'Hi, Kate, lovely to meet you,' she smiles. 'I love your hair! I'm so jell!'

I blush a little and touch it self-consciously.

'Usual?' Matt calls to me from the bar, and I nod and smile. He nods back. My mind is going a mile a minute. Is it definitely too late for me to fake feeling sick now?

'Come on,' Paige says, 'our lane is just about ready. Matt can bring the drinks up.'

He follows behind and puts the tray of drinks down on the little table in our lane. Lager for him, strawberry and lime cider for me, red wine for Paige, and what I'm guessing is some kind of dark fruit cider for Sam.

'Cider too?' she asks me with a smile. I nod. Come on, Kate, use your big girl words before she thinks you're a complete tool.

'I might try one of the cocktails later,' I say. She grins.

'Oh, I think you and I are going to get along just fine,' she says, and I immediately feel a little more relaxed.

We spend most of the first of the three games we've booked just chatting in between our respective turns, and I'm immediately struck with how friendly and bubbly she is, which is great, because it's keeping my mind occupied. We talk about our jobs, exchange the usual stories of how we met Matt and Paige, and then move on to general chit-chat to try to establish if we have enough common ground for this to be a thing. She's into art and travelling and tells me about the backpacking trip to Cambodia and Thailand she took before starting University.

Matt is unusually quiet tonight, and I find myself wondering if Paige has told him to let Sam and I spend time getting to know one another. He normally has loads of quick one-liners to throw into any conversation, but he's barely said more than a few sentences tonight. Maybe he just takes his bowling really seriously, and I'm reading too much into it. He sounded pretty pissed off earlier when one of his shots went straight to the gutter. I don't think I've ever heard him sound even remotely grumpy before.

'Well?' Paige whispers to me, as Sam waits for her ball to be returned from behind the pins.

'Well, what?' I smile. She nudges me.

'You know very well what I'm talking about, lady. What do you think of Sam? How did I do?'

'You did very well,' I concede, still smiling. 'She's nice.'

'Nice?' she raises an eyebrow.

'Nice.' I reply.

'And...?'

'And we'll see how it goes,' I say.

Matt comes back from the bar with another round of drinks. He's still being very quiet. I give him a smile, and he simply passes me my drink. I want to ask him if he's okay, but I don't. I wonder if maybe he doesn't feel comfortable with Sam here. The whole dynamic just feels a little off tonight. He's had a couple of extra beers in between our rounds, but I don't think anyone else has noticed.

Paige is being her usual wonderful self, just buzzing around between us all, making sure everyone is okay and having a good time. Maybe that's what's bothering Matt tonight? Is he feeling a little— I don't know, ignored? Left out? Every time I've tried to engage with him, he's practically blanked me. Is he pissed off that I've been patching them for the last few weeks?

As we finish the last of our three games, one which I finally manage to win, Sam approaches me.

'Hey, I'm not ready to head home yet. Would you like—.' She pauses. 'I'm hungry. Do you want to maybe go and get something to eat?'

I look across at Matt and Paige who are putting their jackets on. Matt seems to be actively avoiding making any eye contact with anyone now. Paige, on the other hand, is smiling and giving me a 'go on' nod.

'Yeah, that would be good,' I say. 'We could head back up into town from here.'

Paige threads her arm through Matt's as we wait outside for the two taxis we've called.

'Thanks for tonight, guys,' I say. 'It was lovely seeing you both again.' Paige pulls me into a side hug.

'We had a great time, didn't we, babe?' she says as she looks up at Matt.

'Yeah. Enjoy your dinner,' he says flatly.

'Give you a message tomorrow?' I say to him as our taxi pulls up.

'Cool,' he says.

'Have fun,' Paige winks.

Chapter Twenty-Four: March 2nd

Paige: The Morning After

Nobody tells you that when you finally graduate with a law degree, the studying doesn't stop. Over the course of my two-year traineeship, I need to complete a minimum of sixty hours of what they politely call 'continuing professional development,' which I'm convinced is actually code for 'the dullest reading material known to man.' Of course, I'm probably sabotaging myself by having the latest issue of Kate's magazine sitting beside my laptop on the breakfast bar in our kitchen, because the cover is tempting me with, amongst other things, Kate's interview with the 'honeytrapper,' and it's all I can do not to shut my laptop over and just lose myself for a little while in gloriously juicy and salacious fluff and nonsense. Lord knows it would certainly be more entertaining than— let me check my notes here, *The Changing Law of Cohabitation.*

Focus, Paige. Show some bloody discipline. This is just three hours of, granted, very dull and dry reading and webinars, and then you can read as much trash as you like for the rest of the day. Put the magazine in the living room and pour yourself another coffee.

And that's exactly what I do. I drop the magazine onto the coffee table for later, come back into the kitchen, top up my 'Live Laugh Law' mug – a gift from Matt – from the machine and sit back down in front of the laptop. Matt is still in bed after our night at the bowling, and as much as I could have stayed in bed with him, it felt like an ideal opportunity to get this little piece of training done and out of the way. Just one more box ticked and another step closer to becoming a fully qualified solicitor.

Last night was fun. I can't remember the last time I went bowling. It has to be before I even went to Uni, probably with a high school boyfriend. Maybe Justin. I bet it was with Justin. Oh my God, that makes me feel so old. I haven't thought about that name in years. What an absolute twat he ended up being. To think all of the girls in my year were jealous when I started going out with him. If only they knew what he was really like. He thought he was the absolute dog's bollocks because he was first in sixth year to pass his test and get a car, even though it was a dung-coloured Nissan Micra which still had a cassette player and reeked of the previous owner's cigarette smoke, no matter how often he got it valeted.

I find myself wondering how Sam and Kate got on after we parted ways with them last night. Sam had mentioned they were going to head back up to town to get something to eat and get to know each other a little more. Matt and I stopped off at our local takeaway on the way home and picked up our usual order – mushroom pakora for him, chicken for me, and a pepperoni pizza to split. Delicious and super unhealthy, and just what the doctor ordered after a few drinks and a fun night with good company.

It was great to see Sam and Kate hitting it off as well as they did. I never doubted it, of course. I knew they'd have a lot in common, despite their different backgrounds. When I see Kate out in that environment, I still find myself wondering what on earth that Steph girl thought she was missing out on when she was with her. I mean, she's absolutely adorable. So fun to be around. She's bubbly, she's very funny, she's a lot smarter than she gives herself credit for, and I know for a fact that Sam thought she was super cute. She made a point of telling me every time Kate went to the bar or the bathroom! I have to admit that I'm seriously having to fight the urge to text one or both of them to see if they have any gossip. I know, I know...

I can hear Matt rustling around in the bedroom, getting up

and dressed. He's not working until later today, so he'll have time for something to eat before he goes – assuming he's not too hungover, that is! I pour a coffee out for him and sit it on the breakfast bar just across from me.

He seemed a little off again last night, but I couldn't quite put my finger on why. I don't know if perhaps he was just a little uncomfortable with Sam there. As far as I know, he hasn't had any problems or major disagreements with her in the past, and it was him who gave me the go-ahead to invite her along last night, so I doubt it could be that. I noticed he did seem a little standoffish with Kate, though, but he hasn't mentioned them having had any kind of falling out either. I don't know. Maybe he was just having an off night? It happens to the best of us.

He walks into the living room.

'I'm in here, babe,' I call out from the kitchen. 'There's a coffee here for you.'

'You are an absolute angel,' he says, and sits down at the breakfast bar opposite me, looking like he still has something on his mind.

He clears his throat and takes a sip from his coffee.

'Look, about last night,' he says.

Matt: The Morning After

I feel like crap. Not the kind of Saturday morning 'I feel like crap' which is normally a direct result of the 'Yes, thank you, I *will* have that sixth pint' kind of Friday night – although I would be lying to myself if I tried to pretend that wasn't also a factor here. It's more the 'I'm an idiot who needs to get his head out of his arse pronto before I lose the best thing that's ever happened to me' type of 'I feel like crap.'

So, yeah. While I do feel a little rough, it's more that I just feel *bad*. I acted like a bit of an arsehole last night – okay, a *total* arsehole, not just a *bit* of one, and I can't pretend to myself that I don't know why. Because I do. I know exactly what it is that's bothering me. But the problem is, I can't say anything or do anything about it without burning everything around me to the ground.

All I had to do was go out, have a good time with my amazing girlfriend and let whatever was going to happen, happen. But apparently I'm not even capable of acting like a sensible adult for any length of time whenever Kate is involved, and the worst of it is that there's no good reason for any of it beyond the fact that I like her because I like her, and I can't just have that and let that be enough for me.

Arsehole.

The Saturday morning 'beer fear' is trying to convince me that I ruined everyone's night because of how I was acting, but I know that's not true. I don't even think anyone else noticed. Paige certainly never mentioned anything to me, either on the way to the kebab shop for our semi-drunken post-bowling munch, or at home afterwards when we ate it in the kitchen before heading to bed. This is all in my head.

The worst thing about all of it is that I genuinely did want to have a good night. I went out with the sole intention of making sure Paige and I had a good night and giving Kate and Sam enough space to get to know each other, because I thought that if I did that, and they hit it off, my brain would somehow kick itself into gear and finally internalise the fact that this is something I can never have, and something I should never even be thinking about wanting.

The trouble is, though, the heart doesn't follow direct orders from the brain, does it? The heart is always going to want what it wants, and the brain can piss off if it doesn't agree. Frankly, the heart is also an arsehole. Write a song about that, Celine Dion.

So instead of just concentrating on having a good time and putting this nonsense behind me, I spent the whole night resenting how well Sam and Kate were getting on, and trying to drink enough to numb myself from feeling what I was feeling, and to prevent myself from saying what I wanted to say more than anything else, which is—

Jesus, Matt. Enough. Don't say it. Don't even think it. This is absolute madness. And more to the point, this isn't you. This isn't who you are. You're completely and utterly in love with Paige, and you're lucky enough that she hasn't realised that she's absolutely one hundred per cent out of your league, in every way possible. How can you lie here even contemplating doing anything to jeopardise that? You could never betray Paige, because you believe in loyalty. Loyalty to your family, to your friends, and most of all to the woman you love more than anything else in the world. That's who you are, Matt, and you need to get your head out of your arse and remember that. And you can start by getting out of this bed and apologising to Paige for being such a gigantic throbber last night.

I get up and throw on my sweatpants and a t-shirt, look out my work clothes for later, and walk barefoot through to the living room.

'I'm in here, babe,' Paige shouts from the kitchen. 'There's a coffee here for you.'

See, here's the thing. There are a million beautiful-looking women in the world, but not all of them will have a coffee sitting waiting for you on a Saturday morning, especially not if you've been acting like a knob.

'You are an absolute angel,' I say as I walk into the kitchen. I sit down at the breakfast bar opposite her, trying to work out what it is that I need to say to her. I clear my throat and take a sip from the best coffee I've ever tasted.

'Look, about last night,' I begin.

'Hmm?' she looks up from her laptop.

I look at her, sitting in the sunlight which streams through the French doors of the kitchen and just bathes her in the most incredible golden glow, and she almost takes my breath away. She smiles at me, and all of a sudden nothing else matters and nobody else exists.

'I think we could use a little time away, babe. Just you and me. Maybe next week or the week after if you can get time off work. We could go through to Edinburgh, make a night of it. See a show, go out for a nice meal, a wee overnight in a hotel and then spend a day out exploring the city? Maybe go up to the Castle?'

'Oh, babe, that sounds brill,' she lights up, and so does my world, even if just by a little.

Kate: The Night Before

I don't look back out of the taxi window as Sam and I leave the Quay and head back towards the city centre, because I'm trying to focus on being present in the moment here with Sam and not thinking about Paige or Matt. There's no awkwardness or tension between Sam and I at all. It's nice. It feels quite natural, like we've known each other for longer than just these last two hours. She smiles at me.

'What do you fancy then?' she asks. 'To eat, I mean. What are your favourites?'

'I'm easy,' I say.

'I'll keep that in mind,' she winks. 'But let's get some dinner first,' and I blush. I hear a little chuckle from the driver who'll no doubt be on the radio to pass that one along as soon as we're out of his taxi. I roll my eyes.

'Chinese or Indian is always a safe bet,' I say. 'And there are plenty to choose from.'

'In that case, I know just the place,' she smiles.

The taxi drops us off on Trongate, and we walk the short distance along Candleriggs until we get to the restaurant Sam has suggested. It's nice. Warm and inviting, not at all pretentious or overly showy. It's a traditional North Indian menu, and I admit to Sam that I'm a little lost without seeing the usual suspects like korma and tikka masala on offer. She talks me through her recommendations, and I eventually decide on a monkfish dish, and smile as I remember the conversation Matt and I had about fish pakora the second time we met, eating a takeaway in the snow on Sauchiehall Street.

We split the bill evenly, and as we step back out into the night, I become acutely aware that, while I don't really know Sam, or if this thing, whatever it is, stands a chance of becoming anything, I also don't want the night to end just yet, because despite my nerves at the start of the night, I really have enjoyed myself, and I've enjoyed her company.

'Are you tired?' I ask hopefully.

'Not at all,' she smiles.

'I've got wine at home. Nothing fancy. Some fruit cider too.'

Oh God, this is it. I've actually done the whole 'do you want to come back to my place for a coffee?' cliché. Except that's not really what's on my mind. Not completely. I'm not trying to lure Sam back to my place for 'coffee' or even for 'wine' or 'cider' or any other metaphor for hot girl sex, especially not with my gross, unshaven legs. All I'm trying to say, as far as I can tell, is that I'm having quite a nice time hanging out with her and I don't want that to stop just yet, and I hope she's feeling the same way too.

'That sounds good,' she says.

After a short taxi ride, with one stop off at an all-night garage to grab some chocolate, we're back at my flat.

'Sorry in advance if there's any random bras, knickers, piles of ironing or empty takeaway boxes lying around. The maid's on holiday and I wasn't expecting company tonight!'

'Sounds like my place,' she laughs genuinely, and it makes me feel happy inside.

I kick off my shoes as we go into the living room, and she walks over to the IKEA bookshelf which houses my small music and book collection while I go to check what I've got in the fridge.

'I apologise for the quality of the CDs,' I say. 'My ex took the good ones when she left!'

'It's the books I'm more interested in,' she replies. 'You really love a cheesy romance, eh?'

'What can I say?' I laugh as I reappear from the kitchen with two bottles of strawberry and lime cider, 'I'm just a romantic at heart!'

We sit on the couch and for the time it takes us to finish the other four bottles of cider I have in the fridge, we exchange more horror stories about the unsuitable girls we've dated, the weirdest places we've had sex, the most embarrassing wardrobe malfunctions we've suffered, and I wonder if we're flirting, and part of me hopes that we are, because if I'm thinking about flirting with Sam and thinking about kissing her, then I'm not thinking about Paige.

I can't believe I'm doing this. My heart is racing as I slowly lean in, closing my eyes. Her lips are right there, I can feel her breath on me. Our lips touch, our tongues brush lightly together, and then... I feel nothing. There's no spark at all. Not the slightest bit of chemistry, not even when I try to imagine it's Paige I'm kissing. It just feels awkward. I pull back, opening my eyes, hoping that I haven't offended her. What's the etiquette here? Do I apologise? Do I make a joke? I sigh.

'We're only going to be friends, aren't we?' she smiles, and relief washes over me.

'I'm so sorry,' I say.

'There's no need to apologise,' she says. 'If you don't feel it, then maybe it's just not meant to be. And that's okay.'

'I really did have a lovely time with you tonight,' I say, feeling like I'm ready to tear up.

'Me too,' she says and hugs me.

As her taxi arrives to take her home, she stops at the door and turns to me, taking my hand.

'Can I say something to you, just girl to girl? A little advice, that's all.'

'Of course,' I say.

'I just wanted to let you know that I know it's hard for you. And I know that sometimes your heart feels like it's being ripped apart. But I promise it'll heal, and you'll get over it. You'll learn to accept that there are some things in life that you can have, and some that you can't, and that's just how it is.'

I look at her, stunned.

'How did you—'

'I used to be in love with her too,' she says and hugs me again. 'Take care of yourself, Kate.'

Chapter Twenty-Five: March 9th

Matt

'I can't believe you've done all this, babe,' Paige says.

Not to blow my own trumpet, but I think I've played an absolute blinder here. With just over a week's notice, I've managed to organise the perfect weekend to give Paige and I a chance to unwind and reconnect. Train from Glasgow through to Edinburgh this afternoon, dinner and tickets to a show tonight, an overnight stay in a hotel – jacuzzi and champagne waiting on ice in the room, naturally – and I still have one last surprise up my sleeve for tomorrow. Well played, Matt. Well played indeed.

'You deserve it,' I say, and hold up my cocktail glass. She clinks hers against it. 'Cheers.'

We're sitting in an amazing Nepalese restaurant just a short walk from the theatre, which will be our next stop after dinner. I'm not the biggest fan of musical theatre, but Paige absolutely adores it, and I wanted this weekend to be about her and nothing else. It took a bit of hunting to get decent tickets at short notice without having to break our necks in the nosebleed seats, but she's worth every bit of it.

One thing I really am enjoying, though, is this dinner. I'd been looking forward to it ever since I saw someone reviewing this place on TikTok. I know, I know. Not exactly the most thorough of research methods, but to be honest, I don't think I've had a bad recommendation from it yet. I've gone for the Himali hot pot, and Paige has pushed the boat out and been really adventurous with her choice of chicken with cashews, coconut cream and powdered nutmeg flower. I didn't know what to expect from it when we did our customary 'offer each other a forkful to taste' thing, but it really was incredibly tasty.

She squeezes my hand as we cross the road towards the theatre.

'I love you so much, Matt.'

'I love you too, babe,' I smile.

I can't believe how lucky I am. Just walking down the street holding Paige's hand makes me so happy. Her hand fits perfectly in mine, like our hands were just designed to hold each other. She looks more beautiful than I've ever seen her tonight. The way her eyes light up when she laughs at my crap jokes just melts my heart. I'm the luckiest guy in the world to have someone as sweet, kind and wonderful as her. We just click on so many levels. I never imagined that I could ever feel this way about someone. She makes me want to be the best version of myself. More than that, though, she makes me want to plan the lifelong memories we'll make together, and as we walk along this damp Edinburgh street tonight, I'm just overflowing with love and happiness.

The show is better than I'd expected. It's got some laughs in places, the songs are catchy, and I have to admit, it's a more captivating spectacle than I thought it would be. I'm even still humming one of the songs – "Let Me Exposit My Back Story (In Excruciating Detail)" – as we step out of the lift in our hotel and enter our room for the night. Paige's eyes light up as she sees the champagne chilling in the ice bucket, the jacuzzi in the bathroom, and best of all, the sight of this beautiful city lit up at night from the huge window.

I put my arms around her waist from behind and kiss the back of her neck softly. She lets out a contented sigh and melts back into my embrace.

'This is perfect,' she says.

'You're perfect,' I reply, and I lead her across the room and into our bed.

The following morning, we sleep late and have a gloriously lazy room service breakfast in bed as the sun streams in through that amazing window. Afterwards, we spend a little time shopping on Princes Street before I put the final part of my plan for the weekend into action.

We stroll, hand in hand, up the winding path on Arthur's Seat, taking in the most breathtaking panoramic view of the city below us, bathed in a golden glow as the sun begins to dip in the spring sky. Near the top, we find a grassy spot to take it all in. To the west, the old town's Gothic spires and cobbled streets, to the east, the shimmering waters of the Firth of Forth, and just off in the distance, the skyline is dominated by the Castle itself. It feels like we're on top of the world. I spread a blanket out on the grass as Paige enjoys the view.

When she turns around, I am down on one knee and my heart is beating so fast I think it might burst out of my chest.

'Paige,' I begin. 'From the first moment I saw you, I knew you were the missing piece of my heart.'

'Matt—' she smiles, clapping her hands over her mouth.

'You're my best friend, my greatest supporter and my truest love. With you by my side, I feel like I can take on anything. You make me want to be the best version of myself. And I promise to always be your number one fan. I'll laugh with you, I'll cry with you and I will love you every single day for the rest of my life if you'll allow me to.'

I reach into my pocket and produce a small red velvet box.

'Paige Marie McKinnon, you are the love of my life, and my entire heart belongs to you. Will you do the greatest honour of becoming my wife?' I smile. 'Will you marry me, babe?'

'Yes! Yes I will!' she squeaks as tears stream down her cheeks, and I somehow manage to slip the ring onto her finger, despite my shaking hands.

My heart is racing as I spring to my feet, and I can hear onlookers whistling and cheering from behind as I put my lips to hers and kiss her. We embrace and I lift her from her feet and spin her around and around.

I am on top of the world, and tonight, it's ours alone.

Chapter Twenty-Six: March 11th

Paige

@TheRealBigSuze
OMG I can't believe it! Congratulations, gorgeous!

@LeahDoesLaw
Stunning photo, stunning ring, stunning girly!

@JennyNailsAndBeauty
#CoupleGoals DM Me for bridal packages

@xPartyGal69x
What an amazing location! He's a keeper!

@JasonLovesBoaby
*Gag. Heavy giving me the boak. Get a room. *vomit emoji**

My phone is already blowing up with congratulations and well wishes, and while I'm still trying to process it all, this ring on my finger reassures me that it's all real. We're engaged! I don't think I'm going to stop staring at my hand or obsessing over wedding plans for a long time. I'm happy, I'm in love, and I want everyone to know. Even if it's super cheesy, this is my moment, and I'm going to enjoy every second of it!

I know it's such a clichéd way to announce an engagement, but I'm just so excited that I want to tell the whole world, and what better way to shout it from the virtual rooftops than to post it on Insta? I know some people roll their eyes at these kinds of social media engagement reveals, but for me it just feels right. Matt and I have shared so much of our relationship online already, and it means that all our friends from near and far can celebrate with us, even if they can't be here with us in person.

Maybe we could have waited and put together a more creative or personal announcement, but honestly, I don't care. The moment was so perfect – everything about it, the setting, Matt's words, the ring itself – that I couldn't wait to tell the world how thrilled I am to be taking this next step with the man that I love. And I love the photo that we took together to capture the moment at the top of the hill. Edinburgh in the distance beneath us, and the way the sun shone on us as I held out my hand, as if it was for us and us alone. It was just beautiful. I couldn't have imagined a more perfect moment if I'd tried. I'm just amazed that Matt managed to keep it quiet for so long. He's normally so terrible at keeping secrets.

My Mum's on Insta, because of course she is, but still, I made a conscious decision to phone her right before I posted it because no doubt she'd have spit the dummy if she wasn't the first to know. She sounded thrilled in her own way, but still managed to take the wind out of my sails for a minute when she sneaked in one of her wee comments about starting the diet to get ready for the wedding dress. I mean, really, what is the need? I'm not letting it get on me, though, I won't let one snarky remark ruin this moment for me.

I look at Matt as we sit facing each other on the train from Edinburgh back through to Glasgow. There's a little table between us and our hands are clasped on top of it. He strokes his thumb over my finger and the ring.

'What are you thinking?' I ask him.

'Just pondering if I'd be able to slip it off and make a run for it,' he winks.

'You'd never be able to outrun me,' I laugh. 'Hey, can I ask you a question?'

'Course you can.'

'How long have you had the ring hidden away? It's not like

you to be able to keep anything hidden from me.'

'You don't know the half of it,' he laughs. 'I've had it for a while. I just wanted to find the perfect moment, because that's what you deserve.'

'I think we can safely say you nailed that part. It was just how I always imagined it.'

'I'm glad,' he smiles.

'Just one more question,' I say.

'Mm hm?'

'When did you know for sure? That I was the one, I mean. Do you remember?'

'Of course I do. It was exactly a second after you said you'd go out on a date with me.'

He grins so widely and brightly that it turns my insides into a ball of hot lava. He always puts himself down in that laughy-jokey way that he does and goes on about how I'm so totally out of his league. But the truth is, I feel like the luckiest girl on the face of the Earth when I look at him. He's handsome, of course he is, but he's so, so much more than that, and I don't think he even sees it. He's the kindest, most generous, selfless man I've ever known, and I think I've believed we were meant to spend the rest of our lives together from the first second we locked eyes across the kitchen at that house party.

I guess that's part of why my mind is already starting to run away from me. I'm so totally invested and excited about the thought of being engaged to Matt that I'm already starting to think about how our wedding will look. Will he wear tartan? Oh god, I hope he does. And my dress. How will it look? Long and flowing, covered in intricate lace detailing? Simple and elegant? What song will we choose for our first dance? Where will we host our reception? Will I be able to take it all in on the big day, or will I be too caught up in the moment? And the honeymoon! Where will we go? I've always fantasised about the Seychelles or Maldives, all colourful, fruity cocktails, and the most Instagrammable photos of crystal clear oceans and beautiful white sand between my toes. I sigh, and then realise I've sighed out loud as I snap out of my daydreams.

Matt is grinning at me.

'Dare I even ask?' he says.

All I can do is smile back at him.

'I'm just happy, babe. Like, the happiest I've ever been. And it's all thanks to you.'

Kate

What. The. Actual?

I can't believe what I'm looking at. Paige and Matt are *engaged?*

I have to re-read it two or three times, just to make sure. When I saw the photo pop up in my Insta feed, I kind of – well, I don't think I wanted to believe it, if I'm honest. I look at the photo again. They're up a hill somewhere. Paige is holding out her hand. That's a ring. There's no mistaking what this is. This really is an engagement announcement, and it feels like the bottom just fell out of my world.

Ugh. Ugh ugh ugh. It's like I've just had a dagger plunged between my ribs. I feel sick.

I know I should have seen it coming, that's the worst part of it. I don't think I've ever seen two people better suited to being together than Paige and Matt. Of *course* they're getting engaged, they're sickeningly perfect for each other. And now I'm going to watch them getting married while I— what? Just pine away in silence?

I know I should be happy for them both. It's wonderful news, and I know that they'll treat each other how they both deserve to be treated, but still, I can't ignore how much this hurts. Dammit, Kate. Why couldn't you have felt something when you kissed Sam? This would all have been so much easier if you weren't, oh, I don't know, completely and utterly bloody obsessed with Paige!

I never meant for any of this to happen. You know, when

Matt and I met at first, all I could think about was that I hoped that he and I could be friends without it jeopardising his relationship. Because you never know, do you? I mean, I know I've been with guys before, even though I've always preferred girls, and although I don't feel that way about Matt – like, at all, but if– IF I was ever going to fall in love with a guy again, he would definitely be the kind of guy I would want to fall in love with. He's just the sweetest guy I've ever known.

Which is what makes this all the more painful and difficult, I guess. I mean, in some ways I wish he was just a complete arsehole who treated Paige like shite. Because if that was the case, I wouldn't think twice about shooting my shot and letting her know how I feel about her. But it's not, is it? He's lovely. And she's perfect. They're perfect. Just so bloody perfect.

Not only did I not mean for this to happen, I didn't even expect it. Like the first time I met her, when I was so intimidated by her that I wanted the ground to open up and swallow me whole. She's not even the kind of girl I normally fall for. Then again, maybe that's the problem! Maybe she's the kind of girl I *should* have been looking for all along, instead of the absolute roasters that I always seem to end up being attracted to.

I can't jeopardise what we've all got. My friendship with both of them. Their relationship. They both trust me completely, and if I act on anything I'm feeling, it will ruin everything. And I don't think I'd be able to live with that kind of guilt if I caused either of them any hurt. I have to keep this to myself. I have to ignore this stupid, hopeless crush, and it will go away eventually. I need to keep telling myself that.

You're a bloody idiot, Kate. Fi warned you about this. Why can't you ever listen to good advice when it comes to relationships? Why do you always find a way to complicate simple things or mess everything up? It's because you're Kate bloody McArdle, the most persistent traveller on the path of *most* resistance!

Come on, you can do this, Katie. Just send a simple

'congratulations' message to let them know that you're happy for them, even though your bloody heart is shattering into a million pieces. Be a friend. Be the woman that Mum and Dad raised you to be. This is the right thing to do. You want them to be happy. You want *her* to be happy. Even if it's not with you.

Maybe one day this won't sting so much. Maybe one day you'll be able to look at them without your stomach twisting in knots.

It's just two words. You can do it.

Congratulations, guys!

Send.

Take a deep breath. You're going to get through this. They're both still your friends, so focus on that and not the impossibility of anything more than that. Their happiness is enough for you.

It has to be.

Chapter Twenty-Seven: March 17th

Matt

I can't believe I've let things go on this long without reaching out to Kate. It's been weeks since that night out with Sam when I acted like a massive arsehole. And as much as I've been busy with planning the weekend break with Paige, and then dealing with all of the celebrations and congratulations that came afterwards, the simple truth of the matter is that I've been avoiding her since that night. I've been so stupid and immature. And once again, I've been a massive arsehole.

No matter what else I should or shouldn't be feeling, the plain fact is that I miss her, even just as a friend. I miss hanging out, going to gigs and having a beer, going to daft pub quizzes and just talking about nothing and nonsense. I should have reached out as soon as we got back from Edinburgh, so it's time for me to man up and make this right. Of course, I can never tell her why I've been avoiding her, but I can at least apologise for going missing and remind her how much I value having her as a friend.

I pick up my phone and swipe open my contacts. Hers is saved under my favourite photo of the three of us together at our New Year's Eve party, where she's sandwiched between Paige and I, and both of us are kissing her cheeks while she pulls the most ridiculous face.

'Matt,' she answers. 'Hey. How have you been? I feel like I haven't seen you in forever.'

'I know,' I say, preparing to lie. 'I've just been snowed under with everything.'

'Everything okay?' she asks, and I have to fight down the

urge to spill my guts.

'Yeah, it's all good,' I lie again. 'How about you? Have you seen any more of Sam?' I ask hopefully.

'Nah. She was nice enough and that, but I just didn't feel— a *connection* with her, you know what I mean?' she says, and my heart sinks like a stone.

'Yeah, I guess. If you don't feel it, you don't feel it. That's a shame, though. I really hoped you two would hit it off,' I say, and it's the first honest thing I've said in this conversation.

'I know, I really wanted that too,' she says, and she sounds genuinely sad about the fact.

'Been up to anything else?' I ask. This small talk feels so painfully forced and awkward, like we're both circling around some unseen and indefinable elephant in the room.

'You know me. Taking on more work than I've got the capacity or the attention span to handle, same old same old. I sometimes think I'll never learn,' she laughs, and my stomach flips over at the sound.

There's a brief, awkward pause before she breaks it.

'Never mind me, though, mister. What about you? Congratulations on your big news! I messaged Paige when I saw the photo on her Insta, but I completely forgot to send you one too. I'm so sorry, you must think I'm dead ignorant!'

'I'd never think that,' I say. 'It's all good. It's been a bit of a whirlwind since then, so, you know, no big deal. But thanks anyway.'

'I'm really pleased for you both, Matt. I love you guys. I've missed hanging out with you both these last few weeks.'

'That's kind of why I'm calling, now that you mention it,' I say.

'Oh aye?' she replies.

'You know what Paige is like,' I say. 'Getting engaged is the ultimate excuse to throw a party, so we're going to have a little get-together at the end of the month. Nothing wild or anything. Just our family and closest friends round at ours for a good dinner and some drinks. I'll make sure Derek and J are barred from getting a karaoke session going this time. It'll be nice.'

'I know it will,' she says. 'I'm in. There's nothing I'd love more.'

'Cool. Brilliant. I'm glad.'

I pause for a moment.

'Kate?'

'Mm hm?'

Another pause.

'See you soon, okay?'

'See you soon, Matt.'

I end the call and immediately wonder what the hell I was thinking. I keep telling myself that she's our friend, *just* our friend, and that's all it should ever be, but part of me can't help but think there's a very real danger that this could still get messy. Part of me was hoping that she would say no, that she couldn't make it, that she was too busy with work, or even that, if she was going to come, she'd come with Sam. Any of those options would have made things so much easier. But of course she happily accepted and sounded genuinely excited for us both.

My first thought is that maybe I could uninvite her. Make up an excuse or something. Tell her the party is cancelled. But I know that won't fly. I can guarantee that Paige will post something on Insta. It's okay. It's fine. This is all my fault. I don't deserve an easy option or a convenient way out.

I can handle this. I'm in love with Paige, and only Paige. I'm marrying her and we're starting an exciting new chapter of our life together. I never meant for any of this to happen. I didn't plan to have feelings for two women at once, but I can deal with it. I just have to push past this and commit one hundred per cent to the life I'm choosing with Paige.

I can do that.

I can do *that*.

I *can*.

Chapter Twenty-Eight: March 30th

Kate

It's a cruel twist of fate, isn't it? Realising that the one person you want more than anyone else in the world is the one you can never truly have. Sorry, that sounds a wee bit overdramatic. What I'm really trying to say is that, well, it's a shite state of affairs.

It doesn't matter how much I try to convince myself that I'm not falling in love with Paige. I'm just not that good at lying, and that's what I've been doing. Lying to myself, lying to my sister, and when I wished them well on their engagement, lying to Paige and Matt too. I keep thinking about that conversation I had with our Fi a few weeks ago. Yet again, she was one hundred per cent on the button. If I don't get my head on straight, I'm going to lose two friends and risk wrecking their relationship, and she's right, Mum and Dad raised me better than that.

So why am I sitting here, getting ready to go to this bloody engagement party or dinner or whatever the hell it is, still wondering whether or not there's a chance that me getting close to Paige might somehow spark something in her? I mean, she's never given me any indication or reason to even suspect that would be the case. Which makes me either completely and utterly delusional, or best case scenario, just a bloody idiot.

There's a completely irrational and reckless little devil sitting on one shoulder, whispering in my ear, and a pissed-off angel on the other one tapping its wee angel foot and glaring at me disapprovingly as I run this theoretical conversation through in my head. The one where I come clean and get it all off my chest, just roll the bloody dice and see what happens in the slim chance that she feels the same way and is just marrying Matt out of obligation or comfort. And no matter how much I tell myself how stupid and unlikely that is, the wee devil is still there, going 'aye, but what if you're not wrong...'

Ugh. I am the actual worst friend in the world. To both of them.

Time is ticking on. I keep thinking about that article I wrote about 'sliding doors' moments a wee while back. You know the ones I'm talking about. That one incident or decision that changes the course of your life forever. Where you miss a train and end up meeting the love of your life as you wait for the next one or turn down a so-called dream job offer and then discover what you were really meant to be doing all along. All I can think about are those moments I've had over these last few months, and I wonder where the other paths would have taken me.

If only I'd never answered Matt's message the morning after that night on Sauchiehall Street.

If only I'd never gone to the Fort that night and started crying in the coffee shop.

If only I'd been a better girlfriend and then maybe Steph wouldn't have dumped me.

If only I didn't feel so bloody lonely all of the time.

If only I'd met Paige in another life.

Paige

I'm a ball of anxiety and wracked with insecurity tonight, and that's not how I'm supposed to be feeling. This is supposed to be a happy night, a special occasion, a gathering of everyone Matt and I love, to celebrate our engagement. I should be floating on cloud nine. Instead, I feel like I did when I was seventeen and getting dressed for my high school prom, or when I was eleven and getting ready for Alison Taylor's birthday party, or any of the hundred other occasions growing up when all I wanted was for Mum to tell me I looked pretty instead of having some snide, catty remark or backhanded half-compliment which resulted in me feeling like crap and not even wanting to leave the house because people would remind me I'm too tall and too skinny and ugly, ugly, ugly and what the hell am I even thinking?

I've got two of my favourite dresses laid out on the bed in front of me, and I'm trying to decide which one says 'I'm a classy future bride-to-be' without trying too hard, whilst also being Mum-criticism proof. The navy wrap dress is cute, but a little revealing, and no doubt if Mum sees any cleavage she'll have something to say about me not having enough up there to show off, or she'll tell me I don't need to dress so 'trampy' anymore, now that I've already landed the man and got the ring on my finger.

Why can't I have a normal mother who can just be excited and happy for me? I watch everyone I know get emotional support from their mums, and mine has managed to turn every special occasion in my life into something to nitpick and control. I'm a grown woman and she still manages to make me feel two feet tall. She drives me crazy at the best of times, but a night like tonight will be like throwing petrol onto an open flame with her. Honestly, if I thought we'd have gotten away with not inviting her tonight, I wouldn't have. Ugh.

You know what, if tonight was just about me, I think I could probably just about cope with her snide remarks. I'm used to it. But I keep thinking back to that conversation we had when I picked them up from the airport, when I mentioned Kate to her, and she started going on about how she'd be raging if Dad became friends with another woman, and how I should be marking my territory so she doesn't get any ideas about Matt, like that would ever happen. Just thinking about what Mum might say to Kate is making my stomach churn. Knowing her, she probably won't even say anything directly, but she'll have some bitchy little passive aggressive comment to make at some point. I swear, if she even insinuates anything inappropriate about Matt and Kate's friendship, I might actually lose it on her. I should probably have pre-warned Kate, now that I think about it. I don't know how she'll react if Mum says anything like that to her.

I feel terrible for saying this, but sometimes I wish I could just have a mother like Marianne, Matt's mum. From the moment I met her, she's never been anything but lovely to me, even with everything she went through losing Matt's dad the way she did. I love that she's happy again with Derek. I never got to meet Matt's dad, but I can see so much of where Matt gets his amazing kind-hearted nature from in his mum.

Right on cue, he sticks his head around the bedroom door.

'You doing okay, babe?' he asks.

'Just feeling a bit anxious,' I confess.

'What's up?'

'Same old same old,' I groan. 'Stressing about what rubbish Mum's going to hit out with tonight. You know what she's like, Matt. I can deal with her giving me crap about how I look or whatever, but I hope she doesn't cause a scene or say something rude to Kate.'

'I'm a step ahead of you,' he grins. 'I texted her earlier and told her to take anything your mother says with a pinch of salt. I explained what she's like. Besides, what does it matter what she's got to say anyway? You're going to look incredible no matter what you wear. You could wear a potato sack and look like you've just stepped off the catwalk.'

God, I love him.

'You're right, babes. Why should I care about what she thinks? I'm an adult. If she says anything snide or out of order, I'll just smile and ask if she wants more wine.'

'And if we run out of wine before she stops, there's always that bottle of gin that's been gathering dust in the cupboard,' he smiles, and I laugh out loud, although I briefly consider the bottle of bleach under the sink instead.

I'm going to wear the emerald green clingy silk dress. I feel beautiful in it, and Matt hasn't seen it on me yet. No doubt Mum will have something catty to say when she gets here, but I'm determined that this is one night I'm not going to let her ruin for me. This is mine and Matt's night, and I'm going to wow everyone and let her stick out like a sore thumb if she wants to with her constant criticism. I'm fed up needing her approval in order to be happy. This is my life, and she can either get on board, or she'll show herself up in front of everyone. And if she does, then after tonight we're going to have a wee talk, whether she likes it or not.

Kate

'Hiya, gorgeous!' Paige says as she opens the front door to let me in.

Oh. My. *God.*

My stomach flips as I look at her. She's wearing the most amazing, daring, beautiful dress I've ever seen, and it looks so good on her that it makes me want to cry, or go home, or pin her against the wall and ravish her.

But I don't do any of those things. I simply smile, hand her the little gift I've brought for them, and follow her into the house.

Despite everyone's best efforts to make me feel part of things, I still feel like the odd one out here. Everyone else is here 'with' someone. There's Paige's parents, Matt's mum and her friend, Matt and Paige themselves, of course, and even Jason and Heather who might not be 'together together,' but you'd never know it to be around them. And then there's me. As if I wasn't nervous enough after the warning text Matt sent me about Paige's mum, I'm still trying to fight off this stupid urge to just take Paige aside and blurt everything out to her. What is it that Gran always says when I get like this? I'm as 'nervous as a long-tailed cat in a room full of rocking chairs.'

I knock back my second glass of red wine in quick succession, despite us not even having eaten yet. I'm not sure if I'm trying to suppress my anxiety or pluck up courage. I even find myself wishing Sam had been able to make it – part of me thinks she made an excuse not to come to save me any embarrassment. But still, although I know there's not going to be anything between us, at least I wouldn't feel like such a spare part, and she'd be another friendly face. Not that everyone here isn't already being friendly and lovely, for the most part, at least. I'm a little intimidated by Paige's mum, and I'm trying to keep out of her way as much as I can. And then, at the other end of the scale, there's Paige. She looks so bloody good in *that dress* that I can't help but wonder how much better she'd look out of it. I imagine us sneaking into the bedroom, my hands all over her, the silk of her dress skimming over her incredible, lean, tanned body as it slips to the floor, and I– *ohhhhh, God.* I bite my lip and wait for the fluttering in my lower abdomen to subside.

Look at them, so completely wrapped up in each other. It's just those little details. The way Matt's hands brush the small of her bare back as he walks past her while she talks to someone else. The way she looks at him without him even noticing. Barely even perceptible to most people, but I see them. And as much as I watch them enviously, and I wish that it could be me, what little courage that I might have had wavers, crumbles and dissipates, and I know that I'm not going to be able to bring myself to do it. Not now. Not ever.

'Good together, 'int they?' comes a voice from behind me which startles me a little. I turn around. It's Carol, Paige's mum. My stomach lurches. From what I've been able to gather from Paige and from Matt, they're very different people in terms of personality, but physically there are a lot of similarities between them. The high, sculpted cheekbones, the thin and delicate nose, the piercing blue eyes and hair like spun gold. She could pass for a woman ten years younger, no questions asked. But she doesn't possess an ounce of the warmth and joy that her daughter does, and I completely get why Paige talks about her the way she does.

'They make a lovely couple,' I stammer. 'Paige is beautiful. Obviously inherited a lot of good genes from you,' I add, trying to curry favour in the faint hope that she'll go away and leave me alone.

'Mm hm,' she nods, a little coldly. Fine. Be like that. She looks me up and down, and I want the ground to open up and swallow me whole.

'Matt's a nice boy,' she continues. Shite. I was hoping we'd already reached the end of our brief and awkward exchange. 'Sometimes too nice for his own good. I'd hate to see anyone take advantage of that good nature of his. I'm forever telling my Paige that she needs to set some boundaries around their life.' She pauses for effect. 'Do you know what I mean?'

She looks directly at me, and I can feel her eyes pierce me to the core. She's not exactly being subtle with the message that she's trying to relay.

'Mm hm,' I nod.

'Nice to meet you, anyway,' she says icily as Matt's mum wanders over to talk to me, and I have no doubt that she doesn't mean a single word of it. Marianne waits until Carol is out of earshot and then gives me a little squeeze and winks at me.

'Don't mind Carol, hen. Between you and me, she's a sore arse,' she laughs, and I almost snort wine out of my nose.

'Thanks,' I say, composing myself.

'That poor lassie must have the patience of a saint,' she says, nodding at Paige. 'It can't be easy having a mother like that. The way she talks to her is terrible, but it's not really my place to say anything. It's just such a bloody shame. I love Paige to bits. I can't get my head round someone treating their own daughter the way Carol does.'

'I know. I don't know how I'd manage without my mum sometimes. My dad, too. I just love them both to pieces.'

'Ach, that's nice, hen. You know, I can see why our Matt

speaks so highly of you.'

'He does?'

'He talks about you all the time. I'm glad he's got a pal like you, Kate. I know how much you mean to him and Paige,' she smiles.

'Did I hear someone mention my name?' Paige says, as she puts an arm around each of us.

'I was just telling Kate how much she means to you and Matt,' Marianne says with a wink.

'Of course she does!' Paige smiles. She nudges me a little conspiratorially. 'Which reminds me, you and I need to talk privately shortly. After dinner, okay?'

'Sure,' I gulp, finishing my third glass of wine, already knowing that I'm not going to be able to eat a single bite.

Matt

I'm sitting on the couch with Derek, still completely stuffed from one of the best dinners Paige has ever put together, just watching her effortlessly be herself as she glides around the room, making sure everyone's glasses are full. I still can't quite believe she said 'yes' when I proposed. There's no way I deserve someone as amazing as Paige. I'm the luckiest man in the world.

'She's a good lassie,' Derek says.

'She's the best, Derek,' I reply with a smile. 'I can't wait to marry her.'

'That's how it should be, son.' he says. 'When you marry the right woman, one who's not just your wife, she's your best friend and soulmate as well, that's all you need in life, really. I'm happy for you, Matt. I'm glad that you're getting to experience what true love feels like. It's the best feeling in the world.'

'And I'm glad you and Mum have found each other too. When my Dad died, I was terrified that she'd just give up and wither away without him, you know?'

'That would be a terrible loss to the world,' he says. 'It's a much brighter place with your mum in it, son. And so is my world. I can't imagine her not being in my life now. You and Paige, too. I always wanted a family, but I didn't think it was meant to be, especially after Jane died. But you and your mum have given me that. So thanks, Matt. Thanks, son.'

'Aw, God's sake, Derek, you're going to have me in tears here. Give me that glass and I'll get you a top-up.'

I walk into the kitchen to top both of our drinks up, and Paige's parents are there. Martin is leaning against the breakfast bar, glass in hand. Carol bounces around from the other side to greet me.

'Matt, darling, come and give your future maw-in-law a kiss, gorgeous boy!'

I wonder if she's already been getting in about that dusty bottle of gin? She's as 'relaxed' as I've ever seen her in as long as Paige and I have been together. She plants a sloppy kiss on my lips and Martin rolls his eyes. I extricate myself from her hug before her hands start wandering. She's got a tendency to get a bit grabby when she's had a few, does Carol.

'Put the boy down, Carol. You alright, Matty?' He extends his hand and I shake it.

'Happiest man in the world, Martin. Never been better. Just in getting Derek a wee top-up.'

I've never been so thankful to have an excuse to get in and out of a room quickly. I like Martin and Carol, I really do, but she's a bit of a handful, especially after a few drinks. I can always sense when Martin's getting a bit tired and ready to throw her into a taxi, and I'm definitely getting that vibe right now. In a way, I'm secretly hoping they will call it a night shortly, as I know that Paige is never completely relaxed around her mum.

I hand Derek his freshly topped up glass and join Heather and Jason over by my record collection. I know I'd promised that there would be no repeat of the New Year's Eve shenanigans tonight, but it's almost impossible to keep Jason away from the music at a party. To give him his dues, though, he always seems to know what just to play to keep the mood up. In another life, I reckon he'd have made a fantastic party DJ.

'What's shaking, big shag-nasty?' he grins at me.

'Wrap that, you,' Hev nudges him. 'He's taken. You've missed the boat and you're gonny have to learn to deal with it.'

'Actually,' I say, 'I *do* have a proposal for my man here.'

'See?' he playfully shoves Heather, 'I told you he wouldn't be able to resist me for much longer. This is him finally about to tell me that he's chucking Paige and me and him have to run away together.'

'Settle yourself down, tiger,' I smile. 'I actually do have a serious question that I want to ask you both. And before *you* even start,' I wink at J, 'It's not related to the measurements of any body parts.'

'Do you two need a bit of private big boy alone time?' Heather asks, rolling her eyes.

'Very funny, Hev,' I say. 'Right, can you two knock it off so we can be serious for just one minute, please?'

'Scout's honour,' J pouts, doing the 'zipping the lips' gesture.

'The three of us have been best friends for longer than I can remember,' I say. 'You two have seen me at my best and my worst, and you're both like family to me. So, it would mean the world to have you both standing by my side on the biggest day of my life.'

They look at each other, and then back at me.

'Are you saying—'

'I'm asking if you two halfwits will be my Best Man. And Woman. Best People? I don't know exactly what I should be calling this. But let's face it, nothing else about our friendship is conventional, so why should this be any different? I just know that my big day wouldn't be the same without the both of you right there with me.'

'Do I need to wear a dress?' Heather asks me, eyes

narrowed.

'Do you even *own* a dress?' I reply.

'Can I wear a dress?' Jason asks.

'Not with those legs,' I grin.

'Bitch.'

'So... you guys in or what?' I ask.

They both pull me into a three-way hug, and I guess I have my answer.

Paige

I breathe a huge sigh of relief as I wave Mum and Dad off in the taxi. Thankfully, Mum managed to behave herself – relatively speaking, of course. At least we made it through the evening without her making *too* many snide comments, and as far as I'm aware she didn't manage to offend anyone else. Still, it feels like a weight has been lifted from my shoulders as their taxi disappears around the corner at the end of our cul-de-sac.

I walk back into the house, close the front door and just take a minute to myself. I hate that I let her get to me as much as I do. Tonight should have been a night for us just to celebrate, but I still felt like I couldn't completely unwind. It's unfair, of course it is, but for better or for worse, she's my mum. What else can I do?

Marianne takes me by the hand and leads me into the kitchen.

'Mon we'll have a wee blether, just the two of us, hen,' she smiles.

'No bother, Marianne,' I say.

I pour us each a glass of wine and we sit across from each other at the breakfast bar. Everyone else is in the living room.

'You having a good night?' I ask her.

'Och, brilliant, darling,' she smiles again. 'Thanks for having us over tonight. It means the world to us. I wish Matt's dad could have been here too. He'd have been so proud of our

Matt, and I know he'd have loved you to bits.'

'Aw, that's so sweet of you, Marianne,' I say, as I feel tears prick at the back of my eyes.

'Look, that's what I want to talk to you about, actually,' she says.

'Mm hm?'

'When our Matt was growing up, I always felt as though we were still missing something from our wee family. I'd have loved to have had a daughter as well, but it never worked out for us. We were only ever supposed to have Matt, I think. Not that I don't love the bones of my boy, but I think I missed out on having that special mother and daughter bond, know what I mean?'

Oh boy, do I ever.

'And then when our Matt met you and brought you home to meet me, I couldn't have been any happier. See if I'd ever had a daughter, hen? I couldn't have wished for a better one than you. So, see from now on? No more calling me "Marianne," alright? If you're comfortable with it, it would mean the world to me if you'd just call me "Mum."'

I can't hold the tears back any longer. The honest truth is, and I hate myself for even thinking this, I wish I had a mum like Marianne instead of my own.

'Aw, I think that's the nicest thing anybody's ever said to me, Mari— Mum,' I sniff.

'Och, don't be silly, darling. C'mere and give us a wee cuddle.'

I hug her tightly and kiss her cheek, then wipe my tears away with the heel of my hand. Thank God for the waterproof mascara and eyeliner I put on as a precaution tonight. I knew at some point I'd be thankful for it.

Kate walks into the kitchen and sees Marianne and I, and the state I'm still in.

'Oh, sorry, I didn't mean to interrupt, I'll leave you to it,' she says.

'No, it's fine, come on in,' I laugh. 'This one's just got me a bit emotional by being so bloody nice!'

'I'll leave you lassies to talk,' Marianne smiles. 'I'll need to go and keep an eye on that daft old goat out there in case he starts harassing Jason to let him sing!'

'Thanks, Mum. Love you,' I say to her, and Kate looks at me with an eyebrow raised.

'That's new?' she says.

'Aye, I suppose it is,' I say. I try to change the subject to stop myself getting emotional again. 'Enjoying yourself? Enjoy dinner?'

'You know I always enjoy your cooking,' she says. 'It's the only reason I come here, you know. Otherwise, I'd just be sitting in the flat in my pants, eating chips and curry sauce straight out of the foil tray.'

'Hot!' I laugh and take a glug of wine. I punch her playfully in the arm.

'I know, right? I'm such a catch.'

'Right,' I say, straightening myself up, 'I think you and I need to have a serious talk, woman to woman.'

'Okay,' she gulps, and for just a moment it looks like the colour drains from her cheeks.

'C'mon, we'll go through here and talk,' I say, as I take her by the hand and lead her into my bedroom.

'I need to ask you something. And I want a serious answer. How do you honestly feel about Matt and I getting married? I mean, really.'

She pauses for a second, as if she's choosing her words carefully.

'I think it's amazing, babe,' she says. 'You have no idea how happy I am for you both. I don't think I've ever known two people who deserve each other more than you two do.' She pauses again, looking a little confused. 'Wait, why?'

I break into a huge grin.

'I was hoping you'd say that. Because I want to ask you something very important.'

I open the drawer of my bedside table and take out the

envelope I'd put there earlier just for this exact moment. I hand it to her and nod. She opens it and takes out the card I had made, with the photo of her and I posing together on New Year's Eve. She opens it, reads the message inside, and then looks at me with her wide, watery brown eyes.

'Are you serious?'

'Yes, Kate. I'm one hundred percent serious. I want you to be my Maid of Honour. I want you standing by my side when I say "I do" to Matt.'

At first, she looks shocked. She looks down at the card again, and then back up at me.

'But— why me?' she asks.

'Because I can't think of anyone I'd rather have with me on the biggest day of my life. It's like Matt's mum was saying about always feeling she'd missed out on something by not having a daughter until she met me. I always felt like I missed out on having a sister until I met you. Say you will? Please?'

I give her my best puppy dog eyes, the ones that always work on Matt.

'I can't say no to you, can I?' she smiles.

'It's bad luck to refuse a bride,' I say.

'Is that even true?'

'Oh, absolutely. It says so right there in the Bridezilla Handbook they give us all when we get engaged,' I laugh.

'Right, well, in that case, I suppose I'm in. I can't afford any more bad luck!' she says, and I squeak with excitement and pull her into a hug.

The emotion of the evening must be getting to Kate too, because as we hug in my bedroom, I swear she's crying.

Chapter Twenty-Nine: May 16th

Kate

Things have settled into a comfortable routine in the seven weeks since Paige asked me to be her Maid of Honour. I'm not even going to lie, I thought my heart was going to shatter in my chest when she asked me that night at their engagement dinner. It felt like any hope that I still harboured that we could somehow be together was being snatched from me, and looking back at it now with clearer eyes, I suppose that really was the case. But time and perspective has also shown me that it's for the best, because now I get to spend time with my two best friends in the world, and I know that things are all going to be okay. I've had more fun days and nights out with both of them together, and Matt and I have gone out to a few gigs ourselves when Paige has been snowed under with work, but what's surprised me most is how much fun I've had being involved in Paige's wedding planning, when it's just been the two of us.

At first, every single piece of preparation felt like a dagger between my ribs. Whether it was the afternoon we spent tasting samples of wedding cakes, the Saturday we spent looking at all of the floral arrangements, or the handful of venues we've scoped out, everything was a constant reminder that she'd chosen the person— the man she wants to spend the rest of her life with. And so I put on a brave face and played the supportive best friend and let myself hurt and heal.

Then the oddest thing happened. Slowly, but perceptibly, things changed. As we've spent more time together, sharing in these silly little details that go into preparing for a wedding, I've felt that childish crush fading, and even though I still feel a tiny sense of loss at what might have been, a comfortable contentment's settled in, and I feel like I'm genuinely sharing in her joy. I've even been able to lean on a few contacts from the magazine and we've managed to secure the services of the most fabulous photographer for their big day.

Today, though, is the biggest day of them all. Today is the day we start looking for The Dress. I'd asked her if she wouldn't rather have had her mum with her for this, but she changed the subject, and I didn't want to push the matter any further in case it upset her.

So here we are, sitting in the early summer sun outside of a coffee shop in the Merchant City, just around the corner from the exclusive 'bridal boutique' where we have an appointment in fifteen minutes. I wonder how she pictured her wedding dress looking when she was a little girl? I know a lot of girls dream about it. I always felt a little weird because I never did. I suppose I just imagined that girls like me didn't grow up to have fairytale weddings. I mean, I guess I still don't, when I really think about it.

'Excited?' I ask her.

'Terrified more than anything else,' she says. 'What if I can't find one that looks right on me?'

'Somehow, I can't see that being an issue. You could tape a bunch of pedal bin liners together and still look better than most people.'

She shakes her head and rolls her eyes dismissively. Her complete lack of self-confidence still staggers me. Her mum really has done a number on her and it makes me so sad.

'Should we head round there now?' she asks.

'Yeah,' I say, checking the time on my phone. 'Let's take a walk.'

I feel like a fish out of water before we even set foot inside the boutique. It's classy. I mean, like, *seeeeeeriously* classy. It's got Paige written all over it, even though she's nothing like the snotty women who eyed me up and down as we walked in.

She's their dream client, though. Elegant, I think that's how I could best describe Paige. I know she's one of those girls that they'd beg to use her photos on their website. And then there's me. We probably look like a gazelle is out shopping with her pet hippo. I digress.

I'm sitting on a gold velvety sofa in what they call their 'Crown Suite,' sipping on a glass of champagne and trying not to fidget as Paige discusses her requirements with her consultant. It's all creams, golds and marble, apart from the rectangular black box in the centre of the rug on the floor, which I recognise from enough trashy reality TV shows as being the platform where Paige will stand to model her dress.

The first two dresses she tries on look absolutely fine to me, and I start to wonder if I'm just immune to wedding dresses and whether I can actually add anything of any value to this conversation. When she steps out of the changing booth with the third dress on, though, I finally get it.

My breath catches in my throat, and I actually feel tears welling up in my eyes. It's stunning. *She's* stunning. The sweetheart neckline, the intricate beadwork cascading down the skirt – it's like this dress was made for her. I can't take my eyes off her as she steps delicately onto the little podium and turns to admire the back in the mirror, and from the little smile at the corner of her lips, I know, I just know, that every time she imagined this day growing up, this was the dress that she saw herself in.

I down the rest of the glass of champagne just to stop myself from ugly crying.

'What do you think?' she asks me.

'Matt's the luckiest man alive,' I reply.

The sun is starting to dip in the Glasgow evening sky as we walk back towards the city centre, Paige's arm linked through mine.

'Are you hungry?' she asks me. 'I want to treat you to dinner as a thank you for putting up with my wardrobe tantrums and letting me drag you around all of these shops today.'

I don't answer. I can't answer, because the bottom has just fallen out of my world. They're walking straight toward us, but she hasn't seen me yet. It's been almost six months, and I really should have been prepared for this happening at some point, but I'm not. I'm frozen to the spot, and it feels like everything around me is moving in the slowest of slow-motion.

I guess that's the girl she left me for. It has to be. They look happy and carefree, laughing, just touching each other casually. I can't move and I can't take my eyes off them. And now it's too late and we're face to face.

'Kate,' she says.

'Steph,' I reply.

Paige

I used to pretend I had an imaginary twin sister who went everywhere with me. It made me feel less alone growing up as an only child. When I asked Kate to be my Maid of Honour at our engagement party, I meant every word I said when I told her I always wished I had a sister. Don't get me wrong, this isn't a 'poor me' pity party. I grew up perfectly happy and well-adjusted. I had lots of friends and I never really wanted for anything, but still, I felt like I'd loved to have had that sisterly bond with someone. Someone to play dress-up with and to share secrets with when the lights went out at night.

As I grew older, I watched friends with sisters and envied the built-in best friend they seemed to have. I tried so hard to create that same connection with my own friends, but it's not quite the same as having a sibling. That blood connection matters. That's why I find the bond I have with Kate quite remarkable. We're not connected by blood. I've only known her for six months. And yet, I feel more connected to her than to friends I've known my whole life, and I don't even fully understand why, except that it just feels like the most natural thing in the world.

I can't imagine having anyone else but Kate by my side today. She's been absolutely fantastic over these last few weeks as we've started making wedding plans. She's definitely got the patience of a saint, I can tell you that. She's managed to talk me down from the Bridezilla ledge more times than I care to admit. It's funny, though. She plays it down so coolly, like weddings aren't really her bag, and like she doesn't get excited about them, but I swear I could see a little wistful look in her eye when we were looking at some ideas for bridesmaid dresses earlier. And, of course, she got so excited when she was able to pull some strings to get an amazing photographer she knows through the magazine to agree to shoot the wedding for us.

This will be the real test of how excited she is, though. I think I've finally found the dress I want. Neither of us were totally sold on the first couple that I tried on, despite the consultant's *ooh*-ing and *aah*-ing over them. I mean, they were both nice enough, but I don't want *nice*. I want my dress to take Matt's breath away when he sees me. I take a deep breath and step out from behind the curtain of the changing section, and Kate looks at me, wide-eyed. I step carefully up onto the little black podium in the centre of the room, so I can see myself in the giant marble-enclosed mirror for the first time.

I almost can't believe I'm looking at myself. This is the one. This is The Dress. This is what I'll be wearing when I marry Matt. For the first time, I can see it all coming together. Walking down the aisle toward him, with Dad at my side. The way Matt will look into my eyes as we make our vows. How this dress will twirl and glide across the floor as we share our first dance. I turn around to look at the cut of the back, *'daring yet elegant,'* the consultant described it as.

'What do you think?' I ask Kate.

'Matt's the luckiest man alive,' she replies.

I link my arm through Kate's as we walk past George Square which is just bathed in the most gorgeous golden evening sun. Or maybe it's just me. Maybe I'm just so happy that this is how

I see the world tonight, cast in a warm glow. The streets are bustling with people either heading home from work or heading out for the evening, and it occurs to me that I'm hungry and I don't want this perfect day to end so soon.

'Are you hungry?' I ask Kate. 'I want to treat you to dinner as a thank you for putting up with my wardrobe tantrums and letting me drag you around all of these shops today.'

Kate stops dead in her tracks, our arms still interlinked, and my first thought is that I've said something wrong. I look at her, about to ask if she's okay, and I see the colour has drained from her cheeks. She's staring straight ahead and has a strange mix of emotions on her face that I haven't seen from her before. It's not wistful or sad. It's more like anger and pain, and I barely recognise her as the Kate that I know.

There are two women I don't know standing in front of us, and it takes a second for the pieces to fall into place.

'Kate,' the one on the right says.

'Steph,' Kate replies. 'Hi.'

So, *this* is Steph. This is the girl that Matt told me about. From that first night in the coffee shop, when she broke up with Kate and publicly humiliated her in the process. My heart sinks looking at the anguish on Kate's face. I think about the party on New Year's Eve, how raw and hurt she still was. I think about the day we spent redecorating her flat in an attempt to help her heal a little. Mostly, though, I think about how hard she's had to work to try and get over this girl, and how their relationship ended, and what I want to do, more than anything else right now, is tell this heartless cow what I think of her. Her eyes flit to me, looking me and up down, and then back to Kate. I sense a little contempt in her, and I immediately feel myself bristle.

'How have you been?' she asks Kate.

'Fine,' Kate replies flatly.

'Aren't you going to introduce me to your new *friend?*' she smirks, with a sneering, snarky emphasis on that last word as she nods at me. Oh, you arrogant, raggedy little bitch.

Someone better hold my earrings because this is about to get very real.

'I'm not her *friend*,' I cut in. 'I'm her *fiancée*.'

I don't even have to look at Kate to know that she's looking at me. And I also know that she's going to say something which gives this bitch the upper hand over her again, and there is no way on earth that I'm letting that happen, even if I'm completely in the wrong for what I've just done.

'Oh,' Steph looks at me, then at Kate, then back at me. 'That's... nice. I hadn't heard.'

I give her my sweetest smile and purposely put my hand on Kate's shoulder, making sure this bitch gets a nice long look at my gorgeous engagement ring. She doesn't need to know that it came from Matt and not Kate. The look on her face is all I needed to see.

'Anyway, it's been *so* nice to meet you, *Stephanie*,' I say. 'But we've still got some wedding arrangements to take care of and we really need to get moving. Come on, babes,' and I make a show of pulling her close as we sweep past them and across George Square. To rub a little salt into the wound, and purely because that I am one hundred percent certain that rancid, salty cow is still staring daggers into my soul, I plant a kiss on Kate's cheek without even looking back to acknowledge them.

'Wh—' Kate is about to say, but I cut her off.

'Shh. Just let her stew. It'll eat her alive.'

My hands are still shaking as we finally get out of sight, and I take a deep breath. She turns to me, eyes wide and glistening wet in the evening sun.

'Why did you do that?'

'Because I absolutely hate spiteful, snotty, vindictive cows like that. Because nobody deserves to be treated the way she treated you. Because you deserve so much better than someone like her. Because you deserve to be with someone who'll make you feel like the beautiful, amazing, funny, sweet person that you are. And mostly, because I meant what I said at New Year. It's her loss, not yours.'

Kate

My phone rings in my hand. It's our Fiona, but I'm in no state to answer it right now. My hands are shaking and my heart is ready to burst out of my chest. Mostly, though, I think I'm in shock. Shock at seeing Steph so unexpectedly. Shock at still feeling as wounded as I did, even after all these months. And I'm not going to lie, shock at how Paige stepped in like that, that she would lie to spare my embarrassment without even thinking about it. That she held me up when I felt like my legs were about to give way beneath me.

'I feel so stupid,' I say, but it's barely audible, little more than a hoarse whisper. 'I can't believe I let her get to me like that. After all this time.'

'Sshh,' she says. 'I've got you. You'll get through this. We'll get through this together.'

I look up at her and rub my eyes with my hands. I must look an actual state.

'Thank you,' I say to her. 'I don't know what I'd have done if you hadn't been here.'

'It's okay,' she says. 'It's all going to be okay, Kate. I promise.'

I close my eyes and rest my forehead on her shoulder. I feel her hand in my hair, cupping the back of my head, and it gives me immediate comfort. My phone pings, but I can't bring myself to look at it. I put it into my pocket. I don't want to move. I don't want to open my eyes. I don't want anything except this moment, right here, right now.

I didn't think it was possible to feel as low as this. I thought I was in a good place. I thought I was doing well. I thought I was over her. Steph, I mean. I didn't think she'd be able to hurt me again. Yet here I am. My cheeks flush with acute embarrassment, and I feel just like I did that night in the coffee shop at the Fort. The only difference is that this time it's Paige who's come to my rescue and not Matt.

'Do you want to go and get something terrible to eat?' she asks me. 'To hell with dinner and to hell with wedding dress diets. I want a big fat slice of cake and a strong drink. I think we deserve it.'

As much as I think she's right, and that we do deserve it, I'm not sure I could stomach anything right now. My insides are churning away like a cement mixer and I feel like I'm about to be sick.

Breathe, Kate. Just breathe. Slowly in, slowly out, just one deep breath at a time. This is going to pass. Just breathe and let this pass.

I compose myself just enough to get my phone out of my pocket. One missed call, one unread message and one voicemail, all from Fiona. I quickly check the time. She can barely even be home from her work. What's so important? I touch the little voicemail icon at the top of the screen.

'Katie, it's Fiona,' I hear her say. She sounds frantic, breathless. 'Call me as soon as you get this, hen. I'm in the Queen Elizabeth Hospital. It's Dad,' her voice cracks and I can tell she's crying. 'They think he's had a heart attack. I'm here with Mum. Please, Katie, call me. Get here as quick as you can. I love you.'

The message ends, and I just look at Paige, blankly. I am unable to form a single word. Unable to move. Unable to do anything except try to process the thought that the hurt I was feeling a few minutes ago is nothing compared to this, and that the very centre of my world is collapsing around me.

Paige

Hospital... heart attack... please...
The noise and the buzz of the Glasgow city centre rush hour traffic passing us makes it hard to pick out exactly what's being

said in the voicemail that has Kate's face turning chalk white, but between what I can hear and the expression on her face, I understand enough to be able to work out that it's not good news. Her hands are shaking so hard that she's barely even able to tap the button to end the call. I have to grab her to stop her from collapsing onto the pavement.

'Oh God... Paige... Oh God... I... No...' she's breathing in short, desperate whoops and gulps, almost on the brink of hyperventilating.

'Breathe, sweetie, just breathe,' I say softly, trying to sound as reassuring and calming as I can. I'm looking directly into her damp, panicked eyes, willing her to focus on the sound of my voice. Her entire body is trembling. 'Just breathe as slowly as you can. In. Out.'

Her breathing begins to slow and steady. Okay. Good. Better.

'I need to go,' she says, but it's as if she has no idea where she's supposed to be or what she's supposed to do. I sit her down on the little wall just along from Waxy O'Connor's pub and get my phone out. I tap on Matt's contact icon, hoping that he's not at work already. It rings and rings and then I hear his pre-recorded voicemail message. I tap to end the call without leaving him a message. It's okay. It's going to be okay. I've got this.

I crouch in front of her, my hands on her shoulders. Her breathing is still a little ragged.

'Listen to me, Kate. It's going to be okay. I'm going to look after you. I want you to tell me exactly what's happened, and then we'll do whatever it is that we need to do, okay?'

She nods, wet-eyed. 'Queen Elizabeth Hospital. My sister called. It's my Dad. He's... oh God, Paige, he can't die. My dad can't die, Paige. What am I going to do if he dies?' I can sense that she's starting to panic again. I hug her tightly until she settles, and then I try to stay as measured and calming as I can for her.

'We're going to go and get my car from the car park, and

I'm going to take you to the hospital, okay? I just need you to take a second, breathe and come with me, okay?"

She nods and I take her hands and help her to her feet. I make sure we walk quickly but calmly for the five minutes it takes us to get the car park at Buchanan Galleries where I'd left the car. She's settled down again for now, but I don't know how long that will last. On a good day, we could get to the Queen Elizabeth Hospital in fifteen minutes from here. But it's a Thursday evening rush hour, and it could just as easily be three or four times that.

My fears are confirmed as soon as we hit the motorway, and it's almost nose to tail. I know that if I show any signs of anxiety or frustration, it will set her off again, and that's the last thing either of us needs right now. I reach across and give her hand a little squeeze and smile as reassuringly as I can for her. We're moving, slowly, at a crawl, but we're moving at least. I think that's enough to keep her at peace for now. I hope it's enough.

'I'm going to call Matt again, just to let him know where we're going, okay?' I say to her.

She nods. Thank God for hands free. I hit Matt's number and I hear the dial tone through the car's speakers. Ringing. Ringing.

'Hi, this is Matt. I can't take your call right now—'

I kill the call again. I don't want to leave that message with Kate in earshot. She's still teetering on the edge as it is, and I don't know what will tip her over at this point.

We're over the Kingston Bridge and south of the river now, and the traffic is thinning just enough for our speed increase to be perceptible. She's quiet, looking out of the passenger window, and her intermittent sniffs are enough to let me know that she's crying, but I won't make a big deal. I need her to stay calm, not for me, but for her family when we get there. I want to fix this for her, but I'm helpless. All I can do is drive and keep us moving forward.

'We're nearly there,' I say to her. 'You're doing great, babes. It's all going to be okay. It's probably just a little scare, that's all. Your dad's going to be fine, you'll see.'

She nods wordlessly. Within a couple of minutes, we're leaving the motorway and the hospital looms large ahead of us. My heart is breaking a little for her, because even if her dad is going to be okay – and I hope more than anything else right now that he will be – this has to be the hardest thing in the world for her to go through. I think about Mum for a minute, about how difficult she can be and the differences that we have, and I start to feel a little guilty that I didn't invite her along to look at dresses today, because despite everything that she says and does, at the end of the day she's still my mum and I can't bear to think about my life without her in it.

We pull into the busy hospital car park, and I pull into the first space I find. She opens the door and gets out. I turn off the ignition and I do the same. She looks at me.

'You don't have to—'

'I know,' I nod. 'I want to. You're not going through this alone. I'm coming with you, and I'll stay as long as you need me to.'

I take her hand and we walk, quickly and quietly, towards whatever it is that comes next.

Kate

My hands are still trembling, but I'm just about able to find our Fi in my contacts and I tap her photo. It rings.

'Hi, you've reached Fiona, I'm sorry I can't take your call right now, but if you leave a message I'll get back to you as quick as I can. Thanks, bye!'

Just the sound of her voice makes me want to cry. I can't. I can't, because if I start, I don't know if I'll be able to stop.

'Hi, Fi, it's me, I'm on my way. I promise I'll be as quick as I can. Look after Mum for me, please. I love you.'

I end the call and Paige gives my hand a little squeeze. I try to smile. I look out of the window and try not to look ahead at the line of traffic that feels like it's never going to move. All I can think about is Dad, and it terrifies me. What if I'm too late? What if he's gone by the time we get there and I never get to remind him how much I love him and how much he means to me, to all of us? This isn't how it's supposed to be. Billy McArdle isn't even sixty yet. He's not old. He's never been sick. Maybe his diet could be a wee bit better, sure. And maybe he could walk a bit more often instead of taking the car. But he doesn't smoke. He doesn't drink anywhere near as much as he did when he was younger, barely at all, really. He never complains unless he comes down with the dreaded 'man flu,' but show me a man who doesn't under those circumstances. I just want to scream and be completely and utterly raging about the unfairness of it all, because Billy McArdle, my dad, shouldn't be lying in a hospital bed after a heart attack. Because we all need him.

I'm trying my hardest not to cry, because I don't want Paige to stress or fuss while she's driving, but it's hard. It's so bloody hard. Maybe if I just keep looking out of this window, and I try not to think about it, the traffic will clear and we'll be there and I can see him and he'll be okay and all of this will be over.

It barely even registers with me that we're at the hospital until I feel the car pull to a stop, and I realise that we're in the car park. I take off my seat belt and get out of the car. I don't know if I'm going to be able to do this. I'm terrified. About what might be waiting for me when I go in there. Even just about going in there. I can't remember the last time I was inside a hospital. It has to be fifteen years. I can just about remember being taken to visit my Grampa before he died, and that smell. That hospital smell.

I can't deal with this anxiety. I'm about to thank Paige for the lift when I see that she's already out of the car on her side.

'You don't have to—' I start to say.

'I know,' she says. 'I want to. You're not going through this alone. I'm coming with you, and I'll stay as long as you need me to.'

I nod and she takes my hand and leads me across the car park. We enter the hospital and Paige scans the various directions and signs.

'Intensive Care Unit,' she says. 'That's where he'll be.'

My stomach lurches and it's all I can do not to be sick. Oh God. Intensive care. That's where my dad's going to die. I think she sees the terror in my eyes.

'He's going to be okay, babes. I promise. Everything's going to be okay.'

I know that Paige only means the best, but she can't promise that. She can't promise that everything's going to be okay, because it might not be.

We get to the Intensive Care Unit, and Paige leads me over to the desk. I just look at the nurse blankly. I know I'm supposed to say something here, but I can't. I don't know what it is that I'm supposed to say. I just want my dad. So I suppose I should say something about my dad.

'McArdle,' Paige says to the nurse. 'Billy McArdle. Can you give us an update, please?'

'Are you family?' the nurse asks.

'Daughter,' Paige says.

'Come on, I'll take you along to the waiting room,' the nurse nods.

Why are we going to the waiting room? Why can't I see my dad? I just want to see my dad and tell him I love him and that it's all going to be okay. She's leading us along this sterile corridor and all I can think is that she's taking us to a quiet room to give us bad news. She pushes open a single door marked 'Family' and I see Mum and Fi. I burst into tears as I run in and grab them both in a hug.

'Mum, I'm so sorry, I got here as quick as I could,' is what I try to say, but I'm choked with tears, and I don't how much of it is intelligible.

'You're here now, hen,' Mum whispers. 'And that's all that matters.'

Paige

The nurse opens the door and Kate falls into the arms of her mum and a younger woman who I assume is the Fiona I've heard so much about, and I immediately become very aware that I'm an interloper, a stranger in the midst of what should be a private family moment. That said, I also don't want Kate to think I've just abandoned her. I stand in the corridor, on the other side of the waiting room door, and make productive use of these few moments by trying Matt's phone again.

'Hi, babes,' he answers. 'Good timing. Just taking a break and I noticed you'd called a couple of times. Everything okay?'

'Yeah. I mean, no,' I say. 'Well, yeah, I'm okay, but no. I'm at the Hospital with Kate.'

'What? Is she okay? What happened? How do you manage to get injured shopping?'

'It's her dad,' I tell him. 'They think he's had a heart attack.'

'Christ, sorry. Do you need me to come? I can get Hev to lock up for me.'

'No, it's fine. Her family are all here with her. I don't know how long I'll be here. I might just hang around to make sure she's okay before I head home. I'll see you there later?'

'Okay, babe. Let me know if you need anything, or if there's anything I can do? And tell Kate I'm asking for her too.'

'I will,' I say. 'Love you.'

'To the moon and back,' he says, and I end the call.

I open the door and enter the waiting room, putting my phone into my pocket. Kate is still crying into her mum's shoulder as they hug. The other woman approaches me. God, she looks so much like Kate, just a little older and more, I don't know. Mature? Serious? It's hard to tell under these circumstances. Maybe she doesn't always look that way.

'Fiona?' I say, extending my hand.

'Aye, and you must be the Paige I'm always hearing so much about,' she says. She gives me a hug, and I'm a bit taken aback, but I give her a little squeeze. 'Thank you for looking after our Katie. And for getting her here safely.'

'Is there anything I can do?' I ask her.

'We don't really know anything yet,' she says. 'They said one of the doctors will be along to talk to us, but it feels like it's been forever.'

'What happened?' I ask.

'Mum phoned me in a bit of a flap. They were pottering about in the garden, and Dad just collapsed out of nowhere. One minute he was just talking away, doing something with one of the plant pots, and the next he was on the ground. Thankfully, Erin next door was out in her garden as well and phoned an ambulance straight away. They were loading him into it when I got there, and I brought her here with me in the car.'

The door opens again and a man who looks like he might be in his early thirties enters. He's got neat, sandy-coloured hair and glasses.

'Oh, Ewan,' Fiona says and hugs him.

'How's your dad, darling? Is he okay? What happened?'

I step back to give them a moment to themselves. I'm thinking about making my excuses and leaving the family to it when I feel Kate's hand in mine.

'Paige,' she says. 'Come and meet my mum.'

'Thanks for looking after my baby, hen,' she says to me with a smile. She has a warm and kind expression, and reminds me a little of Matt's mum, Marianne. No wonder they're such a close family. I sometimes forget that there are parents like these in the world.

'I'd do anything for Kate,' I say. 'Your daughter's one of the nicest people I've ever met. She's a credit to you and your husband.'

Kate looks like she's about to say something, but cuts herself off as the door opens again, and a young woman in blue scrubs enters. Everyone turns to look at her, expectantly.

'Mrs. McArdle?'

'That's me, hen,' Kate's mum says, stepping forward.

'I'm Joanna, one of the doctors looking after William.'

The tension in the room is almost unbearable, and all I can think is that I hope this isn't bad news, because I can see how devastating it'll be for this whole family.

'Is he okay, doctor?' Fiona asks. I pull Kate close to me, just in case.

'He's stable. Tests have confirmed that he suffered a heart attack, but the prognosis for his recovery is positive. We've given him medication to help dissolve the clot that caused the heart attack and he's sedated and resting now. We'll need to monitor him very closely for the next few days and then we'll decide on the next steps from there.'

'Can we see him?' Kate asks.

'The key is not overexerting him – he needs rest more than anything else right now. Given the time now, my suggestion is that you let him rest just for tonight and let us look after him.'

The doctor leaves, and there's a palpable release of tension in the room. Hugs are exchanged, and some tears are shed. I give Kate another little squeeze as she wipes her eyes.

'Do you want me to take you home, Mum?' Fiona asks her mother.

'In all the years your dad and I have been married,' she says firmly, 'we've not spent a single night apart, and we're not going to start now. You girls get home and get some rest. There's nothing any of us can do right now. I'll phone you if there's any news.'

I look at Kate and Fiona and I immediately recognise that they both know better than to argue with their mum.

Kate

'Come on up,' I say to Paige as she pulls her car into one of the spaces in the little car park in front of my block of flats.

'Are you sure?' she asks. 'It's been a bit of a day, and I don't want to keep you from getting some rest, especially if you're going back to the hospital to see your dad tomorrow. You're going to need some sleep if you're going to be strong for them.'

'Yeah, come on. I'll stick the kettle on.'

I don't think I could face wine tonight. Not after everything that's happened today. The emotion of seeing Paige in her wedding dress. Of meeting Steph in the street, and everything that happened there. And then Dad. My poor dad. I'm in no doubt that alcohol would tip me over the edge tonight. A cup of tea, on the other hand, never goes wrong.

'Okay, just for a little while,' she says with a smile. 'Then I'm going to make sure you get some rest, lady.'

'Deal,' I say.

I flick the switch on my kettle, throw two teabags and a spoonful of sugar into mugs and look out of the kitchen window into the clear dark night sky. I keep replaying today over and over in my head. I know the doctor said Dad was going to be okay, but all I can think about is how any of us would cope without him. I know that Mum is the glue that holds our family together, but Dad really is the rock that it's all built on. I can't even begin to imagine a world without him in it. I know Mum wouldn't cope. He's all the love that she's ever known. I don't even realise that I'm crying until I feel Paige's arm around my shoulder, and I bury my face in her.

'Shh,' she whispers. 'It's all going to be okay, Kate. I know today was tough, in every way, but you made it to the end, and when you wake up tomorrow morning, it's going to be a new day and everything will feel better. I promise.'

'I know,' I sob.

'Talk to me,' she says, and it's all that I can do not to spill my guts out and tell her everything that's been in my heart and on my mind for all of these months. But I don't because I can't. That would be the end of everything.

'Why did she have to speak to me, Paige?' I say, wiping at my eyes. 'Why couldn't she just have ignored me and walked past me in the street? I thought I was finally getting over her, but clearly I'm not. Seeing her today with that other girl just brought it all back. All the memories, all the pain. Maybe if she'd just ignored me and walked right past us, I could've convinced myself that she didn't see me, and then I could have gone on pretending that I'm okay.'

'It's okay not to be okay, babes,' she says, and hugs me again. 'Today's just a wee setback, that's all. Do you think Matt and I haven't seen the difference in you from the Kate we met back last Christmas?'

I extricate myself from her hug and pour water into the two mugs.

'It doesn't feel much like progress,' I say.

'Trust me, you're doing better than you know,' she says. Her tone is soft and reassuring, and for a moment, so convincing that I even start to believe it myself. She's going to make an amazing lawyer someday soon.

'Thanks, Paige,' I smile.

'That's much better,' she smiles back.

We take our mugs of tea through into the living room and sit down on the couch. I grab the remote control and turn the TV on, because I need something to distract me from the noise inside my head. There's a new episode of *90 Day Fiancé*. I hit play and take a sip of my tea.

'Oh my God, do you watch this too?' she says. 'I've been trying to get Matt to watch with me, but he says it's too cringey, even for him.'

'Is that not the whole point of watching it?'

'I know, right?' she laughs.

We settle back into the couch and watch, wordlessly, and it feels like everything that I need right now. Hot sweet tea and completely trashy guilty pleasure television. Just comfort. No talk. No drama. No time spent thinking about the love that I had and lost, about the love that I can never have, and most of all, about the two greatest loves that I will ever have in my life, one of them lying in a hospital bed across the city, and the other waiting by his side, never leaving him, not even for a single night.

The episode ends, the credits roll, and Paige stands up, stretches her impossibly long limbs and fishes her car keys from her pocket.

'It's getting late, babe. I should head home and let you get some sleep.'

'Don't,' I say quietly.

'Hm?' she says.

'Don't go, Paige. Please?'

She sits down beside me on the couch again.

'What's wrong, babes? Are you okay?'

'Yeah. It's just— I just—'

Tears prick at the back of my raw, sore eyes again, and I look at the floor.

'I don't want to be alone, Paige. Not tonight. Not after everything that's happened today. I don't think I could bear it.'

Paige

As the show ends, I stand up, stretch, and reach for my keys.

'It's getting late, babe,' I say. 'I should head home and let you get some sleep.'

Kate says something, but it's so quiet that I can barely hear her.

'Hm?' I ask.

'Don't go, Paige. Please?'

I sit down beside her again, a little worried. 'What's wrong, babes? Are you okay?'

'Yeah. It's just— I just—'

She looks upset, like she's about to cry again. I just want to hug her and reassure her that it's all going to be okay. With her dad. With everything, really.

'I don't want to be alone, Paige. Not tonight. Not after everything that's happened today. I don't think I could bear it. I promise I'll never ask again.'

I weigh it up in my mind, but not for long. I know Matt won't mind me crashing here tonight under the circumstances. He knows better than anyone what the thought of losing a dad must be like, and he knows how Kate has struggled with getting over that other bloody cow too. I know he'll understand. I can't leave her in this state. I couldn't possibly live with myself. She needs a friend more than ever right now.

'Yeah, of course I can stay,' I say. 'Let me just text Matt to let him know.'

'Thank you,' she says softly, with tears in her eyes. 'I just—' she sniffs.

'I know, babes. I know.'

I tap out a message and send it to Matt.

> *ME*
> *Going to crash at Kate's. She's really struggling.*
> *I'll be home in the morning to get my things for work.*
> *See you then x*

Before I can put my phone in my pocket, he replies.

> *MATT*
> *Give her a hug from me. See you in the morning x*

He really is the best.

> *ME*
> *Love you xo*

> *MATT*
> *To the moon and back xo*

'Okay,' I say. 'All sorted.'

'I don't think any of my pyjamas will fit you,' she frowns. 'I've got loads of long t-shirts?'

'Anything's fine,' I smile.

She disappears into the bedroom for a few minutes and then walks back into the living room and hands me a folded-up t-shirt. I look at it for a second and then look at her and then back at the t-shirt.

'Hello Kitty?' I raise my eyebrow.

'Shut up, it's comfortable!' she says. 'I'll let you get changed. Just turn the light off and come through when you're ready.'

She leaves again, and I change into the soft cotton t-shirt, which I'm pretty sure was once black and is now washed to a faded charcoal grey. She's right about one thing, though, it is super comfortable. I fold my clothes and leave them on the couch for the morning, and then I turn off the living room light.

I knock on her bedroom door.

'I'm decent,' she says. 'Come in.'

She's got her hair tied back, and she's sitting at her dressing table taking off the last of her make-up.

'Are you sure you're still okay with this?' she asks me. 'If it's weird or uncomfortable, I'll understand, you know.'

'It's fine, babes. I'd have felt crap if I'd left you alone tonight.'

'Thank you again,' she smiles. 'I don't know what I'd do without you.'

I climb in one side of the bed, and she closes the bottle of the lotion she's just finished applying and then slides under the covers on the opposite side. We arrange the duvet around us, and finally, she flicks the switch on the lamp on her bedside table, plunging us into darkness. It takes a few seconds for my eyes to adjust, but they do, and I can make out her silhouette as she lies facing me, and then after a few more, the finer details of her face as a little shard of moonlight breaks through a tiny gap in her curtains.

'Night, babes,' I say.

'Goodnight,' she replies, and gives me a quick hug. Her lotion has the faintest scent of peaches and her skin feels soft and delicate against mine.

She puts her head back down on her pillow, and I do the same. In the silence and the half-light, our faces are so close that I can feel the warmth of her breath on my neck, and it sends a shiver down my spine that I can barely comprehend. I don't know whether it's the unravelling of the coils of today's stress, or the intimacy and comfort of this moment, but I become intensely and acutely aware of one thing, and one thing only; that more than anything else in the world right now, I have the overwhelming desire to kiss her. And not in the way that I planted a kiss on her cheek earlier. This time, it's not driven by a need to protect her, or make someone jealous. This time, it's driven by curiosity, and by desire. And before I even know what I'm doing, that's exactly what happens. My heart races in my chest as I place the lightest of kisses on her soft mouth, my tongue flicking and tasting the cherry of her lip balm.

Almost immediately, my senses are flooded with the most intense, electrifying desire, and then, microseconds later, an overwhelming sensation of guilt, and I pull away from her.

'Shit, Kate. I'm sorry. I shouldn't have— I'm so sorry.'

She places her hand lightly on my cheek and I can smell peaches again.

'Shh,' she whispers. 'Don't be.'

I look at her in the moonlight. For the first time since I've known her, I *really* look at her, and she no longer looks cute to me. Or pretty. In the moonlight, she looks beautiful. I run my hand over hers, and edge my body close, closer, until finally my lips brush her bare neck and I can feel her eyes flutter and close. This time, I kiss her neck more deliberately, with just the merest trace of my tongue, and she inhales sharply. She sweeps my hair back and behind my ear and kisses my neck, and between the scent of the lotion and the sensation of her warm breath on me again, I'm overwhelmed because everything feels and smells and tastes so good that it's making me dizzy.

Her hands skim the hem of the Hello Kitty shirt, as if waiting for my approval, and I slip my hand up the back of her pyjama shirt, lightly tracing her spine with my fingertip, causing her to gasp and shudder. She tugs my shirt gently upwards, still kissing me, and I shift my body to allow her to slide it, first, past my breasts, and then over my head. I wriggle free of it and do the same to her, first with her shirt, and then, hesitantly at first, and then with increasing purpose and urgency, her shorts. We kiss, and kiss, and kiss, and I cannot get enough of her mouth, of the taste, the warm wet softness of it, the way her lips and tongue feel against mine. My hands are in her hair as she trails her tongue softly along my collarbone, around the stiffness of my nipple, down the flat of my stomach, and it feels like my whole body tightens in anticipation as she finally takes me in her mouth, and I shiver again, completely enveloped in the intensity, in the very real rush of this moment.

My eyes roll back and close, and I have no words to express this exquisite pleasure as I lose myself to her mouth, to her hot breath, to her fingers and her tongue, on me and in me, over, and over, and over.

Soon, my breaths become moans, and then cries. Soon, her voice joins mine, and as unbearably hot as it becomes under her duvet, the terrible, unspoken thing that neither of us can say aloud is that it can never be pulled down or kicked off, because as long as nothing can be seen, we can keep lying to ourselves that nothing is happening at all.

When it's over, when every last trace of need in us is sated, we lie in the dark, panting, gasping, our bodies still intertwined and slick with sweat, neither of us speaking, neither of us moving, until exhaustion finally claims us, and we tumble headlong into sleep.

Chapter Thirty: May 17th

Kate

I reach across to silence the alarm on my phone, and I look blearily at the screen. *7.45am.* Ugh. I'm tired. I'm so tired and I have no idea why.

Oh God.

Yes I do.

I know exactly why I'm so tired.

I turn around and stretch my arm out across the cool expanse of my bed, which I realise is now empty. I roll over and sit up. As the sheet slips away from me, the cool morning air hits my boobs and I suddenly become acutely aware that I am completely naked.

Oh God Oh God Oh God.

What have I done?

Maybe it was all just a dream. That's all it was. Right? It has to be. It was just a vivid, filthy, exciting, dangerous dream, and I haven't just completely burned three relationships to the ground and lost the two best friends that I have.

'Paige?' I call out, but there's no response.

I reach down to the floor beside the bed and pick up my discarded pyjama shirt and shorts and slip them on under the covers. I kick the duvet off and get out of bed. I walk through to the living room, and it's empty. The only sign that she's even been here is the neatly folded Hello Kitty t-shirt on the couch. Well, at least now I can be sure that it wasn't a dream. Shit.

I check the kitchen and then the bathroom, but deep inside, I know that she's gone, and a million and one panicked, chaotic thoughts are already jostling for attention in my brain.

How could I have been so selfish? Yes, I wanted last night to happen, I wanted it so much that it hurt, but still. What if she's at home confessing everything to Matt right now? What if we've just done something so terrible that none of us will ever recover from it?

I'm trying to justify this to myself, to find some excuse for what happened last night. She started it. She made the first move. And what, Kate? You were so weak and powerless that you couldn't protest? That's bullshit and you know it is. You can lie to yourself all you want, but you could have stopped it when she pulled back and apologised. You could have said any one of a million things right there and then that could have put it all to rest without making her feel bad, or awkward, or uncomfortable. But you didn't. You didn't stop it. Yes, she made the first move. But you made the next one, and that's one hundred percent on you.

There's no escaping this cold, hard truth. I knew exactly what I was doing. I knew what the potential consequences would be, and I still chose to ignore them, to prioritise my own desires above everything else. Because that's what I do, isn't it? I'm so selfish. Steph was right.

I pick up the Hello Kitty t-shirt and go back into the bedroom to get my phone. Maybe I'm blowing all of this out of proportion. Maybe she's just gone home to get ready for work. Maybe she understands it happened in the heat of the moment, at the end of a bad day, and that it doesn't really have to mean anything if we don't want it to. I can call her. This doesn't need to be a big deal. We did something we shouldn't have, no matter how incredibly hot it was, but it doesn't need to ruin the rest of our lives.

The call goes straight to voicemail. That doesn't mean anything, though. Maybe her phone died. Maybe she's still driving. There could be a perfectly simple explanation. Right?

I bring the Hello Kitty shirt to my face and inhale. I can still smell her perfume on it and a small, terrible part of me secretly wishes that it could be last night all over again.

My brain is still whirling. I'm thinking about Matt, and how devastated he's going to be. How betrayed he'll feel. He will, right? Maybe. Maybe he won't. I know that I'm trying to somehow justify this to myself, but I find myself wondering if it would turn him on. Maybe he'd even want to join in next time. What am I even saying? Next time? Oh my God, there can't be a next time. Can there?

I'm thinking about our Fi, and how she warned me – over and over again – that this was a bad idea from the beginning. I'm thinking about how she reminded me that Mum and Dad raised us to be better than this, and how I've proved that completely wrong.

Dad.

Oh, Dad.

I've let everyone down, but nothing could hurt me more than knowing that Mum and Dad are going to be disappointed in me. All I've ever wanted was to make them both proud, not feel like they've failed me as parents. Fiona's right, just like she always is. This isn't the person they raised me to be. The kind of person who causes someone to cheat on their partner. And worse still, a friend. I don't think I could face looking in my dad's eyes and seeing him disappointed in me, and my selfishness, and my complete lack of morals.

And the worst part of all of this, the thing that makes me the *actual* worst person in the world, is that even above all the regret and shame and deep self-loathing that I'm feeling right now, every time I think about what we did, red hot ripples of excitement flash through my entire body and make me shudder. Whether it was just the illicit nature of what we were doing, or the intimacy of the bond that Paige and I already shared, there's no denying this one fact.

Last night was, without a shadow of a doubt, the best sex that I have ever had.

Paige

So, this must be what a Walk of Shame feels like. Or a Drive of Shame, if we're being pedantic. It's just a little after six in the morning, and I'm on the way home from Kate's, trying to make some kind of sense out of what last night was all about. I feel like the worst person in the world this morning, because make no mistake about it, last night was one hundred per cent all my fault, and I can't even explain why.

Mr. Kohli, the tall, gregarious man who owns the local convenience store, recognises me and gives me a friendly wave as I drive past, and then I see him do a kind of little double take as he realises what time it is, and my sense of shame intensifies. I thought my days of doing this – and feeling like this – were behind me. I think about the few one-night stands that I've had in my life, and I can't believe I've been so stupid and reckless. The memories are coming back in short flashes, and my cheeks are burning with the sheer embarrassment of it all.

Was it completely spontaneous? Yes.

Do I regret it? More than anything I've ever done in my life, I think.

Did I enjoy it?

Well?

Oh God, yes. And I'm almost positive it's just because it felt so forbidden, so wrong, but everything about it in the moment felt new, thrilling, dangerous, and so very, very ridiculously *hot*. I've never looked at Kate the way I did last night. I've never even thought about it before, not with her, not with anyone. I've never felt the slightest attraction – not in that way, at least – to another woman. Not until last night. And now, in the cold light of morning, it's the only thing I can think about and I don't know if I'm certain of anything anymore.

I shouldn't have left the way I did, and I'm racked with guilt. I should have woken Kate so we could talk about this. About what happened. About how it was a mistake, and it was all my fault, and more than anything, how we can never talk about it again and how it must never happen again. But I didn't do any of those things because I am a bloody coward.

Instead, what I did was wake up, look across the bed at Kate, sleeping, and looking just as beautiful this morning as she did in the heat of the moment last night, and then completely freak out. I picked up her t-shirt from the bedroom floor, crept naked into the living room, folded it neatly and placed it on her couch. Then I put my own clothes from last night back on, and left quietly, like a mouse, like a thief in the night, terrified that Kate, my friend, would catch me leaving and realise that I'm fleeing from more than just her flat.

I couldn't do it. I couldn't stay. I couldn't wake her up, because I can't face the inevitable question that I'm so not ready to answer. And now, I hate myself so much that I can't even look at myself in my rear-view mirror as I pull into my driveway.

Matt is still asleep when I get in, having closed the front door quietly behind me. I think about putting the kettle on and making myself a coffee, but I don't think I could even face one right now. My stomach is churning with shame, anxiety and regret, and all I really want is to get out of these clothes and wash last night's terrible mistake away in a hot shower.

The steam is already rising to meet me as I step under the water, as hot as I can stand. I close my eyes and tilt my head forward, hoping for two things. That the heat will seep into my muscles, relaxing the tension I've been carrying in my neck and shoulders all the way home, and that the water will be enough to wash away the regret as easily as it has last night's sweat.

I slip into the white towel robe I'd hung on the back of the bathroom door and look in the mirror as I brush my hair back, and I see the guilt and shame still written large across my face, like my own personal Scarlet Letter.

I try to be quiet as I tiptoe into our bedroom, conscious of every single creak of a floorboard. I just need to get my work clothes for today out of the wardrobe and then maybe I can get out of here before Matt—

'Hey babe,' he croaks, groggily. My stomach lurches and I close my eyes. Shit.

'Morning, babes,' I say, my eyes still closed. I can't even look at him. How in the hell am I going to be able to hide this from him?

'How's Kate?' he asks. 'Was she okay last night?'

I want to say she was more than okay, so *much* more, but I can't. I can't ever say that, and I shouldn't even be allowing myself to think it. I shouldn't be thinking that she made me feel things that nobody else ever has. Not even Matt.

'Fine,' I choke. 'Good. Just a rough day, you know?'

'She's lucky to have a friend like you,' he says. Ugh.

'Mm hm,' is all I can muster.

'You feeling okay?' he asks, and all I want to do is cry and tell him everything and beg for his forgiveness, because I don't know if I am built to carry this secret.

'Just feeling a little under the weather this morning,' I lie.

'Probably didn't get the best sleep, right?' he says. God, if only he knew.

'I think I might be coming down with something. I haven't felt myself since I woke up. Probably just a bug or something.'

Ugh. I hate lying to Matt. He doesn't deserve any of this. I've betrayed him, and I don't know how I'm going to be able to live with myself.

'Maybe you should just call in sick and come to bed? I'm getting up for work, anyway.'

'Yeah, I think that's probably best. I wouldn't want to pass it on to anyone else.'

I climb into bed, still wearing the towel robe, and curl up into a ball. He leans over and kisses my forehead and then gets up. I just want to tell him how much I love him, and how I promise I'll never do anything to hurt him, but I know I can't, because no matter how hard I try to get it out of my mind, the fact of the matter is that last night was, without a shadow of doubt, the best sex that I have ever had.

Chapter Thirty-One: June 3rd

Matt

The air is thick with the smell of steaks and sausages coming from Derek's barbecue and my mouth is watering. It's a gorgeous summer evening, and we're at Mum's— Mum and Derek's place – I'm still getting used to saying that – for a family barbecue to celebrate Derek and Mum finally becoming 'official' and Derek selling his little place to move in with her.

It's not like any of us didn't see it coming, really. They were spending more and more time together, and no matter how much they tried to keep it low-key, it was becoming increasingly obvious they're absolutely besotted with one another. I love Derek. I love the joy he's brought back into Mum's life. And as much as he'll never replace Dad – and he's never tried to – I love having someone like him in my life again.

'Matt, son,' he whispers, conspiratorially. 'Keep a wee eye open for your mum, I promised her I wouldn't have too many of these pork and leek sausages, but they're too good to resist.' He winks and grins at me, and I do the same. As secrets go, there are worse ones to have to keep. You enjoy your sausages, mate.

'Mum, he's in about these sausages again!' Paige shouts over her shoulder as she steps out onto the back decking with more beers for Derek and I. My mum follows her out through the French doors and tuts as she rolls her eyes at Derek. I smile as I look at Paige and she smiles back. She looks fantastic tonight. Summer weather suits her more than anyone I've ever known. With her blonde hair, her long legs and how naturally she takes a tan, she has the look of a Californian in the summer, and it drives me nuts. No matter how hard I try, my Scottish genes remain undefeated, and my summer colour spectrum is pale white to lobster red and back again. It's just as well that summer only lasts for the three days in the west of Scotland.

She plants a kiss on my lips as she passes me my beer, and kisses Derek's cheek as she gives him the other one.

'Sorry, Derek,' she winks.

'Clipe,' he smiles back at her and munches the illicit sausage freely now that he's been caught in the act. He clinks his bottle against mine. 'Cheers, son.'

'Right, Derek,' Mum says as she puts plates down on the circular glass-topped patio table. 'I think it's time, don't you?'

'Oh, aye, right enough, Marianne. Coming.'

He hangs his tongs on the handle of the barbecue and walks around to stand beside my mum.

'What's going on?' Paige asks.

'Sorry to spring this on you both,' Mum says, 'but we've got something else that we need to tell you.'

'What is it, Mum? Everything okay?'

'Neither of us are getting any younger, and now that we're living together and not sneaking about keeping secrets like a pair of teenagers—'

Paige and I look at each other and smirk. 'You weren't doing a great job of keeping it secret,' I laugh.

'Shoosh, you! Don't interrupt your mother,' Paige scolds me and nudges me in the side.

'So, anyway,' Derek says, looking adoringly at Mum. 'I've asked this amazing lady if she'll do me the honour of becoming my wife, and I'm delighted to say that she's accepted.'

Mum brings her hand round from behind her back and shows off a lovely ring. Paige squeals and springs to her feet to hug my mum. I stand up, shake Derek's hand and give him a big hug of my own, and then give Mum a hug and a kiss.

'That's amazing news,' Paige bubbles. 'We're so excited for

you both! When's the big day?'

'We've not booked anything yet, but it'll be soon. It's not going to be a big wedding like yours or anything, so there's no point in us messing about,' Mum says.

'And it would mean the world to us if you'll both be there for us,' Derek says.

'Paige, darling, I was hoping you'd be my bridesmaid,' Mum says to her.

'And Matt, son, I'd be honoured if you'd be my best man.'

'We'd love it!' Paige and I say at exactly the same moment, and as the four of us hug, I have an entirely new appreciation for what love means, and I don't think I've ever been so happy.

Paige

The most exciting – and at the same time stressful – thing about entering the second year of my two-year traineeship is being able to appear in court on my own. It's not without some limits, of course. Even though I've now been admitted into the Law Society and granted a restricted practising certificate, I still sometimes feel like I've got training wheels on my bike. There are only certain types of work I can handle, and I have to ensure that clients fully understand that I'm a trainee. Still, though, it's exciting, and with every day that passes now, I feel like I learn something new and get one step closer to finally fulfilling my ambition.

The downside, of course, is the serious increase in my workload. And as the evenings start to draw shorter, the nights where it's beginning to get dark when I finally arrive home will become more and more frequent. Matt, to his eternal credit, though, has been incredibly understanding and supportive, even though nights out are becoming an increasingly rare luxury for us. In some ways, I guess that's not necessarily a bad thing. Especially when it comes to— you know. The workload is a welcome distraction if it cuts down the amount of time that

I have to spend thinking about her.

Am I burying my head in the sand instead of dealing with my mess like a functional adult? Absolutely.

Do I feel guilty about it? I'd be lying – yet again – if I said that I don't.

The truth of the matter is that I miss her terribly, and I feel like I've ruined everything that we had. I can't count the number of times I've picked up my phone to call her, or text her, or send a message on Insta, and then just put it back down again. I was a coward when I snuck out of her flat that morning, and I'm even more of a coward now, no matter how much I try to convince myself and everyone else that it's all just because of my workload.

I'm torn. That's all there is to say, really. No matter how hard I try, I can't get that night out of my mind. And then I think about Matt, and I'm devastated all over again that I betrayed his trust every bit as much as I betrayed Kate's. That's the thing, though. As much as I know that I'm still in love with Matt, when I think about the feelings I have for Kate, I don't think I can distinguish the difference. It's not like I can say it's a different *kind* of love. Because deep down, I don't believe that it's different at all. That's what makes me a truly bad person.

Which makes it all the more difficult knowing that, whether I like it or not, I need to reach out to Kate, and soon. There are still so many wedding plans to make, and I need to know whether or not she feels like she can still be involved, after—everything. I don't know if I even have the right to ask, or expect anything from her, after what I did. If I don't do something soon, though, Matt will start to ask questions, and one way or another, I need to find answers.

He's going out with Heather and Jason to see a couple of bands playing on Friday night. I've already told him that I'm not going to be able to make it due to work, so this might be the last chance I get to make things right. For all of us.

I pick up my phone and steady my shaking hand long

enough to call her. It rings, and rings, and I'm just about to end the call before her voicemail message kicks in when—

'Hey.'

'Hey,' I say. 'Can you talk?'

The pause seems to last forever.

'Yeah, but not right now. I've got a deadline to meet.'

'Are you free on Friday night? We need to talk this through.'

'We do,' she says. 'I've missed you, Paige.'

My heart floods with emotion just at the sound of her saying my name.

'I've missed you, too.'

Kate

'Stop fussing and just come and sit down, pal,' Dad says to me.

'Stop bloody giving me reason to fuss then, Dad,' I reply. He smiles, knowing full well that I'm right. His recovery has been going well, due in no small part to the system Mum, Fiona, Ewan and I have contrived between us to ensure he doesn't overdo things – despite his best efforts to the contrary. That's my dad, though. He's never been out of work for more than a week in the forty-plus years since he left high school with nothing but a handful of failed exams and the knowledge that he would happily spend the rest of his life loving my mum. Throughout my life, he's been the very definition of the words 'stable' and 'provider,' and I know how hard it's been for him to slow down and take things easy.

I sit down on the couch beside him. I've been dividing my time between working back at the flat and being here to help with Dad, and I have to say that it's been good for me. Spending time with my family, I mean. I needed that more than anything lately. Maybe not *anything*. But still, it's been amazing. I know Mum and Fiona have been happy to see more of me, and I feel the same. Friends are great, but my little family unit is the centre of my universe, and I guess I forgot that for a little while somewhere along the way.

'How's your wee pal doing?' Dad asks me. 'You've not mentioned her for a while.'

Dad's an expert at this. Navigating conversations that need to be had at just the right time. You hear about men with zero emotional intelligence who just charge in with the big boots on. For a man of his age and background, my dad is as shockingly opposite to that as it's possible to be. He's sensitive and intuitive and knows exactly what to say and when, like he has a radar constantly scanning over his family looking for ships that might be in danger of drifting into troubled waters.

'We've just been busy, that's all. I've had a lot of work on, and she's been busy with wedding plans. Loads to get done, you know?'

I feel bad. Bad for not being honest with Dad, yes, but also bad for how poorly I've behaved with Paige since— that night. I've been making excuse after excuse to distance myself from her, because I don't know where we stand, and I'm not sure I could stop myself from spilling my guts, telling her how I really feel about her, and begging her to scrap the wedding. I've had this stupid idea circling in my head about pitching a thinly veiled version of our story to the magazine, because I know that she reads it, I know that she'll see it, and then I'll be able to say all of the things I want to say without having to, you know, actually *say* them. Ugh.

My phone buzzes in my pocket. I take it out.

Paige.

I think about letting it go straight to voicemail. Yet again. I know in my heart that I need to face this, though.

'I need to get this, Dad,' I lie. 'Work call.'

I walk through the kitchen and step out onto the decking in their back garden.

'Hey,' I say.

'Hey,' Paige replies. 'Can you talk?'

I want to. More than anything. I've missed the sound of her

voice. I've missed the time that we spend together. I've missed the conversations that we have. I've just missed *her*.

'Yeah, but not right now,' I lie again. 'I've got a deadline to meet.'

'Are you free on Friday night? We need to talk this through.'

'We do,' I say, and I feel so completely choked up that I can barely speak. 'I've missed you, Paige.'

'I've missed you, too.'

I end the call, because if I don't, I'm going to cry, and I'll have to tell Dad everything. And that is a conversation that I don't think I'm ever going to be ready to have.

Chapter Thirty-Two: June 7th

Paige

I'm already second guessing my decision. Perhaps the safest, the most sensible thing would have been to arrange to meet somewhere public, rather than here at home. Sure, we'd have run the risk of either or both of us getting embarrassingly emotional or angry, but maybe that would have been easier to handle than this— tension? This thing between us, whatever it is. You can't really call it 'unresolved sexual tension,' can you? Not when it's already been *resolved*. Multiple times, as I recall.

Focus, Paige. You're making this so much more difficult than it needs to be.

'How's your dad?' I ask, trying to find some kind of comfortable ground for us both while we figure out how on earth we're going to navigate this. But I'm fully aware that there's really no such thing, is there? Everything is just charged now, loaded, one way or another.

'Better,' Kate smiles. 'He's back to his old self. One day at a time, really, you know?'

One day at a time. I get that. Completely. That's how I've survived these last three weeks.

'Good,' I nod. 'I'm glad. I'm happy for you all, babe.'

'Paige, I—' she starts.

'Kate, I—' we cut each other off and stop awkwardly. I hate that this is what our relationship has become.

'You first,' I say. She smiles. I've missed her smile so much.

'About the wedding,' she says.

'Look, I'll understand if you feel it would be too much,' I say. 'After everything that— you know. I can tell Matt that you've had to pull out because of your dad, or work, or something. The last thing I would ever want is for you to feel obliged to—'

I can barely even bring myself to finish the sentence. I can't bear the thought. All I want is for us to be able to take that night back and go back to the way things used to be. When it was the three of us. When we were— whatever it is that we were before we were *this*.

'I don't want that, Paige,' she says, and I can see in her eyes that she means it.

The trouble is, though, what are the alternatives? Are either of us capable of putting what happened that night behind us and moving forward with the rest of our lives? Are we capable of just being good friends? Because I'm not sure that we are. I'm not sure that we ever were *just* good friends. I think the honest truth is that we were— we *are*, lovers with shit timing.

She reaches across the breakfast bar, looks into my eyes and puts her hands on top of mine. I don't want to cry, but it's getting harder by the minute. I'm scared that if I do, she'll comfort me, and her touch, her embrace, will be more than I can stand, and then neither of us will be able to control what happens next.

Kate

'I don't want that, Paige,' I tell her.

I reach across the breakfast bar and put my hands on top of hers.

'About that night,' I say to her.

'Don't—' she begins, but I need to say this to her. If I leave any of this unsaid, neither of us will ever be able to heal or move forward, and then what will there be left of us?

'I didn't plan for any of that to happen,' I say. 'You have to believe me, Paige. The last thing I ever wanted to do was to hurt you or Matt. When you pulled away from me, I should have told you that it was okay, and we could have just gone to sleep and none of this would have happened. We could have gone on just being friends, and that would have been enough.'

She looks down, unable to meet my eyes. Is it guilt? Shame? Regret?

'Would it, though?' She looks up. 'Be enough, I mean? Could we have gone on just being friends?'

At first, I don't fully understand what it is she's trying to say.

'Aren't we?' I ask. 'Just good friends?'

'I don't think we are, Kate. I don't think we were ever meant to be *just* friends. That's why I kissed you. Not because it was the heat of the moment, or because of everything that happened that day, or any of the other million lies that I tried to tell myself in order to justify doing what I did. What we did. I did it because I needed to. Because I *wanted* to. Because, in spite of everything that's happened, and despite all of the consequences if I do, I *still* want to.'

And in a split second, I am off my stool, around the breakfast bar, and we're tumbling backwards into her living room, and spilling onto her couch, all hungry, wet mouths, sucking, nibbling, biting, and desperate clawing hands, tearing away not just at our clothes, but at the last shreds of what we were, leaving only that which we're becoming. There's no self-consciousness this time, no duvet, no hiding in the vain pretence that nothing is happening. There's just this sheer animal lust and the two of us, naked and lost in the searing heat of it.

Her breath is hot and wet as her lips close over my willing, searing, sensitive flesh, and I feel my eyes roll into the back of my skull at the sweet, delicious ecstasy of it all. That gorgeous pressure building, wave upon wave, until I can take no more and it breaks, fast and hard, like a champagne bottle smashing against the hull of a christened ocean liner, an eruption of such ferocious, unbridled intensity that neither of us even register the sound of the key in the door.

Matt

'You can't be serious,' Jason says to me, still trying to process what I've just said, like I'd offered him an ancient Babylonian scroll to decipher, instead of simply telling him, as I had, that I wasn't really feeling the gig, and that all I wanted to do was head for home instead.

'You hearing this, Hev?' he laughs. 'The auld yin here can't hack gigging with us now that he's all fitted for his ball and chain.'

I don't know if that's exactly how I would phrase it, but the truth is that not a million miles off the mark. As much as I love going out and discovering new bands, and as much as I love Heather and Jason's company, I think I'd trade it all in a heartbeat to be with Paige, even if we're just sitting quietly in our own company, her buried in work and me reading a book, or listening to some music with my earbuds in. Just the feeling that she's there with me is all I need in the world sometimes, and I guess tonight is one of those nights. I was hoping she'd have been able to come out with us tonight, and when she said that she was laden down with work, I don't think my heart was really in it after that. I'd have been just as happy sitting at home with her and splitting a takeaway while she works. Maybe that's boring, and maybe I'm a dull, smug, married suburban man just waiting to happen, but I don't care, not a jot.

'Not even staying for the headliners? You're a shell of the man you were, Matt,' Hev laughs.

'Just youse young yins go on and enjoy yersels, hen,' I joke-croak like an old man. 'I'll go home and get my slippers on in front of the fire.'

'Say hi to Paige for us,' J says. 'Tell her she needs to park her work for one night and get out with us!'

'Will do,' I say, as I hug them both and make my way through the SWG3 crowd and out into the warm evening.

I think about giving Paige a call to tell her I'm on the way home but decide to score myself some brownie points instead. I'm going to grab some Chinese before I get a taxi back home and surprise her with a late dinner. I know she won't say no to that. Hey, she might even be convinced the rest of the work can wait until tomorrow.

'Just here's fine, mate,' I say to the taxi driver as he pulls into our little cul-de-sac. Hev and J are right. I'm so suburban, these days. What I'm not, though, is expecting to see Kate's car sitting in one of the spaces in front of our house. And as much as I'm excited to see her and looking forward to catching up with her, I'm doing some quick mental calculations to work out if there's enough food for the three of us. If I'd known Paige had arranged something for them for tonight, I probably wouldn't have gone out in the first place – or at the very least picked up enough food for us all. It'll be fine, though. We'll manage.

What I see when I open the living room door is enough to make me drop the bag I'm holding, and I don't notice that it's burst open all over the redwood floor at my feet. Every fibre of my being screams in protest, but when I open my mouth, no sound comes out.

Paige

Kate is yanking at my hair, and at first I think she's still in the throes of passion, but when I look at up her wide, scared eyes and chalk white face, it becomes apparent that something is wrong. Something is very, very wrong.

'What the fuck?' Matt screams from behind me, and I've never heard him so angry.

Shit shit shit shit shit.

'What the fuck is going on here?' he shouts again, and I spin around from between Kate's thighs and tumble from the couch onto the floor, scrambling to get to my dress, which I clutch to my naked body in an attempt to— what, I'm not quite sure.

There's no covering this up.

A million thoughts are running through my head all at once, yet everything around me seems to have slowed to a crawl, and the only thought that I can discern from all of it is that I am in serious trouble. My heart is racing, and my stomach feels like it's tied in knots, and I have no idea what it is that I'm supposed to say or do now. How can I possibly explain this? There's no way that I can justify what he's just walked in on.

Finally, I look at him, and it breaks my heart to see his expression. I see the shock, the hurt, and the disgust in his eyes, and I am so devastated with shame that I can't move.

'Oh my God, Paige, put something on, for fuck's sake,' he says, in a tone I've never heard from him before.

I realise I'm still standing in the middle of the floor holding my dress against myself. I slip it quickly over my head. Out of the corner of my eye, I see Kate is still frozen in shock on the couch, covering herself with her hands. I grab her t-shirt from the floor and throw it onto her.

'Matt—' I gasp, trying to breathe, trying to compose myself.

'Shut up! Just shut up— I—' he stammers.

His hands are in his hair. I can't tell if he's still trying to process everything, or if he's going to explode. I feel like I'm suffocating, like every last molecule of oxygen has been sucked from the room. I can't look at him. I look at the floor, at the bag torn open, at the noodles all around Matt's feet and what looks like sweet and sour sauce on his trainers.

'Let me get a cloth—' I start, as I bend over to attempt to pick up as much of the mess as I can.

'Just leave it!' he snaps.

'But your shoes—'

'I said fucking leave it, Paige!' he yells, and I flinch. He looks and sounds nothing like the man I know and love, and it's all my fault.

I step back and say nothing. I look at Kate, who is looking back at me, the expression on her face one of silent pleading with me to tell her what to do next. The truth is, though, I have no idea. Whatever happens next is going to be no more or less than I deserve, because I can't begin to explain any of this, and even if I could, what explanation could possibly make any of it okay? There's no excuse for any of it.

'I didn't expect you home so early,' I say, because it's all I can think of, despite it being the worst possible thing I could have said.

'Clearly,' he spits, and there's no answer for that.

What else can I possibly say right now? That this isn't what it looks like? That's the cliché that normally gets rolled out when you see this scene unfolding in movies, isn't it? I can't possibly say that because this is *exactly* what it looks like. He's walked in on his fiancée cheating on him, and with their mutual best friend, just to rub salt into the wound.

I want to reach out to him, to beg for his forgiveness, to turn back time and undo all of the damage that I've caused. But I know that it's too late for any of that, because I've crossed a line, there's no doubt about that. In fact, I've gone so far past the line that I can't even see the line anymore. I've ruined everything, for all of us. That first time it happened, that night in Kate's bed, I instigated it and she simply responded. It was a moment. But tonight, there's no excuse. We were talking, and I could have taken the conversation in a million other directions than the one I chose. What happened tonight, what we did, is completely my fault, and I hate myself.

Kate stands up from the couch, now wearing the t-shirt that I tore from her body just minutes ago. Tears are streaming down her cheeks. She may have been a willing participant, but I'm in no doubt whatsoever that I am the cause of all of this.

'Matt, I'm so sorry— I swear I didn't mean for any of this to happen,' she pleads with him.

He turns to her angrily, the three of us now standing in a triangle in the middle of our living room. His face is etched with hurt and disbelief, and I know that we've broken his heart.

'Sorry? You're sorry?' he snarls at her. 'How long has this been going on, Kate? How could you do this to me? After everything I've done for you, how could you do this to me?'

'Matt, please—' she cries. She looks at me, her eyes begging for me to say something, say anything, anything at all, to come to her assistance. But I can't. I can't say anything. I can barely breathe, let alone speak.

'I wish I'd never met you,' he says coldly to her, and I swear that I see her heart break right in front of me.

Kate

Fuck.

I can't speak. I can't think. I can barely move, except for the effort that I somehow manage to muster to bunch my still-shaking hands, still buried in Paige's hair, into fists and pull, causing her to yelp in pain.

'What the fuck?' Matt bellows as he looks at us, naked, entangled, and breathing heavily.

Paige looks up at me, but my eyes are fixed on Matt. I feel her head turn around.

'What the fuck is going on here?' he shouts.

Paige scrambles from between my legs and falls from the couch onto the floor, and then quickly grabs her dress and gets to her feet. I shut my legs and put my arms over my boobs in a panic, but I can't move. I can't do anything except watch in mute horror.

'Oh my God, Paige, put something on, for fuck's sake,' Matt says to her. She slips her dress quickly over her head, and then looks at me. She grabs my t-shirt from the floor and tosses it in my direction. It flutters and lands on my thighs. I pull it over my head and then reach down and grab my pants from the floor just at my feet.

'Matt—' Paige says, and it looks like she's about to pass out from the panic.

'Shut up! Just shut up— I—' he says to her.

Everything is spiralling out of control, and I have no idea

what I'm supposed to do about any of it. My heart is racing so fast that I think it might explode. Breathe, Kate. Just breathe. Oh my God, I think I might actually throw up. I look at Paige, hoping she has an answer. Something. Anything. Tell me what to do and I'll do it, Paige. Do I need to get my things and go and leave you two to try and salvage something from this wreckage? Do I sit here and face whatever awful consequences are coming my way? If that's what it takes, then it's all that I deserve. But just say something, Paige. Please. Say something now.

'I didn't expect you home so early,' she says to him.

'Clearly,' he says.

I feel sick with regret and shame. How could have I been so stupid – again! Why did I think that even coming here tonight was a good idea? Ugh. I'm such an idiot. I'm so pathetic, and needy and desperate for someone to love me, and now I've ruined everything. Fiona warned me right from the start that this would happen, and I somehow managed to convince myself that the three of us had this special connection that would keep us all safe from being hurt.

I wipe the tears from my cheeks with the heel of my hand and stand up. I face Matt.

'Matt, I'm so sorry— I swear I didn't mean for any of this to happen,' I sob.

He turns to me, and his eyes are burning with rage. He looks so hurt and betrayed that all I want to do is run, away from here, away from everything, and never look back. I'm angry at myself. I'm embarrassed and ashamed of what I've done.

'Sorry? You're sorry?' he snaps at me. 'How long has this been going on, Kate? How could you do this to me? After everything I've done for you, how could you do this to me?'

'Matt, please—' I plead.

I look at Paige, trying to will her to say something. To tell Matt that we're both to blame for this, to say something that will somehow magically make all of this okay. But she can't because there's nothing that can be said that will fix any of this.

I look back at Matt, and I know he's right. How could I have done this to him? How could I betray him like this? No matter what part Paige had to play in any of it, I can't escape the fact that I've broken Matt's heart just as much as she has.

'I wish I'd never met you,' he says to me.

There. That's the consequences of your actions, Kate. Right there.

But no matter how much he hates me right now, though, I hate myself more.

'Matt, please,' Paige says, and he glares at her. 'It's complicated. I— we never meant to hurt you.'

'Complicated?' he says to her, and then looks at me and back to her. 'How is cheating on me with our friend complicated?'

'We never meant to hurt you, Matt,' I plead with him. 'It just happened.'

'It just happened,' he says, picking up the small, silver framed photo of the two of them in Edinburgh. The day he proposed to her. He throws it violently to the floor, and the glass shatters around his feet. I flinch. I've never seen him like this.

'You both made a choice,' he says. 'You betrayed me, Paige.'

'Please, Matt, just listen to me,' she says to him. 'It was a mistake. It's all just a terrible mistake. We never meant to hurt you, I promise.'

'No, you just never meant to get caught, that's all. This isn't a mistake. A mistake is forgetting to pick up milk on the way home. A mistake is forgetting to set the alarm for work in the morning. A mistake is locking your keys in the car.'

He's right. He's completely right. There's no defending what Paige and I have done to him. We knew exactly what we were risking when we made the choices we did, and yet we carried on. Maybe they'll somehow be able to come back from this, I don't know. I've been where Matt is right now, and I don't think I'd be a big enough person to forgive this. I brought all of this on myself, and I deserve everything that's coming my way.

'And as for you,' he says, turning back to me. 'Do you want to know why this breaks my heart so much?'

Matt

The three of us stand facing one another in the middle of the living room. I can barely bring myself to look at either of them because I don't think I'd be able to disguise the bitterness and disgust I feel for them both.

'Matt, I'm so sorry— I swear I didn't mean for any of this to happen,' Kate says, wiping her tears with her hands. I look at her in disbelief.

I can't believe her nerve. Does she really just think she can say 'sorry' and expect everything to be miraculously okay? As if it'll erase everything I'm feeling right now. The truth is that I don't care if she's sorry because I want her to feel terrible for this. I need for her to feel just a fraction of the pain that I'm in right now. I think back to that night in the coffee shop, when Steph broke her heart and I was there to pick up the pieces. Then I think about the night in G2, and the walk along Sauchiehall Street afterwards. When she was at her lowest. And about the hundred and one times between then and now when I was there for her, even when it meant pushing my own feelings down into the pit of my stomach.

'Sorry? You're sorry?' I snap. 'How long has this been going on, Kate? How could you do this to me? After everything I've done for you, how could you do this to me?'

'Matt, please—' she begs.

'I wish I'd never met you,' I tell her, and right now, despite everything I still feel about her, despite everything she is, everything she's been to me, I mean it.

'Matt, please,' Paige says and I turn back to her. 'It's complicated. I— we never meant to hurt you.'

What bullshit. There's nothing complicated about any of

this. That's just a vague excuse designed to avoid taking any real responsibility for the lies and the betrayal. There's no context here. No mitigating circumstances. Just flat out cheating. If she can't own it, she should at least have the decency not to downplay my totally justified resentment at what she's done to me, what she's done to *us*.

'Complicated?' I say. 'How is cheating on me with our friend *complicated?*'

'We never meant to hurt you, Matt,' she says. 'It just happened.'

'It just happened,' I say.

I take a moment, trying to get my bearings. I see the little silver frame on the shelf. The photo we took together on Arthur's Seat when I slipped the engagement ring onto her finger. I wonder if it was going on between them back then, and it feels like everything is mocking me. The photo. Kate. Paige. It's all a big joke, and I'm the punchline. Well, no more. I hurl the frame to the floor and the glass explodes from it. I glare at Paige.

'You both made a choice. You betrayed me, Paige.'

'Please, Matt, just listen to me. It was a mistake,' Paige pleads with me. 'It's all just a terrible mistake. We never meant to hurt you, I promise.'

'No, you just never meant to get caught, that's all. This isn't a mistake. A mistake is forgetting to pick up milk on the way home. A mistake is forgetting to set the alarm for work in the morning. A mistake is locking your keys in the car.'

I turn back to Kate. I can't hold it back any more.

'And as for you. Do you want to know why this breaks my heart so much?'

She looks at me. Whatever she thinks I'm about to say to her, I know that it's not this.

'Because I'm in love with you.'

Her eyes widen and her jaw drops. I can't even look at Paige right now, because I know if I do, the heartbreak in her eyes – if she still feels anything for me, that is – will stop me from being able to finish what I've started.

'Because I've been in love with you, on some level, whether I wanted to admit it to myself or not, since the first time I set eyes on you in the coffee shop. The night that Steph broke your heart. And I didn't think anything more of it, because I assumed that I'd never see you again, and then we ran into each other at the gig in G2.'

She's staring hard now, a lump in her throat, her eyes wet and glistening.

'And afterwards when I walked along Sauchiehall Street with you in the snow, it wasn't just because I wanted to make sure you were okay. I mean, I did want that, but that wasn't the only reason. We sat on that bench, just talking, and I felt a connection with you like I've only ever felt with one other person in my life.'

I look at Paige, white as chalk. I turn back to Kate.

'And that was when I knew. But I also knew that I couldn't just let you walk out of my life, because my life feels better with you in it, Kate. Even if I couldn't allow you to be what I so desperately wanted you to be. Even if I had to swallow the hurt that I feel every time I'm with you, because I knew you would never look at me and see what I do when I look at you.'

All of the anger that I felt when I walked in on them is gone now, drained from me, along with every ounce of adrenaline I had, and all I'm left with is a sense of hollow deflation, and the heartbreaking realisation that nothing is ever going to be the same between any of us again.

'We can talk about this,' Paige says after what feels like an eternity. 'Maybe we can work through it, the three of us.'

'There's nothing left to say,' I say to her. 'Because even though I love you, I've betrayed you just as much as you've betrayed me by feeling what I did— what I *do*, for Kate.'

I look at them both, in turn.

'The only difference between us is that I didn't do anything about it.'

Chapter Thirty-Three: October 31st

Paige

'Trick or treat,' my next door neighbour's wee girl says as she stands on my doorstep holding her bag open.

'You look absolutely gorgeous, Sophia— sorry, I mean Princess Elsa!' I say, and I wink at Susanne, her mum, who's standing at the end of my front path. I take one of the little bags of sweets and treats I pre-packed earlier and drop it into her bag. She gives me a big, gap-toothed grin, and it warms my heart. I've tried to keep things as close to normal as I can since Matt moved out. It's all I can do to stop myself from going nuts. If you'll pardon the Halloween pun.

The first few days were the hardest. Watching him pack up all of his stuff and load what was left of his life, box by box, into the back of his car. And the silence. There were no more fights after that Friday night. There was no fight left in any of us. He didn't even really say goodbye. Just took out the last box, closed the boot, got in his car, and left. And just like that, with neither a bang nor a whimper, Matt and I were over.

Mum cried when I broke the news to her, more out of how much she'd miss Matt than out of any sympathy for me, I suspect. Not that I deserve any sympathy. I didn't tell her what happened that night. I just couldn't. I couldn't bear to see the self-satisfied look on her face knowing that she'd been right about our relationship with Kate, about the whole situation. I just told her that it hadn't been working between us and we'd parted ways amicably. For the first couple of weeks, she kept trying to convince me to call him to see if we could patch it up, and in the end I had to firmly but politely tell her to keep her nose out.

I guess if there's any kind of silver lining to this cloud, it's that it's allowed me to completely immerse myself in work. Oh, and Connor bloody McCauley finally got his comeuppance and found himself being unceremoniously dismissed, which just proves that sometimes bad things do happen to bad people. Although, I guess I found that out in my own way too. The good news is, though, that in just over six months, I'll finally be a qualified solicitor, and the partners have assured me there's a permanent place ready and waiting for me. It's a relief that there's still one thing in my life that I haven't managed to completely cock up.

Talking of which, I still think about Kate almost every day, but it doesn't hurt quite as much now. It gets better by increments, day by day. We haven't spoken since that night. Matt went into the bedroom, I went into the kitchen, and she gathered the rest of her clothes from the living room floor, got dressed and left. When I heard the front door click, I went back into living room with a dustpan and mop and cleaned up the takeaway on the floor. After that, I just lay down on the couch and cried myself to sleep.

A little part of Kate is still with me, though. I still buy the magazine to read her articles, and I can hear the words in her voice. I know that sounds sad and pathetic, but that's what my life is now. Again, not looking for sympathy that I don't deserve. Just saying. I unfollowed her on Insta a few days after it happened, and she did the same with me. I think just the thought of seeing each other on there was too hard for us both. I know it was for me, at least.

I'm trying to be kinder on myself, even if I don't really deserve it. Relationships end, that's a part of life. Just because I caused it doesn't mean I'm not allowed to feel sorry that it happened. And I'm not thinking about jumping back into the dating pool any time soon. For now, I need to heal, process things, and try to work out who I am again. Or more importantly, who I want to become. A better person, that much I know at least. Not the kind of person that impulsively sets fire to everything good she's been lucky enough to have in her life.

I still think about the times we had together, the three of us, and despite how it all ended, I don't regret what we had. It burned bright for a little while, and then it burned out. I know, that seems like I'm being awfully philosophical about it all. The truth is, if I think about the good times, it helps me forget, even if just for a little while, my role in the bad times.

There's the door again. I've only got a few more bags left in the dish to give out. Once they're all gone, I'll blow out the candle in the pumpkin at my front door, turn out all of the lights, and run myself a hot bath. Tomorrow is a whole new day, after all, and with every one that passes, this gets a little bit easier.

'Trick or treat,' the wee girl from along the street says from under her mask, and I drop one of my little packs into her bag.

'Happy Halloween, sweetie,' I say.

Chapter Thirty-Four: November 5th

Kate

I crane my neck to gaze up at the clear, dark sky. I'm bundled up in my thickest wool jumper, mittens, and a knitted hat that I've got pulled down over my ears. My breath fogs out in front of me in the crisp night air. All around me, the sounds of Bonfire Night are filling the air. Small explosions echoing off the buildings, whistles and crackles piercing the brief moments of quiet, and the smell of gunpowder mixing with the aroma of burgers and sausages wafting from Dad's barbecue, which Ewan has commandeered for the night.

'It's not right making a grown man sit here with a plate of rabbit food when there's burgers on the go,' Dad grumbles as he forks at his salad. I sit down beside him at the patio table.

'You know what the doctor told you, Dad,' I say. 'Besides, look at how well you've been doing with the diet. You're like a new man, you skinny legend.'

He pats his shrinking belly. 'Aye, I suppose you've got a point, pal. Your mum can't keep her hands off me,' he winks.

'Ew, Dad, no. That's plenty!' I laugh. 'You've a bad heart, I'm telling her she's to keep her hands to herself from now on.'

'What's that you're saying about me?' Mum shouts from the garden just below where Dad and I are sitting.

'I'm saying you've to stop trying to interfere with Dad while he's recovering!' I grin.

'God's sake, Katie, that's enough of that,' Fiona says as she walks out from the kitchen. 'I've not had anything to eat yet, and the thought of that is putting me off! It's hard enough keeping anything down thanks to your wee niece,' she adds, rubbing at her neat little bump.

'Or nephew!' Ewan calls out from behind me.

I link my arm through Dad's and put my head on his shoulder. I don't think I'll ever be as grateful for anything as I am for the fact that he's on the mend now. I can't imagine how I'd have coped over these last few months if I'd lost him too. I haven't told him or Mum anything about what happened with Matt and Paige, but our Fiona knows. I broke down one night just after it happened, and she made me tell her everything. She didn't judge me, she didn't remind me that she warned me about the dangers or say that she told me so. She just wrapped her arms around me, told me that everything was going to okay, and then let me cry in her arms until I was done, because that's what big sisters do.

Work has been going well. I can't remember a time when I was as productive as I have been lately. The tips that Paige gave me about setting up a blog and tying it into my Insta have really been paying dividends. I'm getting more and more requests to write freelance pieces for different magazines and websites. At this rate, I might even be able to think about breaking out and going completely self-employed in the new year. If only I knew a good solicitor who could give me some advice.

While we're on the subject of the magazine, I pitched the idea about writing a piece about a three-way relationship between a couple and their mutual friend – completely hypothetical, of course, and not at all based on personal experience – and to my surprise, they loved the concept, and gave me free reign with it. As much as I hate lifting up the veil to shatter the illusion of journalistic integrity, a fair percentage of the stories that appear in magazines like ours are completely made up, with photos posed by models. I know, right? So, whilst my story, when it appeared in print, was about characters who were figments of my imagination, the events and emotions might have borne more than a passing similarity to real life. Keep that just between us, though, eh? Just our little secret. As far as the editors and readers are concerned, it's just a story. For me, and for one other reader, should she still be reading the magazine, it's my apology, my love letter, and maybe, just maybe, a chance to heal some wounds.

I head for home with a belly full of burgers and a heart fully recharged and topped up with the love that only a family can provide. The flat is dark and still when I get home. Nothing has changed because nothing ever changes. I've adjusted to it now, though. In a way, I even take a little comfort from it. At first, when Steph moved out last year, the quiet was deafening, and the flat felt cold and hollow, like an empty nest. Now, though, there's a certain peace and sanctuary in being by myself. My office space is perfectly organised, and I've got my cooking and cleaning routines down to a tee. Life is okay. Mostly.

There's still one thing I've been meaning to do. I open the dating app on my phone and look at my profile picture. The one that Paige took for me that night when we all had dinner together. It makes me smile when I look at it, because I remember her sorting my hair, talking about the perfect angle, and the magic spell she cast over it afterwards when she tweaked it to make me look my best. I haven't looked at the photo in forever. I haven't had the app open in forever. There are no messages, and I don't even mind.

I close the app and hit the 'uninstall' icon.

Everything is going to be okay.

Chapter Thirty-Five: December 23rd

Matt

These midnight finishes are starting to catch up on me now. I remind myself that tonight is my last shift until the day after Boxing Day, and I immediately feel a little better. Three whole days of not having to listen to the same playlist of Christmas songs on repeat and blaring through the speakers outside. Three whole days of the only coffee that I need to pour being my own. I'm looking forward to it, I'm not going to lie. I'm exaggerating, of course. A little. It's been a relatively incident-free run up to Christmas, and all of the extra hours have allowed me the luxury of being able to book myself a wee holiday. For the first time in my entire life, I'll be travelling on my own – even if it is only for a week in Tenerife in January.

It's taken a while for me to really get used to being on my own again. To a certain extent, anyway. I'm not actually living on my own as such. After everything that happened that night, I moved out of Paige's house and back home with Mum - and Derek, of course. Just until I get back on my feet properly and save enough for my own place again. It's been good for all of us. Mum's enjoying having an extra pair of hands to do things around the house, the extra money comes in handy, and Derek– well, Derek just enjoys having another man around the house to talk football with, I think.

I've even started writing again. One of the unexpected challenges of suddenly having so much free time, is that – well, you suddenly have so much free time that you need to fill. I found myself sitting in my old bedroom one night after finishing work, and I just opened up my laptop and started typing. Maybe it will end up being something. Maybe it won't. We'll just have to see where it goes, I suppose. I'm enjoying having one creative outlet in my life that doesn't involve doodling holly sprigs and berries into the foam on top of our special range of Christmas-themed coffees.

'Oi, daydreamer,' Hev says, nudging me. 'Pretend you're at work, you're not on holiday yet.'

Heather and Jason have been absolute rocks since everything happened. Not that I expected anything less from them, but still. I told Hev everything the next day. About what happened when I walked into the living room that night. About my own confession, and how everything was over between all of us. She rightfully gave me a good dressing-down about my part in it all, and how stupid I was, but I think what Paige did shocked her more than anything else. I know she thought the world of Paige, and she was furious. She was surprised when I defended Paige despite everything that happened. What can I say? None of us are perfect, and we all make mistakes, you know? Things could just as easily have played out differently, and I could have been the one making those mistakes. But I'm grateful for the support of my best friends. Even if J was secretly devastated that his plans for my stag weekend never came to fruition.

'Hev,' I whisper. 'Check this out. Look, over there.'

I give her a little nod in the direction of a mini drama which is beginning to unfold in front of our very eyes. Over at one of the tables by the shop's front window, a young couple are deep in discussion, and it looks like tensions are rising between them. I could tell something was off with them the moment they walked into the shop. Her eyes looked puffy and red-rimmed behind her wire-framed glasses as she slid silently into her seat. The guy shuffled in behind her, running his hands through his messy brown hair, sighing loudly as he sat opposite her.

'I know you care, Sarah, but you know as well as I do that this just isn't working,' he says, his voice drifting off.

Hev raises her eyebrow as she looks at me, and we both pretend to wipe the counter as we strain to pick up snippets of their conversation. I know, I know. I've learned nothing.

'I just need a wee bit of space, some time to figure myself out,' he's saying to her. That old chestnut. Lots of words that don't really mean anything. I swear, if he follows this up with 'it's not you, it's me,' I'm going to have to throw a mug at his head.

'But we've just moved in together,' the girl says, between heaving sobs, burying her head in her hands. 'Why now? Why are you doing this to me now?'

Okay, I am now officially uncomfortable with the scenario. The guy whispers something to her and then pushes his seat back and stands up. She doesn't even lift her head from her hands to watch him leave before they've even ordered anything. The door closes behind him and I can see him walk off into the Glasgow night.

Hev and I look at each other, and I shrug my shoulders. Before I can do anything else, she grabs a piece of red velvet cake from the display cabinet.

'You can just stay right where you are,' she grins. 'You're not to be trusted with this kind of thing.'

I just smile as she brushes past me and over to the table where the girl is still sitting with her head in her hands. I don't hear any of the words which are exchanged between them, but I see the confused look on the girl's face as she sees Heather at first, and then the change in her expression when Hev puts the plate with the slice of cake down in front of her. She smiles and says something to the girl, and the girl motions for her to sit down, which she does.

She looks back over at me and winks as if to say, *I've got this.*

Chapter Thirty-Six: December 24th

Kate

Did I ever mention that I'm a Christmas person?

This is my happy place. This, right here, right now. It's freezing cold in George Square in the centre of Glasgow, but I just pull my wool coat a little tighter around me and take a sip from my cup of mulled wine. For the record, I ended up just Googling it. Mulling, apparently, just means 'to heat, sweeten and flavour with spices.' Every day's a school day, right? I take another bite of my German sausage. I just love that little snap you get from the skin when they're cooked properly. Dad says that's the *wurst* feeling. Yes, that is very much a Christmas-themed Dad Joke. And no, I'm not even sorry.

I get my phone out and take a selfie, making sure I get the mulled wine and the beautifully lit big wheel behind me into the shot. I post it on Insta immediately, no filtering, no nonsense, not even caring how I look, because I'm happy. I think about this time last year, and how different I feel tonight. Last year on Christmas Eve, I was in tears on Mum's couch, getting horrendously drunk to Dirty Dancing and a roast pork chow mein because She Who Will Not Be Named had just moved out of our flat. This year, I'm still alone, and I'm completely okay with that.

See, that's the thing, really. It doesn't matter whether or not I get my miracle, because I'll never lose my faith in Christmas. I'll get up tomorrow morning, open up the presents that I've treated myself to, and then I'll head over to Mum and Dad's and be with the people who mean the most to me in the world. Mum will feed us all until we're fit to burst – she's even giving

Dad a break from his diet for the day. Dad will take great pleasure in telling us the joke from his cracker. Who knows, maybe I'll even get to feel my little niece – sorry, Ewan, we all know she's another feisty McArdle girl – kick my hand through Fi's belly. Maybe I'm looking at it all wrong. Maybe I already have my Christmas miracle. Maybe they've been there all along.

I wander from stall to stall, picking up some extra little last minute gifts for them all. A cute little raggy elf doll for Fiona's baby. Some cinnamon scented Christmas candles for Mum. A miniature bottle of Christmas liqueur for Ewan. And for my favourite person in the whole world, a mug which reads 'World's Best Dad.' Because that's what he is.

The lights just feel magical tonight, and I feel like the little girl who used to dance around the Christmas tree with Mum and Dad while Chris Rea sang to us. I'm just people watching now. I'll be getting ready to head back to the flat soon enough, but I want to squeeze just a little more pleasure out of this moment before I leave. These last twelve months have been tough, in ways that I could never have imagined. There were days when I didn't know how I'd make it through to the end. But here I am, still standing, celebrating another Christmas. God, I'm feeling extra sentimental tonight. Blame the mulled wine.

Next year's going to be better. I can feel it in my bones. I've got so much to look forward to. My career is taking off. There will be a new member of the family to welcome. Everyone is happy, everyone is healthy, and we're all—

My heart stops in my chest. I can't believe it. I have to look twice to make sure.

It is.

Paige.

She's unmistakable. Even from across the crowded square, I could pick her out. The lights catch her golden hair, and it's almost like she has an aura glowing around her. She looks more beautiful than I've ever seen her.

I think about heading for the exit. I don't think I can face an awkward scene. Not here. Not tonight. Not at Christmas in my happy place. But before I can, we lock eyes.

What else can I do?

I smile.

And now she's heading across the square. Through the crowd.

Straight to me.

Paige

I have to admit that I did feel a little twinge of sadness when I walked past the bridal boutique in the Merchant City earlier. A serious case of 'what if,' you know what I mean? I couldn't bring myself to go in and cancel my dress in person after Matt left. I took the easy way out and did it over the phone. I don't think I could have faced it, having to go in there again. Seeing all of those beautiful dresses. Seeing mine. I think it would have made it feel so much more real, seeing it again, if that makes sense. And the questions. The pitying look from the sales consultant. It would all have been too much to bear.

The last of the Christmas shopping is done, though, so that's a positive. Not that there was a lot to buy this year. It makes it so much easier when you're pretty much shopping for yourself. I wouldn't describe it as a luxurious haul, not by any stretch of the imagination. Functional, more than anything else. A couple of suits and some new shoes for work because that's where my focus is now. And I'm okay with that. Maybe I do feel a little sorry for myself when I see loved-up couples in town on Christmas Eve, gazing in shop windows, or sitting in coffee shops with hot drinks, or even skating on the ice rink in George Square, and then I remind myself that I had all of those moments. Once upon a time. I had them all, and I threw them away.

It's cold and it's dark, and I just want to go home now. I've left my car, as I always do, in the car park at Buchanan Galleries. It's only a few minutes from here by foot, and it gives me a chance to stroll through the Christmas market in George Square one last time. Am I a glutton for punishment? Maybe a little. What can I say, though? I like to look at the twinkly lights, and I could pick up a hot chocolate for when I get home. Sounds like a plan to me.

It's crowded. Probably the busiest I've seen it over the entire festive period. It feels like the entire city all got together and had the same idea tonight. Maybe this wasn't the best idea after all. I could probably pick up a hot chocolate somewhere closer to home. I bet the queue at the stall is a mile long too. I'm doing a pretty good job at talking myself out of it, and then—

Kate?

Of course she'd be here on Christmas Eve. She is literally Buddy the Elf.

I know things ended badly between us all, but God, my stomach is churning. It feels like no time at all has passed. Would it be a terrible idea if I go over and say hi? It would, right? And what would I even say anyway? 'Oh, hi, fancy running into you here?' Too breezy. Too casual. Maybe an apology? It's too late for apologies. Maybe this is just the universe telling me that it's time to let go of the past for good.

But I can't. Not now that our eyes have met.

And she's smiling at me.

And finally, there's no more confusion. No lingering doubts. I know exactly what it is that I want, and nothing else matters.

I start weaving through the crowd, which seems to be getting thicker with every second that passes. People laden down with shopping, happy families with young children desperate to ride the rides one last time before heading home for bed, the queues at the stalls and the people browsing the scented candles and wreaths. My heart is pounding, but I have tunnel vision and my eyes are locked on the girl in the long, crimson wool coat with the gorgeous chestnut hair. The girl with the pretty, honest, wide brown eyes. The most beautiful girl I've ever known.

The girl who owns my heart.

I weave around a couple holding hands and gazing at one another. I sidestep a man with a sausage in one hand and a coffee in the other. A group of chatty teenagers move aside, and the path between us finally clears. She's still smiling when I reach her, face to face for the first time since that night, and without a word spoken, I drop my bags at my feet, I place my hands on her cheeks, and under the sparkling Christmas lights in George Square, I kiss her like I've never kissed anyone before.

There are fireworks. Literal fireworks.

Somewhere, off in the distant Glasgow night, someone is celebrating early, but in this moment, this beautiful perfect moment, I know that they're for us and us alone.

Chapter Thirty-Seven: December 31st

Kate

'It was exactly a year ago tonight, you know.'

'What was?' Paige asks me.

I'm lying back amongst a pile of plush cushions on her couch, stretching my legs out with my feet resting in her lap. I wiggle my toes, a little ticklishly, as she applies a new coat of cool, glossy lacquer to my nails. I love the feel of her fingers against my skin and the tiny brush strokes as she paints the colour on. I inhale the faint chemical scent and sigh, contentedly.

'The night we first met. Here. Your party.'

'We both had the same top on,' she says. 'You were so embarrassed, I felt awful for you.'

'I almost went home, right there and then,' I laugh.

'I'm glad you didn't,' she smiles, squeezing my foot, and my heart flutters. It's been a week now since we met again in George Square, and we've barely spent a second apart since. We both decided that we'd already wasted far too much time. We agreed that there would be no more recriminations, no regrets about everything that happened. And it's been good. It feels right. Natural. No awkwardness or tension. It's been everything I could have wished for, really. And there I was thinking that I'd never get my Christmas miracle.

Christmas was good. I mean, really good. Surprisingly so. We came back here to Paige's place, and we just sat and talked until the early hours of the morning. She told me that she had read the story in the magazine, and she knew that I'd written it for her, *to* her, but that she just couldn't bring herself to reach out to me. We went to bed, we cuddled, I told her that I love her, she told me that she loves me, and it was... perfect. In the morning, I made two phone calls. One to Fiona and one to Mum. Well, it wouldn't have been right just turning up for Christmas dinner with an extra guest – even though Mum had predictably made so much that I could literally have turned up with a harem, and no-one would have gone hungry.

And I know what you're thinking. I bet Fiona gave you an earful, right? She's my big sister, and as much as I know she just wants to protect me from ever getting hurt, her first priority is, and has always been that I'm happy. And no matter what happened in the past, she knows in her heart that Paige makes me happy.

As for Mum and Dad, they might have been a little shocked at first, but that didn't last long. I think Mum and Fiona both still appreciate Paige being so amazing when Dad had his heart attack, even if they've never really said it out loud. They've definitely warmed to her, even if Fi is still a little bit guarded. Paige will win her round in the end, I know she will. She's too nice for everyone to not fall in love with her as much as I have.

Dad? Well, that was love at first sight. He's fascinated with her work because he thinks everything to do with law is like it is in those American TV legal dramas he and Mum love so much. And Paige thinks he might be the most hilarious man she's ever met, despite Mum's constant telling her not to encourage his nonsense.

Carol, though. That was another story altogether. We picked them up on Boxing Day to drive them to the airport for their annual holiday in Gran Canaria and I could actually feel the knives she was staring into me. Paige picked up on her resentment, and as they unloaded their cases from the car at Glasgow Airport, finally stood up to her, and although I had to pretend I that didn't hear what was being said, I've never been so proud of her.

Now here we are. The sun is just about ready to set for the last time on what's been the most intense and wild year of my life, and if I'm being honest, I'm beginning to feel a little reflective and emotional. It's been a lot for us both to process, but we survived it, and we get to wake up tomorrow and start a new year planning the rest of our lives together.

But there's still one thing I feel like we never properly resolved.

'Paige?' I say.

'Mm hm?'

'Tomorrow is a new year. A chance to start fresh, clean slate, all that stuff. Right?'

'Riiiiight?' she says slowly, eyeing me.

'You can tell me if you think this is a terrible idea, and I'll totally understand and I'll never mention it again, okay?' I say.

'Let me guess. You're going to suggest that we reach out to Matt to try and make amends, aren't you?'

'How did you—'

'I know you, babe,' she smiles. 'I know you still feel like crap for what we did to him. I know that we're okay now, but I also know that will never be completely enough for you, not until you know that he's okay, and that he can forgive us. You're just like your dad. That's the kind of person you are. The kind of person whose heart is so big and so full of love that you can't bear the thought that you've caused anyone even the slightest bit of hurt or pain.'

'So what do you think?' I ask hopefully.

She looks up at the clock on the living room wall.

'Well, if we're going to do it, I think now is as good a time as any, don't you?' she says.

Matt

The shop is empty. Finally. The last customer has gone, I've locked the door and I'm finishing up the last of the cleaning. I pour myself out one final cup of Americano and lean my elbows on the counter. Mopping the floor can wait. For a few more minutes, anyway. I'm in no rush. I savour the smell of the coffee and take a little sip. It's dark outside. When the sun comes up in the morning, it'll be a whole new year. I wonder what it's got in store for me.

I already know what tonight has in store for me. A large portion of mushroom pakora and a couple of bottles of beer to see out the year in Jools Holland's company. Yes, I know it's pre-recorded months in advance, and no, I don't care. That'll do me just fine tonight. Mum and Derek are off out to their first New Year's Eve party as a married couple, and I have a standing invite to Hev and Jason's for what would no doubt be a fun, eventful night, but I'm quite happy to chill at Mum's, wake up tomorrow morning hangover-free, and get my suitcase packed for Tenerife the day after. Once I've enjoyed an amazing steak pie dinner, that is. There are still some traditions that you just can't give up, after all.

I finish my coffee, wash my cup and get the floor behind the counter mopped. A few last little touches to straighten up here and there, and I'm officially a free man for a whole ten days. I put my jacket and scarf on, turn off the lights and set the alarm. I'm so happy to be locking up and making my way home that I haven't noticed the two figures waiting outside of the shop.

'Hi, Matt,' Paige says. I turn around. Her breath fogs in the air in front of her.

'Paige? What are you doing here?'

'How have you been?' Kate asks me. I put the shop keys into the pocket of my jeans.

'Good,' I reply, still a little puzzled at why they're here, together, waiting for me.

'Can we talk?' Paige asks.

'Sure,' I shrug. I look at them both and make a little motion between them with my finger. 'Are you two—'

They look at each other and Kate nods. She looks guilty, a little afraid, like she's not sure how I'm going to respond. What am I going to say? What can I say, really?

'Okay,' I say. 'That's good. I'm happy for you.' I look at

Paige. 'Both of you.'

Neither of them say anything, like they're scanning what I've just said for sarcasm. I get it. *I'm happy for you* could mean any one of a hundred emotions in these circumstances, but as it happens, in this case it legitimately just means that I'm happy for them.

'Really?' Kate asks. I nod and smile.

'I'm sorry, Matt,' Paige says. 'We both are. More than you'll ever know. We know that we hurt you, and we'd both completely understand if you told us that you never wanted to see either of us again, but—'

'I felt that you at least deserved the courtesy of knowing a couple of things,' Kate says. 'That what happened wasn't for nothing. It wasn't just a cheap, tawdry impulse.'

'And we're okay, now, Kate and I,' Paige continues. 'Better than okay, really.'

I nod. It's cold. I blow on my hands to heat them up a little and then stick them into the pockets of my jacket. I look at Paige.

'I'm glad. For what it's worth, I don't regret anything. You and I, Paige, we were great together. And in another lifetime, we'd have married and had a long and happy life together. I'm sure of that. But in this one, our story just wasn't meant to end that way. If it was, neither of us would have felt the things that we did. That we *do.* And that's okay.'

'I'd like it if we could still be friends, Matt,' Kate says.

I think about it. The truth is, I would like that too. But in the real world, too much water has passed under our own little bridge, and as much as I've forgiven them both, seeing them would just be a constant reminder of what we had.

'I love you both,' I say to them. 'And a part of me always will.'

'But?' Paige says. I smile. She knows me so well.

'But as much as I love you, I could never have shared you. Either of you. I just couldn't. I'm not made that way.'

'I get it,' Paige replies. 'And I suppose I feel the same way too.'

'I'm in a good place,' I say. 'And as much as I care about you, about both of you, I need to move on with my own life. But I mean it from the bottom of my heart when I say this. I wish you nothing but the best together.'

'Thank you,' Paige says, a tear running down her cheek.

'Come on,' I say, nodding towards the car park. 'It's cold and it's getting late.'

Kate

Paige, Matt and I walk slowly around the crescent of the Fort, back towards our cars, our arms linked like it's the most natural thing in the world. Almost like the way we used to be. Even though all three of us understand that it will never really be the way it used to be. I'm in the middle. Matt's on my left and Paige is on my right. One by one, the shops are closing and the staff are emptying out into the cold night. The car park is quiet already, and so are we, as if none of us want to break this spell, as if doing so would be our tacit acceptance that we've finally reached the end of our road together.

I feel something cold and wet brush my cheek, and I look up. It's snowing. The streetlights glow softly, creating halos of light that seem to blur as the swirling snow passes through the beams. I feel their light, feathery touch on my upturned face, each one like a tiny, cold kiss. I look at Matt and Paige in turn, and they're both looking up at the sky too, completely lost in it. I think I could stay in this moment forever with them. I wish that I could capture it and keep it in a snow globe on my shelf.

'This is the part where we say goodbye, isn't it?' I say to Matt.

'It is,' he replies, with the most wistful of smiles.

The three of us embrace for one last time. I can feel a tear on my cheek as my head rests on Paige's shoulder, one of my arms behind her back and the other behind Matt's. I close my eyes as the wind whips and whirls little flurries of soft snow around us.

I think about the night we met here, when I had my heart broken and Matt was there to pick up the pieces. And about the night when we sat on that bench on Sauchiehall Street, a snowy night like this, and we told each other our life stories over the most unforgettable kebab I think I'll ever eat. I think about the selflessness and the kindness that he's shown me since the moment we met, and about all the good times that we've had between then and now, when the three of us together, for a short, beautiful, wonderful time, became greater than the sum of our parts. And as heartbroken as I am that that time is about to end, I know that I'll be forever grateful that we shared it.

'Thank you, Matt,' I say, as we release each other from our embrace, and I wipe the tears from my cheeks with the heels of my hands. 'For everything.'

Paige puts her arm around my back and pulls me close to her. The snow is getting a little heavier now, and it really is time to go. Matt looks at her, and then at me.

'Look after each other,' he smiles, and then he turns and walks away.

Chapter Thirty-Eight: Two Years Later

Matt

When I finish reading, I sit back down in front of the display which features an unnerving and freakishly oversized photo of my head and the cover of my book, *Three's Company*.

Of all the bookstore appearances that my publishers have been kind enough to line up for me, this is the one which means the most, because it's right here in my hometown. And even more pleasing, it's just around the corner from the coffee shop, and my old boss Dom is a friendly face in the audience, which I appreciate so much. In fact, he texted me right before I arrived just to wish me good luck.

The other good luck message I received this evening came from Kirsten. We met through my literary agent, hit it off almost immediately, and whilst it's still early days, I've been enjoying getting to know her, one date at a time. If I've learned one thing over the last few years, it's that you can't take anything for granted.

'First, I'd like to thank you all once again for joining us here at Waterstone's Glasgow Fort this evening,' the store's manageress says into her microphone. 'And of course, a huge thank you to Matt for reading us that little section from his book, which I hope you all enjoyed. Now, before we bring tonight's event to a close, Matt has kindly agreed to answer some of your questions, after which he'll be available to sign some copies of his book, which I know you're all desperate to get your hands on.'

A few hands spring up, and the manageress points to a pierced, blue-haired, artsy-looking girl in a goth rock t-shirt who looks to be in her early twenties.

'Hi, Matt,' the girl says. 'I found it really refreshing to read a story about people like me, and set right here in our own city, too. I was just curious about why you chose to structure it like you did, with all three of the main characters narrating alternating chapters.'

'That's a great question. I've read so many love triangle stories and seen so many movies about them over the years, but where they always seem to fall down is that there's inevitably an obvious "wrong choice" or "bad guy" who loses out in the end. Sometimes it's the cold-hearted girlfriend of a nice guy, or a boorish bully or cheating lowlife of a boyfriend. The point is, there's always someone who makes it far too easy for the reader to root for the good guy – or girl. But real life's never really that black and white, is it? We're all just shades of grey. So, I think I really wanted the reader to fall in love with all three of the main characters and root for them all, despite – or perhaps *because* of all of their flaws. Because really, they're just three good, kind-hearted people who happened to find themselves caught in a weird situation.'

The next question comes from a middle-aged blonde woman in a denim jacket.

'Without giving away any spoilers for anyone who hasn't read it yet, how did you decide which two of the three characters got together in the end? And how hard was it writing the ending for the one who lost out?'

'Look, I'm not going to lie, I actually got really upset over it!'

There's a smattering of laughter and a few sympathetic nods from the audience.

'When you spend as much time with people as I have with these three characters, you get so attached that all you want is for them all to have the happy ending that they deserve. But just like my answer to the last question, life's not like that. I wrote and re-wrote it, again and again, and with every draft, it ended differently. I think that's more like real life, anyway. In any other parallel universe, we could all end up living a completely different life, couldn't we?'

'We'll take one more question before Matt starts signing some books,' the manageress says. 'I can see a hand up at the back. What would you like to ask, dear?'

'Thank you,' the person says, and I don't even have to see her face in order for me to recognise the voice which has just brought a huge smile to my face. 'I just want to say, big fan of the book. My girlfriend bought me a copy for my birthday, and I couldn't put it down. It's just so true to life. I have a two-part question for you if that's okay?'

'That's absolutely fine,' I say, still smiling.

'So, my first question is about the scene where Rob and Amy have just met for the second time when she spills his drink over him, and they're telling each other their life stories over a takeaway on a bench on Sauchiehall Street. Why on earth would you have him eating mushroom pakora? I mean, really, does anyone actually enjoy that stuff?'

It's just about all I can do to stop myself from cracking up with laughter long enough to answer her question.

'Ah, see, I think you're missing the most important point. When you're sharing a moment like that with someone, it's not about the food. It's the person you're enjoying it with that makes it so special.'

'That's very true,' she says.

'What's your second question?' I ask her.

'Do you think Rob regretted any of it in the end?'

I smile again and shake my head.

'Not a single moment.'

ACKNOWLEDGMENTS

Maggie. My compass. My north star. My Donkey.

Tammy, Scott, Amanda and Logan. A wise man once said, "writers write in order to converse with those who remain after they are gone." Whilst this book is something I wanted to leave behind after I'm gone, I'll never be as proud of it as I am of you.

Oliver. You are, and will forever be, my guy.

Thank you to everyone who lent their eyes to this, especially my amazing CritiqueMatch team: Kirsty Cunningham, Steph, Ashley Snyder, Dee and Felicity Beaumont. Your insights into the story and the characters were invaluable as I edited.

Thanks to Dave Pirner. Five words from a song were the seed from which all of this sprung. But what great words they were.

Thanks to Sophie Gravia for opening the door and proving that this can be done. It's a shame that more love/relationship stories aren't set in modern, urban Scotland, instead of the picturesque highlands, all full of kilts and castles, leaving us with 'gritty' stories about crime lords, poverty and the general grimness of life in Central Scotland. I wanted to tell a story that showed that fun and love don't have to be off-brand for Glasgow. I hope I did you all proud.

Finally, to you, dear reader – my most heartfelt gratitude. I hope you cared about Matt, Kate and Paige as much as I do.

All is love... and love is the fing.

ABOUT SCOTT BISSETT

Scott Bissett lives in Lanarkshire, Scotland with his wife, children and an assortment of defective pets. He enjoys cheesecake, cheeseburgers, cheesy rom-com books and cheesy rom-com movies. He spent over twenty years dreaming about one day being able to write the kind of book he enjoyed reading, and started and stopped more times than he'd care to admit. He cries every time Clarence gets his wings.

You, Your Girlfriend & Me is his first novel.

Reach out to Scott at:

Facebook: ScottBWrites
Instagram: ScottBWrites
Twitter/X: ScottBWrites
Threads: ScottBWrites

Printed in Great Britain
by Amazon